Race to the Kill

HELEN CADBURY

Allison & Busby Limited
12 Fitzroy Mews
London W1T 6DW
allisonandbusby.com

First published in Great Britain by Allison & Busby in 2017.
This paperback edition published by Allison & Busby in 2018.

A CIP catalogue record for this book is available from
the British Library.

10 9 8 7 6 5 4 3 2 1

ISBN 978-0-7490-2261-7

Typeset in 10.5/15.5 pt Sabon by
Allison & Busby Ltd.

The paper used for this Allison & Busby publication
has been produced from trees that have been legally sourced
from well-managed and credibly certified forests.

Printed and bound by
CPI Group (UK) Ltd, Croydon, CR0 4YY

HELEN CADBURY wrote fiction, poetry and plays. She worked as an actor before becoming a teacher and spent five years teaching in prisons. She grew up in Birmingham and Oldham, lived in London for many years, then went north and settled in York with her family. Her debut novel, *To Catch a Rabbit*, was the winner of the inaugural Northern Crime Competition. Helen passed away in 2017.

helencadbury.com

By Helen Cadbury

To Catch a Rabbit
Bones in the Nest
Race to the Kill

Dedicated to the memory of Sue Matthews
friend, musician, librarian

PROLOGUE

Sarah

The smell of newly laid tarmac gets stronger as she gets closer, until it eliminates all the other scents of late afternoon on a hot June day. She carries a bottle of water, straight from the fridge. Beads of water coat the plastic and run over her fingers. The lazy turn of the concrete mixer, grit hurling against its sides, slows and stops. He's seen her coming. He wipes his hands on the back of his trousers and his eyes dance with a smile. She hesitates, unsure whether she should cross the trench, lined with orange and yellow cables. She holds out the bottle, but he won't be able to reach it from the other side. She is watching a bead of sweat run down his neck from behind his ear. It trickles along his clavicle and down the centre of his chest where it soaks into a stain on his vest.

He steps over the trench, his legs longer than hers, and lands right in front of her, teetering on her side, right on the edge. She can smell him now, see the thin red blood vessels lining the whites of his eyes. He's too close. She holds the bottle of water against her chest, as if it will protect her. His mouth is open, showing his broken teeth. The muscles along his arms are taut as he reaches his sinewy hands out, like a hawk's talons.

Half a second before he touches her shoulders, she screams, and the sound bounces off the breeze-block wall beyond the trench. It echoes off the solid mass of the building behind her. His face changes and his grip tightens, as if he's going to shake her. A door opens, and she hears feet at the top of the metal fire escape. She is still screaming, trying to push him off, but she is not strong enough. This time, though, someone is coming to rescue her.

CHAPTER ONE

Friday night

The petrol gauge had been nudging red for nearly an hour when PC Sean Denton finally persuaded his partner, PC Gavin Wentworth, to pull into the petrol station close to the Chasebridge estate. Gav stayed behind the wheel, while Sean got out to fill the car. Beyond the spot-lit petrol pumps the woods loomed in the dark. It was just after midnight. Fuel glugged into the empty tank and an owl hooted somewhere over the rough fields. The heat of the day had evaporated and Sean wished he'd put his jacket on.

He returned the nozzle to the pump and went to pay at the window. He asked the young lad on duty to get him a couple of bags of crisps and a can of pop. Pocketing the receipt for the petrol, he handed over a five pound note for the snacks. The cashier's eyes darted up from the money, over Sean's shoulder. A flicker of white in the reinforced glass was enough to make Sean spin round, one hand on his baton. But it was just a woman, dishevelled and pinch-faced, with greasy bobbed hair. Probably no more than thirty, but looking fifty. She took a step back, startled. She'd have to be desperate to try and rob a police officer in full view of the cashier and a police vehicle, so what was her game? She covered her open mouth with the sleeve of her dirty-brown jumper and began to cry.

'All right,' Sean said. 'Do you want to tell me what's happened?'

She gulped a breath.

'You've got to come,' she said.

She reached out and grabbed his wrist. He could have broken her hold, but he didn't want to drop the crisps and the can of pop. Besides, there was no strength in her fingers.

'Everything all right?' Gav was out of the car and walking towards them.

He felt her grip loosen as Gav approached and pulled his arm away, but she wasn't going to let him go that easily. Her fingers darted out and grabbed the sleeve of his shirt.

'You've got to come with me!'

Her voice cracked, the volume out of proportion with how close they were standing.

'Now then, why don't you let go of my colleague, love, and we'll see how we can help you?' Gav said.

She took no notice and tried to drag Sean towards the road.

'You have to come!'

Gav didn't try to talk her round a second time. He might have been pushing for retirement, but he still had the moves. Before she knew what had happened, the woman had lost her grip on Sean and found herself up against the window of the garage shop, Gav's hands firmly on her shoulders.

'Now, if you have something to tell us,' he said, 'I suggest you spit it out, and then we can all go about our business. But if you lay one more filthy little finger on my colleague, I will arrest you for assaulting a police officer.'

She looked at Sean for support.

'What's your name?' Sean said.

'Mary.'

'Mary what?'

'Just Mary.'

'Okay, Mary, why don't you come and sit in the back of the car and tell us what the problem is?'

She shook her head violently and a gobbet of snot dislodged from her runny nose. Gav stepped back to avoid catching it in the face, and Mary seized the opportunity to pull away from him. She ran to the edge of the garage forecourt, but hovered there, unwilling to leave.

'Well?' Gav said. 'Are you going after her or shall I?'

Sean sighed. 'Can we get her in the car?'

'Do we have to? She stinks.'

'What do you suggest?' Sean said.

'She wants you, Sean. She wants you bad.'

'Knock it off.'

'Well, maybe you should go with her,' Gav said, 'and see what's up?'

'Do I have to?'

'I'll follow in the car. Go on.'

Sean looked at Mary, standing there, dark eyes watching him under her greasy fringe.

'Okay,' he said. 'Let me find out where we're going first.'

He walked over to her, while Gav hung back by the kiosk window.

He heard the cashier say: 'Does your mate want his

11

change?' and looked back to see Gav pocketing the money. Nice one. He'd have to remember to get it off him later.

'Where are we going, Mary?'

'The old school.'

She turned away, setting off across the dual carriageway with a limping gait that didn't appear to slow her down.

'Gav!' Sean called. 'Chasebridge School, the old site, not the Academy.'

'I'll be right behind you.'

Sean knew that wouldn't be entirely true. Gavin would have to drive to the next roundabout and double back, then he'd be restricted to the vehicle access to the estate, while he and Mary would be taking the shorter, pedestrian route, between the flats, on cracked paved paths studded with bollards.

'I'll be on the radio,' Sean said.

'Don't worry, she won't hurt you.'

Gav waved him off and went back to the car.

Sean had to run to catch up with Mary. He tried to get her to talk, but she walked on, head down against the light rain that had begun to fall. They came to the four tower blocks at the top of the estate. Out of habit Sean glanced up to the second floor of Eagle Mount One, where his father lived. The windows of Jack Denton's flat were all but dark. Just a light in the kitchen. Maybe Chloe, his half-sister, was still awake. Sean felt a pang of guilt. He hadn't been to see his dad for nearly two weeks. The old man had been in and out of hospital since Easter and although there was no love lost between them, Sean still felt he should do the right thing and go round occasionally.

'Shit!' He'd trodden in a deep puddle, caused by a faulty pipe on the corner of Eagle Mount Two. The muddy water seeped over the top his boot and into his sock. After the run of hot days they'd had, he could only imagine where this water had come from. It definitely wasn't rainwater.

Mary turned to check he was still following.

'It's all right. I'm still here,' he said. 'I don't suppose you want to tell me what's happening, do you? I could have some backup ready, if I had a clue what we're actually doing.'

'I ran out when it started,' she said. 'I didn't see.'

'What started?'

She looked away and carried on walking.

'Something started in the old school?' He said. 'Is that where you've been living?'

Her pace slowed and he came alongside her. The warmth of her body gave off the gagging scent of unwashed skin, tobacco and alcohol: the cocktail odour of the rough sleeper.

'Mary, you need to tell me. Is someone in danger?'

'If you're quick you can run.'

'And if you're not?'

She winced at the question. 'You have to pay.'

He reached for his radio.

'Victor Charlie Four Three.'

'Go ahead, Four Three.'

'I'm heading for the site of the old Chasebridge School, Disraeli Road. We've been stopped by a member of the public. Possible incident, risk to persons sleeping rough in the school premises. Proceeding on foot, with the informant. Victor Charlie Three One is en route, via the main entrance. We may need backup.'

13

'Yes, received, Victor Charlie Four Three,' the call-handler's voice crackled out of the radio.

He saw the face that went with it. Lisa-Marie, dark hair, big brown eyes. They'd had a quick cuddle at an office party when he was still a PCSO. It came back to him, with a blush, every time he heard her voice.

'I'll update when I'm closer,' he said, forcing his mind back on the job.

'Other patrols are committed, Victor Charlie Four Three. There's a big fight in town. I'll get back to you as soon as I can.'

Great, Sean thought. *We're on our own.*

CHAPTER TWO

Friday night

Chloe had no memory of her father as a child. She might have seen him a hundred times and never realised it. He was one of many men who drank in the pub on the estate, one of several who'd been her mother's boyfriend over the years. She sometimes wondered if her mother even knew which one of the men she served drinks to in the Chasebridge Tavern had got her pregnant. Chloe used to ask her often enough, but she always got a different answer. Her mum liked to tell Chloe that her father was a sailor, or sometimes a soldier. Once he was a travelling salesman, and on another day, a fairground worker. By the time she was in secondary school, Chloe knew these were just stories, but she never understood why her mother made them up. Now Jack Denton was real, and her mother long dead, it occurred to Chloe that her mother had known all along, but wouldn't have wished the real Jack on her daughter. Not that he was a bad person; he was just a drunk. *Had* been a drunk, she mentally corrected herself. Jack was sober now. He was also seriously ill with cirrhosis of the liver.

Chloe fumbled for the bedside lamp, trying not to knock

it off the suitcase that stood in for a table. The first time she'd suggested to Jack she might occasionally stay over, this room had been so full of junk that she hadn't realised there was a bed in it. He'd grudgingly let her clear enough space to reveal the old bed-base, which once belonged to her half-brother. It was so narrow she'd struggled to find a mattress to fit it, until one of the girls at work gave her a child's mattress she was throwing out. Chloe's feet already hung over the end if she stretched full length, but after a while, she'd decided it wasn't worth paying rent anywhere else, so she'd given up her own flat and moved her few possessions in here.

It was 2 a.m. and she wondered what had woken her. She lay back on the pillow and listened. Jack coughed in his room across the narrow hallway. The cough came again and tailed off into a chesty, wheezing moan. Chloe sat up. This time the cough and the moan were followed by another sound, a high-pitched whine like a child's cry.

She got out of bed, pushing open the door of Jack's room, and let the light from the hallway spill across the floor to his bed. She'd left him propped up on the pillows, the way the community nurses had shown her, but he'd slipped sideways and lay bent over, crooked, his head tipped towards the edge of the bed, knees drawn up. His face was wet with tears.

'Aagh!' He clutched at the edge of the duvet with his good hand, while the twisted fist of his old injury flailed in the air.

'Where are your tablets?' she said, turning on the overhead light.

She could see now what had woken her. In his pain, he'd swiped everything off the top of the bedside cabinet. The water glass was shattered, shards spread over the carpet, and the cardboard packet of painkillers lay in a pool of water.

She didn't know what to do first. The fog of sleep was still with her, slowing her movements, until he cried out again and she snapped into action.

'Come on, now,' she said. 'Let's get you back up on those pillows. This must be the stomach acid the nurse talked about. You need to be sitting up.'

She lifted him under his arms. Even though his body was tense, Chloe was strong, and it required very little effort to move him. She settled him back on the pillows and stroked the back of his hand. His breathing came in fast, sudden gasps.

'I'm going to get you another glass of water and then you can have a tablet. Will you be all right?'

He gave an almost imperceptible nod. His eyes were closed and his jaw was tight. She knew he hated to show how much it hurt, and would be ashamed of his tears. She picked up a box of tissues from where they had fallen and placed one in his clenched fist.

'Back in a moment,' she said.

She took the soggy packet of tablets into the kitchen, found a tea towel to pat them dry, and reached under the sink for the dustpan and brush.

A terrible shout from the bedroom startled her and she ran out of the kitchen, dustpan and brush in hand.

Jack was lying on the floor, next to the bed, clutching his stomach.

'Jack!' she cried.

She reached under his armpits to lift him, but it was harder this time. He was struggling against the pain and against her. Her hand slipped underneath him to get a better hold and she felt a sharp sting. Broken glass in the side of her hand. Crouching over him, she managed to get him up, onto the edge of the bed, and dragged him back towards the pillows. There was something under her foot and she pulled away, just before the glass punctured the sole of her foot. She realised Jack hadn't been so lucky. A thin line of red on his arm swelled with fresh blood, pulsing to the surface. There was more blood on the duvet cover, but she couldn't tell if it was his or hers.

'I'm going to call an ambulance, Jack, can you hear me? I need you to hold on, try not to move.'

His eyes were no longer focusing and his head lolled back.

'Stay with me, Jack, don't pass out on me. Jack? Dad?'

A flicker of his eyelashes. *Call me Dad*, he'd said, the first time they'd met, and she'd struggled with it, pretending she hadn't heard. She'd called him by his name ever since, and although in her head she thought 'my dad' or 'my father', whenever she opened her mouth it was always *Jack*. His eyes closed.

'Dad?' she said.

His body went slack, but the eyes flickered open again. They stayed open, red-rimmed and watery, but looking at her, focusing. He was still there.

'Lie still, okay? I'm going to get my phone from my bag, then I'm going to sit here and call the ambulance. I'm going to stay right by your side until it comes.'

'Say it again,' he whispered.

'What?'

'Call me Dad.'

CHAPTER THREE

Friday night, Saturday morning

The playing fields had been sold off as soon as the school roll dropped below five hundred. There'd been a bit of a protest, but the local authority said it had no choice. A new housing development was built where two-thirds of the football pitch used to be. Private houses, with their backs turned away from the main part of the Chasebridge estate, clustered around closes and cul-de-sacs. A high fence was built on the boundary. Three years later, the school closed for good, and the remaining staff and pupils reluctantly joined the new Academy, on the other side of The Groves. More fencing appeared, and the ground-floor windows were boarded up. Sean had hated most of his lessons here, but he'd had some good times too. Like everyone who'd grown up in the area, he felt a belated sense of loyalty to Chasebridge Community High School, now it was falling to pieces and awaiting demolition.

Mary hesitated on the edge of the school site, where a row of plywood boards were attached to the metal fence.

'I'll show you where to get in,' she said.

'Wait a minute.'

He wasn't going in without Gav. He looked along the road. There was no sign of a vehicle, but there was something else moving towards them in the shadows. It was a man with a large dog. He was walking close to the high fence bordering the back of the new houses in Springfield Gardens. He stopped and bent down to the dog, unclipping its leash. The dog rushed forwards, barking furiously.

'Police!' Sean shouted, reaching for his baton. 'Get your dog under control!'

Mary screamed and began to run, which gave the dog something to run after. Sean raised his baton, ready to knock the dog back when it drew level with him.

'Mosley! Here boy!' the man called, and the dog skidded to a halt, ears flicking back towards its owner, eyes still on Sean. It was a German shepherd with a mouth full of very sharp-looking teeth. For several seconds it held Sean's gaze, as if trying to decide whether to obey its master, or sink its fangs into Sean's face.

'Mosley. Here!'

It was enough to break the spell. The dog sloped back to its owner and Sean lowered his baton. He looked around, but Mary had disappeared.

'Sorry about that, mate,' the man said. 'Didn't see your uniform.'

He was in his mid-thirties, Sean guessed, a tousled look to his receding hair, which may have been a styling choice, or simply because it was the middle of the night. Sean resisted the urge to point out that he was not the man's mate and wouldn't have thought twice about bringing his baton down on the dog's skull, had it got close enough to bite.

'Bit late for dog walking,' he said.

'Just doing my bit for the community,' the man said.

'By walking your dog?'

'Keeping an eye on things, you know.'

'I'm sorry?' Sean said.

'Isn't that why you're here? We keep phoning the police, it's getting ridiculous. There was a load of them earlier, swarming out into the road, like fucking zombies.'

'When was this?'

'Twenty minutes, half an hour ago, tops.'

Enough time for Mary to have made her way to the petrol station. Perhaps she was one of his zombies.

'Did you see them yourself?' Sean said.

'Aye. A load of junkies and fucking immigrants. They've been using the school as a squat. I won't let my kids come down here.'

'I'll need to take some details, and we'll look into it. Can I have your name and address?'

'John Davies, 39 Springfield Gardens.'

Sean pulled out his phone and made a voice recording, saving it with the date and time. John Davies gave him an odd look, but Sean wasn't about to explain why this was his preferred method of making notes that weren't scrambled by his dyslexia.

'Are you going to do something about that place?' Davies said. 'It wants burning down.'

'I can pass on your concern, but at this precise moment, I'm waiting for my colleague.'

'That woman?'

21

'Eh? Oh, no, she was . . .'

Sean wasn't sure what Mary was. A civilian, just like the dog-owner, worried about what was going on in the disused buildings? Only not like him at all. A different tribe. But she'd wanted him to help her. He thought of her summoning up the courage to speak to him at the petrol station, shivering in her thin, baggy jumper.

'It's a bloody disgrace,' Davies was saying. 'Been boarded up all this time and the security's no use. That lot have been dossing in there for months.'

'You saw a group of them?'

'Some running, the rest sort of milling about. I thought it was a fire or something, but there wasn't any smoke. They spread out and some of them headed up this way towards Springfield Gardens. They better not be dossing down in my fucking shed, or I'll set the dog on them.'

'I wouldn't do that, sir. You're legally obliged to keep your dog under control.'

John Davies looked as if he was about to object, when Gav pulled up in the squad car. Sean opened the door on the passenger side.

'We'll be in touch, Mr Davies, and thank you,' he said.

Sean got into the car and slammed the door shut.

'Neighbourhood watch?' Gav asked.

'With vigilante tendencies. Arsehole. What took you so long?'

'Stopped at the top of the road for a chat with a couple who were pushing their worldly goods along in a supermarket trolley. I thought it was odd for this time of night, and sure enough, they'd come from the school, but they wouldn't tell me anything. Someone or something scared them off.'

Sean told him what Davies had seen.

'We'd better take a look,' Gav said. 'Nobody leaves home in the middle of the night unless they have to. Where's Hairy Mary?'

'Disappeared when our friend turned up.'

Gav called in to say where they were.

'Another unit's on its way,' the call-handler said. 'Sarge says to proceed with caution.'

From the rear-view mirror, Sean watched John Davies and his dog making their way back to Springfield Gardens.

'Received,' Gav said. 'We'll take a look.'

'It seems quiet enough,' Sean said, getting out of the car, 'and we won't be on our own for long.'

'I'm right behind you, Scooby-Doo.'

Sean ran his torch across the boards that were lashed to the steel fence and quickly found the unofficial entrance to the site. One section of plywood had been detached and then leant back into place. When Sean lifted it aside, he could see two sections of metal fencing behind it. They'd been forced apart and by stepping sideways into the gap, he could squeeze himself through.

'Come on, Gav, suck your belly in, and you should just fit.'

'There must be an easier way,' Gav said. 'I can't see a shopping trolley getting through that.'

He moved further down the pavement and Sean could hear him testing the boards for movement, until he reached a gap.

'That's more like it,' Gav called and Sean saw him step through on to what had once been a flower bed, but now was just a patch of dry earth.

The front entrance was fully boarded up, but as a pupil Sean had hardly ever used that door. There was another entrance round the side, which was ramped. It used to lead to the special needs classroom. It was closest to the car park, but furthest from the lights of the new housing development. Sean had a hunch that residents leaving with their possessions in a supermarket trolley might also prefer ramped access.

'This way,' he said.

Sure enough, as he came round the building, a door stood open. A metal grille lay discarded on the grass a few feet away. Sean shone his torch into the entrance and went inside. The smell was unmistakable: human waste, backed up in toilets after the water had been turned off, or just left wherever people had the urge. Very little light made its way through the boarded-up windows. Sean and Gav stood in the dark corridor and listened. It was quiet, except for the dripping of water nearby.

The beam of his torch played across the doors to abandoned classrooms. The tangled hieroglyphs of graffiti tags covered the walls, impossible to read.

'Doesn't sound like there's anyone about,' Gav said. 'Did she give you any clues about what she thought had happened? I mean, beyond some people walking away, which frankly I don't blame them, what are we actually investigating here?'

'She said something started. I assumed she meant something kicked off. A fight of some kind.'

'Why don't we get Marshall's, the security firm, down here, get the place secured and then leave it for the morning? Report a break-in to the owners and threaten them with legal action for allowing a public health hazard on their property. I'm telling you, there's no one here.'

Sean knew he had a point, but there was something in Mary's fear that made him want to look further. He flicked his torch up the stairs. From outside he'd noticed that some of the first-floor windows still had glass in them. He wondered if that would make it a more comfortable place to sleep.

'I'm going to start up here,' he said. 'We can work our way along the top corridor, then come back down the stairs at the bottom end.'

'Hang on,' Gav said. 'Let's keep control informed. There's still no sign of any backup. Maybe we should wait?'

'What for?' Sean said. 'You said it yourself, there's no one here.'

He started up the stairs, craning to hear any sounds, but there was only Gav's voice and the response on the radio, echoing off the concrete. Another unit would be with them in ten minutes, if required, meanwhile they should investigate and report back.

The upstairs corridor was empty, except for the puddles that punctuated the peeling linoleum. The roof had always leaked, even when the school was still open, but now the buckets to catch the drips had gone and the water had pooled in interconnecting lakes. Sean tried a classroom door, but it was locked. Further along another door stood open. There were blankets and clothes piled on the floor, a half-eaten packet of biscuits and some empty beer cans. There was no furniture left.

Gav carried on up the corridor, picking his way between the puddles.

'No one around,' he said.

The next room had more piles of clothes and plastic bags, odd shoes and discarded newspapers.

'Look at that,' Sean said. 'Someone's left a decent-looking radio.'

'Must have been the last one out, or one of the junkies would have had it.'

'I'm not sure they're all junkies, Gav. Mr Davies said something about refugees.'

'Well, whoever it was, they left in a hurry.'

They came to a junction where a second flight of stairs led down to the ground floor, while the upper corridor split along two wings.

'Which way?' Sean said.

They listened, but there were no clues in the silent building.

'What's down here?' Gav said.

'The main hall, then beyond that there's more classrooms and the gym. The science labs are on this level,' Sean said, 'and there's another flight of stairs at the far end.'

'Okay, we'll go down and check out the hall and beyond, then up the far stairs and back along this way.'

'What about the toilet corridor?' Sean said.

'We'll wait and see if anyone comes to join us, and let them do that.'

'Good plan.'

Gav lead the way down the stairs and they were back in the gloom of the ground floor, lit only by their torches and pale slivers of light from the boarded-up windows. Gav opened the door of the hall. A line of windows, just below the ceiling, let in a little more light. Looking up, Sean could see the clouds had cleared and the moon was almost full. For a moment, he saw the school hall as it used to be: red velvet curtains gathered in swags at either side of the stage and the headmaster at the lectern, trying his best to inspire the kids of the Chasebridge estate to make something of their lives. Sean blinked and focused on reality.

His torch picked out burnt patches on the parquet floor and he could see that the stage curtains had been ripped down and used by the new residents as bedding. A bundle in the centre of the room caught his eye, a pool of water spread round it. He trained his torch at the ceiling, but there was no sign of water damage. He shone the light across the rest of the floor. It was all dry. He went closer, the light from his torch more intense as the beam shortened. The bundle was a human shape, cocooned in a sleeping bag, and the water wasn't water at all. It was blood.

CHAPTER FOUR

Early Saturday morning

'It's been boarded up for three years, awaiting demolition,' a female voice rang out from the far end of the corridor.

Sean watched his girlfriend, Crime Scene Manager Lizzie Morrison, adjust her bag on her shoulder and pick her way between the puddles, followed by her colleague, Janet Wheeler. Lizzie was now the senior Crime Scene Manager for the Division and Janet had been appointed Exhibits Officer. Together they made a powerful team.

'Christ, what a stench!' Janet's Edinburgh accent seemed even stronger than usual as she pinched her nose.

He opened the door of the school hall for them.

'Different smell in here,' he said.

Lizzie stopped to put on her shoe covers.

'Thanks,' she said. She caught Sean's eye for a moment. 'CID are on their way.'

They seldom worked the same job, but when they did, they followed the rules, both written and unwritten, tried to keep it professional and leave the relationship at home.

Sean stood just inside the door watching Lizzie and Janet

assess the scene, while Gav sat on the bottom of the stairs, outside the hall, filling in the incident report.

'He wouldn't have stood a chance,' Lizzie was saying to Janet. 'His forehead and nose are completely caved in. The pathologist might be able to work out if he'd been awake at the time of the attack, but I hope for his sake he wasn't.'

Janet was taking photos from every angle, while Lizzie began to mark out the blood pattern. Sean was confident that he and Gav had done a good job of keeping their feet out of it.

'Janet, can you just get a shot here?' Lizzie said. 'I think the suspect must have been standing behind his head. There's a break in the spatters.'

She took out a tape measure and made a note of the point at which the pattern appeared to split. She stood up and looked around the room.

'What a place to live,' she said, and whistled through her teeth.

Or die, thought Sean.

'I suppose they prefer to come here rather than a hostel,' Janet Wheeler said. 'More space and freedom, but also more risky.'

'If they can get into a hostel,' Lizzie said. 'I know Saint Bernadette's won't take them if they're still on drink or drugs.'

'Poor guy,' Janet sighed.

Sean was thinking about what it took to slip into this life, sleeping rough, always in danger. Not much, if you started in the wrong place.

'Sean?' Gav opened the door a crack. 'Khan's here. I don't think he ever sleeps. Ask your missus if she's ready for him.'

'She's not my missus.'

'Whatever.'

'The boss's here,' he called to Lizzie.

'He's early,' she said. 'Okay, let him in.'

DI Sam Nasir Khan liked to put in the legwork, even when the job threatened to keep him chained to his desk, so it shouldn't have been a surprise that he'd turned up as Senior Investigating Officer three hours before he needed to. He'd accepted the permanent role of DI on the Major Crimes Team, instead of going back to Sheffield as a DCI, precisely because he missed the operational side of the job.

Sean stood up straight, holding the door open, a rush of awkwardness as he tried not to catch Khan's eye. Lizzie took one more measurement and marked the area with a yellow numbered cone. Khan stood in the doorway in full protective gear, taking in the scene. He turned to Sean for a moment and his eyes smiled above the face mask.

'Good to see you,' he said quietly. 'You did a good job on Wednesday.'

Sean nodded, his mouth too dry to speak. Khan let the hall door close behind him and left Sean in the corridor with Gav.

'What was that about?' Gav said. 'I thought you were at the dentist's on Wednesday.'

Sean decided not to answer and followed Khan back into the hall. He wanted to be there, to listen, watch and learn. What he hadn't told Gav, or even Lizzie, was that he'd had an interview on Wednesday, with Khan and the Chief Superintendent. An interview for CID. A letter would be in the post by the end of the week, they'd said. And now Khan was smiling, telling him he'd done a good job. He didn't want to hope too much. He had to wait to see it in black and white, but all the same, he felt a little surge of excitement.

'We've got a severe facial injury, impact from a heavy blunt instrument and good markings indicating the direction of assault,' Lizzie said, looking over her shoulder at the DI. 'No sign of self-defence. His arms were still in his sleeping bag. As far as I can tell, he's male, under six foot, south Asian or Middle-Eastern, olive skin, brown eyes, but that's about all I can say for now.'

Khan nodded, taking in the room with a slow, sweeping gaze, the blackened marks on the floor, the abandoned bedding, the plastic bags and newspapers.

'Hotel California,' he said.

'Something like that,' Lizzie said.

'Right,' Khan turned to Sean. 'I need a full search of the premises. See if anyone's still here. Another unit's just arrived and they're checking the grounds. If you find anyone, I want a name for the victim, last fixed address, anyone who knew him.'

This meant Sean and Gav would have to cover the reeking toilets after all.

'There's a couple of old dossers hanging around by the door,' Khan continued. 'PCSO Jayson is down there. She's asked them to wait. Get their statements.'

Sean led the way down the corridor. The sound of water dripping from the roof was soon accompanied by Gav muttering behind him.

'Manners cost nothing. Please. Thank you,' Gav said. 'Never mind that I've spent twenty minutes writing up an incident report, which he hasn't even looked at.'

Sean decided to ignore him.

31

'Come on,' he said. 'Upstairs. Let's cover the bit we didn't get to earlier, and leave the worst till last.'

The stairs up to the first floor were faintly illuminated by the moon, shining through a broken window. Sean was hit by another memory of his time here, the crush at change of lessons, with one class trying to get up the stairs and another trying to get down. It was never a very large school, anyone who had a choice went somewhere else, but it always seemed crowded enough in the narrow corridors and staircases, especially if you were trying to avoid the random kicks or punches from the school bullies. Sean stood still. For a moment it was as if he could still hear the clatter of feet.

'Are we going up or what?' Gav said.

'Coming,' Sean said, and the ghosts vanished.

They climbed the stairs together, stepping over piles of rubbish, their torches picking out needles and bloodied tissues.

Along the top corridor they forked left and stood in the doorway of one of the science labs, torches playing across wooden benches scarred by generations of students' initials and battered by a haphazard attempt to break them up for firewood.

'Hello!' Gavin called into the dark room, but no one answered.

'How many people have been living here?' Sean said.

Gav shrugged. 'Hard to say, there are bits and pieces left behind in virtually every classroom.'

But not their owners, Sean thought. The place was as quiet as the grave.

An old map of Europe was still hanging in the geography classroom. One corner had come away from the wall and was drooping over to hide Poland and half of Germany. More evidence of people's lives: sleeping bags, plastic shopping bags, milk and orange juice cartons. It looked as if everyone had left in a hurry.

'Bloody hell!' Gav's voice came from across the corridor, from what Sean remembered as a domestic science classroom. 'Looks like they've had the plumbers in.'

The old classroom had been wrecked, sink units torn from the walls, and more gaps where there had once been cookers and fridges.

'House clearance more like,' Sean said.

'Or someone with a taste in copper piping.'

'Hardly surprising. Whoever's been in charge of security on this site has done bugger all.'

'Or turned a blind eye,' Gav said. 'It explains all the water in the downstairs corridor, any road.'

'Wait,' Sean said. He couldn't be sure, but it sounded like someone was stifling a cough in a room close by. 'Listen.'

Apart from the gritty scrape of Gav's shoes moving back towards the door, there was no other sound. Then it came again, a stifled cough. Gav and Sean moved together towards the next classroom, their torches picking out the sign, *History*, on the closed door.

'Hello,' Gavin said. 'Anyone in there?'

There was no reply, and nothing seemed to move beyond the door. There was a narrow window at eye height. Sean trained the beam of his torch on more rubbish and personal possessions strewn across the floor, the chairs and tables long gone. Whoever was inside was keeping themselves out of sight. He nudged the door open with his foot.

'Police. Show yourself!' Sean said, but there was no reply.

He could feel Gav's breath on his neck and took a step forward, edging the door open with his elbow. Something flickered in his peripheral vision and he felt a sharp shove in the middle of his back. He stumbled forward. Glass smashed on the floor at his heels. Regaining his balance, he turned to see Gav jumping away from the fragments of a broken bottle, bouncing across the floor. Behind the door was a thin, dark-haired man, with light-brown skin. His raised hand was empty, his face aghast.

'You can thank me for saving your life later,' Gav said to Sean. 'First we need to make an arrest.'

Sean reached for his cuffs and the man began to sob.

'Sorry, sorry, please,' he raised his hands in supplication.

'I'm arresting you on suspicion of attempted assault on a police officer,' Sean said.

The second response unit had come with a cub van. It was parked in what remained of the school car park. Gav and Sean led the man outside and opened the cage in the back of the van.

'Don't take me to police station,' he said, and looked Sean in the eye for the first time. 'I am afraid of police. In my country, they are murderers.'

'Oh, so you do speak English,' Gav said.

'What's your name?' Sean said. 'You can tell us, then we can help you. This is the British police you're dealing with, we're not so bad.'

The man looked at him for a moment. Sean tried to read his expression, but all he saw was defeat.

'My name is Elyas Homsi,' the man said. 'I am from Syria, where I was a teacher in a secondary school.'

'And now you're living in one!' Gav laughed at his own joke, but Elyas Homsi didn't smile. 'Right, have you got any sharp objects about your person? We'll need to search you before you get in the van.'

Sean put on a pair of purple latex gloves and patted Homsi down. He was thin under his cotton bomber jacket and loose T-shirt. The pockets of his tracksuit trousers were empty, but from an inside pocket in his jacket, Sean pulled a folded piece of paper.

'My letter. Please don't take it. This explains who I am. It says I can stay here.'

There were dark smudges on the paper, which might be blood.

'Gav, get us an evidence bag, will you?'

The man's face was hollow and his dark eyes were underscored with heavy shadows.

'What's that on your hands, sir?' Sean said.

Homsi looked at his hands as if he had only just noticed them.

'My friend is hurt, badly hurt.'

'Did you see what happened?'

Homsi shook his head. 'Bad men came. I was too late to help him.'

Sean bagged the letter, while Gav helped Homsi into the cage.

'My paper,' the man cried. 'Will I get it back?'

'Don't worry, sir, it'll be logged and kept for you at the station.'

Homsi said nothing. He sat back on the bench and let his head drop onto his chest, all the energy in his body melting away.

'It doesn't make sense,' Sean said, when he and Gav were out of earshot. 'The whole place is deserted apart from a dead body and him. Everyone else did a runner, but for some reason he hid.'

'Maybe he just didn't get out in time.'

'Or maybe he had nowhere else to go.'

'Or maybe,' Gav said, 'he's the killer. Fortunately, we don't have to make that call. You go and tell the boss we've got someone and a CSI needs to check him over, see whose blood he's got on his hands.'

As Sean walked back towards the side entrance, he noticed two men huddled under the splintered, plastic porch. A female PCSO was barring their way into the building.

'All right, Carly? Are this lot residents?' he asked.

PCSO Carly Jayson gave him a smile. They'd known each other ever since he'd worn the same blue uniform as her, partners as community support officers on the Chasebridge estate.

'I don't know,' she said. 'They were just hanging around when I got here.'

The two old men, drinkers by the look of them, shuffled forwards as Sean opened the door.

'Did you see what happened?' Sean asked them.

'No, nothing,' one of the men said. His friend shook his head in agreement.

'Someone banging on the doors and telling us to get out. We've been sheltering under there. I thought it was going to rain.' He pointed a shaking finger at the corrugated lean-to that had once been an area for cycle parking. 'I said, didn't I? It's going to rain. Can we go back inside yet?'

'Sorry,' Sean said, 'you'll have to wait out here, and it's not going to rain. See, the sky's clear.'

'Go on, copper, we won't get in your way, just need somewhere to kip in the warm.'

'In case you've missed the news,' Carly said, 'this is a murder enquiry, now you can either help by giving us a statement, or you can get lost.'

Sean left her to it and made his way back along the corridor, careful not to breathe through his nose as he passed the toilets. He knocked on the door of the hall and opened it. DI Khan was crouched over the body, carefully unzipping the sleeping bag. Lizzie matched his position on the opposite side of the victim.

'Yes, what is it?' Khan said, without looking up.

'We've got a guy in the back of the van, we found him hiding upstairs.'

'What's he doing in the back of the van?' Khan still didn't turn round.

'Gav, I mean PC Wentworth, has just arrested him for attempting to assault a police officer.'

'Really?' Khan sighed. 'I'll leave this one to you,' he said to Lizzie, and stood up. 'The pathologist is on his way.'

'We need a CSI to take a look at him,' Sean said. 'He's got blood on his hands. No sign of a wound on his body.'

'Janet?' Lizzie said, without looking up.

Janet Wheeler picked up her bag.

'Denton, take Miss Wheeler out to the van. The rest of my team are on the way. You and PC Wentworth are well over the end of your shift, so get back to the station and we'll take it from here.'

'Yes, sir.'

Sean glanced over at Lizzie, but she was focusing on the victim.

He'd like to see the job through, but he knew Khan was right. It wasn't his business any more, and their shift should have ended an hour ago. The flutter of excitement he'd felt earlier was fading, he wasn't part of CID, not even close. *Get back in your box, Denton.* There would be more paperwork when they got back to the police station, but they weren't needed here.

'The guy in the van,' he said, as he stood in the doorway. 'He's Syrian, a refugee.'

'Much obliged,' Khan said, but he wasn't looking at Sean, he was focused on the blood pattern on the floor.

Sean let the door shut behind him.

'Come on, son,' Gav said, as they got into the car. 'I'll log this back at the station and check on our prisoner. I'll drop you off at your place on the way past.'

Sean was going to protest, but found he didn't have the energy.

'Thanks.'

Before Gav turned the engine on, a black Ford Mondeo pulled up next to them and a tall, slim man in a grey suit got out.

'Who's that?' Sean said.

'New DS up from London. Ivan Knowles. He's only been here three days and he's already got two nicknames, let's see which one sticks.'

'Go on?'

'Ivor Biggun, or Ivan Know-It-All.'

'You're slipping, Gav,' Sean said, 'if that's the best you can do.'

Gav put the car into gear and began to turn it round. 'Who said I instigated them?'

'Who else?'

Gav chuckled.

'Hang on,' Sean said. 'Let's go back through the estate.'

'What for?'

'It's not much of a detour.'

'I know that,' Gav said, 'but why?'

'I just want to see if there's anyone unusual hanging about. Anyone from the school who we might have missed. There must have been twenty or thirty people living there by the look of it. They can't all have vanished.'

'Have it your own way.'

Gav put the car into reverse, with a grind of the gears, and pulled left into the one-way section of Disraeli Road. They passed the post-war semis with their lights out and curtains closed. He made an illegal turn and drove the car up on to the pavement and back down, until they were on the access road for the low-rise, four-storey maisonettes, which ringed the centre of the estate.

Gav swung the car right, past the playground. The moon cast shadows from the swings across the cracked asphalt.

'Someone's about,' Gav said.

Sean saw it too, an ambulance parked up on the pavement in front of the main entrance to Eagle Mount One. Instinctively he looked up to the first floor of the block, to the corner flat where his father lived. The lights were on in every room.

'Shit!' he said. 'Pull over.'

'What is it?'

'My dad. That's his place. Lit up like a bloody Christmas tree.'

Gav accelerated round the corner, mounted the kerb and jammed on the brakes. They came to a sharp stop directly behind the ambulance. Sean jumped out. Jack Denton had been ill for years, as long as Sean could remember, although in his childhood it didn't seem like an illness, just a collection of bad habits. An injury during the miner's strike, before Sean was even born, had damaged Jack's hand, put him out of work and led to the drinking that was finally claiming his liver. Things had never been easy between father and son but, deep down, Sean still cared for the old bastard.

He pushed open the heavy door and stepped into the lobby of Eagle Mount One. The smell never got any better. Piss and rancid fat. He could hear voices from inside the lift shaft and the lift doors opened to reveal a group, frozen like a framed picture, looking out at him: a shrunken man, yellow-skinned and wrapped in a blanket, strapped to an evacuation chair, a paramedic on either side of him, and behind him, the pale, drawn figure of Sean's half-sister, Chloe, pressing a bloodied tissue against her hand.

'Sean!' she said, as the group poured out towards him. 'That was quick!'

'I was in the area,' he said, guessing that he'd missed a text or a phone call somewhere along the way.

He turned back towards the front door and held it open for Jack to be wheeled outside. The old man had barely been discharged from hospital a fortnight, and here he was going back in again.

'His breathing was terrible,' Chloe said. 'Then he woke up in so much pain.'

'What happened to your hand?'

40

'He dropped his water glass. It smashed on the floor.'

'Are you all right?'

'Yes, I'll be fine, it's just a scratch.'

'Sure? He didn't . . . ?'

'What are you saying, Sean?' She looked surprised. 'He wouldn't lay a finger on me.'

Lucky you, Sean thought. Jack Denton's violence had escalated when Sean's mother died. Not long after that, at the age of twelve, he'd packed a bag and gone to live with his grandmother.

'Do you want to come in the ambulance,' Chloe said, 'or do you want to meet me there?'

His jaw ached with tiredness. He didn't want to do either. He wanted to go home to his nice clean flat. Lizzie's flat, technically, but he paid his way. He wanted to have a shower, lay his head on a clean pillow, breathe in the scent of fresh cotton, and go to sleep.

'I'll ask Gav to take us both,' he said finally, knowing that this was the right answer. 'We can blue light it and get the old man seen to a bit quicker.'

He let the front door swing shut behind him and watched the paramedics lift Jack into the back of the ambulance. They didn't have to strain, there was nothing to him.

CHAPTER FIVE

Saturday morning

Regent Square was only a short walk from the centre of town. The birds were singing as Sean trudged round the corner and up the steps to the front door. His legs were heavy and it felt like a long way to the top-floor flat.

He let himself in, careful to let the door close softly, and tiptoed to the bedroom, but the bed was empty. Lizzie must still be at the crime scene. He went back into the kitchen and ran the tap. Yesterday's dishes were stacked up, waiting to be washed. He was dog-tired, but not ready to sleep. He rolled up his sleeves and plunged the plates into hot soapy water, but he couldn't get the dirt and squalor of the old school out of his mind.

He was drying his hands on a tea towel when he heard a key in the front door.

'Hi!' Lizzie called.

'I'm in the kitchen.'

She came through the doorway. Shadows were gathering under her eyes.

'Use the hand towel,' she said, 'not the tea towel, it's not hygienic.'

'How was it?' he said.

She put her bag down on the side.

'He'd been dead a couple of hours. Whole place full of junkies, by the look of it.'

'Definitely murder?'

'Probably, unless he smashed a blunt object into his own face,' she said. 'I'm frozen.'

He went to give her a hug, but she moved away.

'Don't. I stink of that place. I need a shower.'

'Shall I make you a sandwich?' he said, opening the fridge and scanning the contents. There was a packet of ham and the remains of a bag of salad.

'It's all right. Ivan had some protein bars. I've had two of those.'

'Ivan?'

'DS Knowles. New guy from London. Good detective, very thorough.'

He was about to ask if Ivan Know-It-All had got anything out of Elyas Homsi, the guy who'd tried to bottle him, but she wouldn't have heard. She was already in the bathroom with the water running. He thought about getting in the shower with her, but she didn't look like she was in the mood.

He stretched his shoulders back and felt his neck click. He needed to sleep, but Lizzie would complain if he got into bed without washing. He wandered into the living room. The settee had a soft, blue blanket folded over one arm. She was taking her time in the shower, and he didn't think he could wait any longer. Sleep was overcoming him. He loosened his belt, undid his trousers, and lay down on the settee, pulling the blanket over him. He didn't hear Lizzie come out of the

43

bathroom, and didn't hear her sigh when she saw his sleeping face pressed into one of the silk pillows her mother had bought her as a flat-warming gift.

When he woke up, it was fully light and the cushion had slipped to the floor. He checked his watch. Two and a half hours sleep at most. At least he'd come to the end of his run of night shifts, but it was like jet lag; he'd have to try to keep going until later tonight, to get his system back to normal.

He got up and put the kettle on. He thought Lizzie might like a cup of tea in bed and if he was quick, he could be showered by the time the kettle boiled. He stepped under the water, but once there, he didn't want to rush. He let the water wash the images of the night from his mind: the body, wrapped in its sleeping bag; the pool of blood; the smells of human lives and human death. He wrenched his mind away and on to his father, swaddled in a hospital blanket, being wheeled away to the ward, after the long wait to find him a bed. Too much in one night, it made his head ache. Forget the tea, perhaps he'd just surprise Lizzie by snuggling under the duvet and kissing the back of her neck. God, he thought, that was a beautiful idea.

'Sean!' Lizzie was knocking on the bathroom door. 'I need to clean my teeth, I'm going to be late.'

He scrambled out of the shower cubicle and grabbed a towel.

'What time is it?' he said, as he let her in.

She went straight to the sink and glanced at him in the mirror, before concentrating on squeezing toothpaste on her electric brush.

'Eight-thirty,' she said. 'I'm in a briefing at nine.'

He didn't feel like shouting over the noise of the electric toothbrush, so he went to get dry in the bedroom. She'd made the bed, neatly smoothing the duvet like a field of untrodden snow. *Sod it*, Sean thought, and pulled it back to climb in.

'Bye,' Lizzie said from the doorway.

'Mm,' Sean said. 'See you later.'

Sean turned over and pulled the duvet over his head. He heard the click of the front door closing. He hadn't had a chance to tell her about Jack being taken into hospital and as for the other secret he'd kept from her, well, that would have to wait until he had something more concrete to say.

He lay there, hoping to go back to sleep, but the memory of his interview on Wednesday made his heart race. He replayed the questions and answers in his head and wondered if he really had done okay, as Khan said. But maybe the DI was just being kind? They'd got to know each other on the Terry Starkey case, and got on well, in fact it was Khan who'd suggested he apply, and offered to recommend him, but the Chief Superintendent was a different matter. He hadn't cracked a single smile across his polished face for the entire interview. *So why do you want to be a detective?* Sean had practised his answer over and over again, but when it came out of his mouth, it sounded ridiculous. *Because I want to see the bad guys put away and the victims get justice.* Like he was some kind of comic book hero. He reached for the radio on Lizzie's side of the bed and let a chart song take his mind off waiting for the letter, and off the thing he feared most, the possibility of being turned down.

CHAPTER SIX

Saturday morning

Sarah lies awake, too tired to move, trying to block out the sound of the birds going mental in the scrubby trees. The walls of the static caravan are too thin and it's as if those damn birds are in the room with her. She's had the dream again, someone holding her down, heavy hands on her shoulders. She woke up wondering if she'd screamed out loud.

There's a crash of her front door bursting open, its plastic frame hitting the side of the worktop in the kitchen, a few feet from her bedroom door. She sits up, grabs her cardigan from beside the bed and swings her feet onto the cool laminate floor.

'Sarah?' It's Tommy Heron's voice. 'Did you know your door's unlocked?'

'It's not,' she sighs. The catch must have slipped again. She needs to get hold of a screwdriver. She can't have a door that isn't safe. 'Why don't you ever knock?'

She stands up and looks around the room for a moment. She notes the black bin bag of laundry that she'll take across to the washing machine in the stadium kitchen.

When nobody's looking, she'll slip her laundry in with the bar towels and tea towels.

'Sarah?'

'Coming.'

She has to face another day of this life she's made for herself, a world away from the one she grew up in. Outside the caravan there's the scrapyard, and beyond the scrapyard is the greyhound stadium, where she cleans, sells burgers, and pulls pints for Tommy Heron's Aunt Lou. There are worse jobs, she knows that, and the family are good to her, despite her being an outsider, but she can't stay for ever.

Tommy is standing by the kitchen table, his bulk filling the small space.

'You okay?' he says.

'Of course I am,' she says, wishing he hadn't asked.

'You know something, Sarah,' he says, twisting his fingers around each other. 'I will always protect you.'

'I know,' she says and forces a smile. 'Did you come for anything in particular?'

'Oh! Yes, I did. You haven't forgotten, have you?' he says. 'Did you do the sign and everything?'

'Of course I haven't forgotten. It's tied over the window so the paint would dry. I did the bunting too.'

She follows him through to the lounge end of the static caravan and watches his face as he takes in the banner, lips moving, reading the words she's carefully stencilled on the vinyl.

GRAND RE-OPENING! CHASEBRIDGE GREYHOUND STADIUM
50 YEARS TOP QUALITY RACING

The fabric bunting reads WELCOME, repeated along a line of coloured triangles. She sat up for several nights, stitching the lettering on pink and blue gingham, and sewing them onto a length of pink binding. She hopes the vintage effect will make the stadium cafe seem more welcoming, less sterile. She's even persuaded Lou to get gingham tablecloths to match. She knows they need to keep the numbers up and she's got some ideas about bringing in a different kind of punter.

'And guess what?' Tommy says, his bright eyes and soft lips belying his eighteen years.

'How can I guess?' she says.

'Our lass is coming!'

'Your sister?'

'Yeah! Joe's going to pick her up. And she won't have that nosy cow of a social worker with her this time.'

Tommy is the source of all her information about the family. The others – his Aunty Lou, her husband Derek, and Tommy's brother Joe – keep things to themselves, and keep her firmly on the outside. It suits her fine. Families are trouble. They can suffocate you, like animals who lie on their young. If there's anything she needs to know, she has Tommy. She can get him to tell her anything, as long as he doesn't expect anything in return. She can't bear the thought of those soft lips near her skin.

'How come she's not coming with her social worker? I thought that was part of the deal.'

'Social worker doesn't know, neither does Aunty Lou. It's a surprise.'

'Oh,' she says.

In the few months she's been here, she's learnt that the Heron boys, and their aunt and uncle, have their own set of rules, and they don't care very much for anyone else's.

'Did you know Aunty Lou's applying to adopt her?'

'You said.'

She waves him out of the way so she can fill the kettle. She's going to need strong coffee to get through today.

'Aunty Lou's got to go and ask my dad, get him to sign the papers and that.'

Tommy's dad is in prison. She's not sure what he's done, but she gets the impression it's violent and the sentence is a long one. Their younger sister slipped into the care system years ago, when their mother died or disappeared. She is never mentioned.

'It's down to me and Joe, you know,' he says, opening and closing his big hands. 'If we hadn't seen her working on that market stall, we would never have known she was back in Doncaster. But she looks just like our Aunty Lou did as a lass.'

Lou is a big woman in her early sixties, and it's hard to imagine her as a young girl, but there's a framed picture of her in the stadium building, from when she was first married, wearing a mini-dress and knee-length, white leather boots. She has a seventies hairdo piled on top of her head.

'What about the foster parents? Won't they ask where she is this evening?'

She gets the milk out of the fridge and the jar of coffee from the shelf.

Tommy shakes his head and looks as if he's going to tell her more intricate details about his sister's life. She hasn't got time.

'Can you make my coffee, Tommy, while I get dressed?'

She goes back into the bedroom and closes the door,

shoving the chair under the handle, just in case. She checks the curtains are fully closed. Taking off her cardigan and then her pyjamas, she shivers, although it isn't cold. There's no chance of a shower with Tommy out there. She pulls on jeans and a T-shirt and shoves her feet into a pair of fake purple Crocs. She checks the mirror and runs a comb through her cropped hair, rubs wax into her fingertips and runs her hands across her scalp, spiking the hair up. Her roots are getting longer. Her mum would hate this haircut. Too masculine, she'd say.

'Well, that's too bad,' she says, under her breath, driving her mother's unbidden presence away.

'What you doing in there?' Tommy calls from the kitchen. 'Or shouldn't I ask?'

He laughs a dirty laugh, which doesn't suit him. It sounds more like something he's copied off his brother, Joe.

'Coming.'

She applies eyeliner, thick on her top lid, thinner underneath and a quick swipe of mascara. That will have to do. Most days she doesn't even bother with that amount of make-up, but she doesn't want to look too tired today.

In the kitchen she adds cold water to the mug of coffee, which Tommy has managed to finish making for her, and drinks it as quickly as she can. She lays the bunting, carefully folded, over Tommy's outstretched arms, and scoops up the banner in one hand, while holding tight onto her bin bag of dirty clothes with the other. As they leave the caravan, she does her best to twist the key, so that the bolt will engage in the strike plate, but it's still too loose. It's not that she has anything to steal, but she needs to feel safe when she's back in her bed tonight.

They weave their way between old buses and vans, dumped here to sell on, at some unspecified time, by Tommy and Joe's dad, Levi Heron. His name is over the high, heavy gates to the yard, which open onto a track they call the Horse Road. Except the gates are never open, they're locked shut with a rusty chain and padlock that doesn't appear to have been touched in years. There's another caravan too, an old holiday static like hers, lifted from some campsite that was falling into the sea. This is Joe and Tommy's home, where they lived with their father before he got put away. It's close enough to hers that she can hear them talking, hear every word if they're shouting.

Their way in and out of the yard is a gap in the fence, a little wider than a car, leading directly onto the car park of the Chasebridge Greyhound Stadium. The hub of Derek and Lou O'Connor's business is the stadium building, a long, low construction with a two-storey section in its centre, standing in a potholed car park, the race track opening out beyond it. To the left of the stadium are the turnstiles and along its windowless rear there are two doors, like black eyes in an unsmiling face.

When she first arrived, Sarah thought it was derelict, even though she was told there were still three race meetings a week. Now there are visible signs of improvement. The back wall of the main stadium building shines with a fresh coat of white paint, and an attempt to resurface the car park has begun. On the far side of the car park, to the right of the main building, is the new kennel block, not quite finished, surrounded by the detritus of construction work.

As she and Tommy cross the car park towards the main

building, everything is quiet, just the insistent birds in the buddleia bushes, which cling to the rough soil around the base of the scrapyard fence. The builders would normally be here by now, but there's nobody on the building site. Lou and Derek won't be happy when they find out.

'What's up?' Tommy has stopped and is looking at her, his soft face puckered with concern.

'Nothing,' she says.

She quickens her pace. She needs to start work, keep moving, stop thinking. That's the best way.

CHAPTER SEVEN

Saturday morning

Sean drifted in and out of sleep, until the sound of an incoming text forced him to pick up the phone. It was Chloe. He put it down and turned over. His limbs ached with tiredness. He looked at the text again and realised he couldn't ignore it any longer.

Jack in bad shape. Will u come?

He pictured her in the hospital alone, his quiet half-sister, taking responsibility for a father she'd only known for just over a year. He should go, if not for Jack, then for her.

He texted back: *On my way*. But didn't move. He lay on his side and listened to the sounds of the flat. The fridge hummed in the kitchen. A carriage clock, left to Lizzie by her grandmother, ticked softly on the mantelpiece in the living room. He considered how often he was alone here. Since he'd moved in six months ago, his and Lizzie's shift patterns had forced them to pass like ships in the night. Sometimes a few words passed between them, but mostly just a Post-it note on the fridge. Most of the Post-its were for him: *Your turn to wash up. Lizzie xx* or: *Please clear your mess off the bedroom floor and hoover round the flat. Lx*

He thought about staying under the duvet – he could just snatch another hour – when his phone pinged with Chloe's reply.

C u soon. Thnx.

'OK, I'm coming,' he said to the empty flat and threw the duvet off.

At the hospital he followed a nurse with squeaky-soled shoes along a corridor lined with paintings. He'd noticed them last time Jack was here, walking with Chloe on the way to the cafe. She'd stopped to admire them.

'I did some paintings in prison,' she'd said. 'Landscapes, seascapes and escapes, I called them.'

She'd laughed, softly, at her own joke. He wasn't sure what to say. He didn't like to ask her about her time inside, in case it upset her. Ten years, and never once speaking up to defend herself. He couldn't imagine what it must have been like.

When Sean got to the ward, Chloe was sitting next to Jack's bed, a peeled tangerine on her lap. Her hands were wiry and birdlike. She separated a segment of fruit and put it in Jack's mouth and Sean felt a flash of gratitude towards her.

'Look who's here, Jack,' she said. 'It's Sean come to see you.'

Jack grunted and kept his eyes fixed on a piece of tangerine in her fingers.

'Is he all right eating that?' Sean said. 'Isn't it too acidic?'

'They've got him on some new meds, haven't they, Jack?'

Jack didn't answer, just waited like a baby for the next mouthful. He didn't look good, but Sean was sure he hadn't lost the gift of speech, just the will to use it around his son. Beyond the bay of six beds, Sean could see the corner of the nurses' station. He recognised the doctor they'd met the last time, chatting to a staff nurse behind the desk.

'I won't be a minute,' Sean said, but Jack didn't seem to notice.

He approached the doctor and waited for a lull in his conversation with the nurse.

'Excuse me, I'm Jack Denton's son, we met when he came in last time. What's the . . . I mean, how should we, what should we expect, from now on?'

'Hello, again.' The doctor smiled with straight, bleached teeth. 'I had a word with your sister this morning. She'll fill you in. Rest assured we're trying to make him comfortable.' The smile flashed brighter and Sean sensed the conversation was over. He turned to go, but the doctor called him back.

'Mr Denton?' he said. 'I hope this isn't too awkward, but Staff Nurse Tura has just reminded me, your father asked us to alter the records we hold here.'

'Sorry?'

'He's decided to name your sister as next of kin. We thought you'd want to know, to avoid any confusion.'

He turned away to read some notes, leaving Sean staring at his back. Nurse Tura kept her eyes down, tapping at a keyboard. Cowards, he thought, the pair of them.

When he got back to Jack's bed, the old man had fallen asleep.

'Do you fancy a coffee or something?' he said to Chloe.

She nodded and stood up, neatly sweeping the tangerine peel into the bin. They walked down towards the lift and he wondered if he should raise the next-of-kin thing. He didn't want her to think he was annoyed, but he was.

'What did he say, the doctor, when he did his rounds?' he asked, as they waited for the lift to make its way to their floor.

'Honestly?' she said.

The illuminated sign counted eight, seven, six, five. The door opened and half a dozen people shifted their formation to allow them space to get in.

'Yes, honestly,' he said.

The door closed.

'He's got weeks at most,' she said and concentrated on picking at a callus on the palm of her hand.

Sean sensed the lift passengers averting their eyes, as they descended together in silence.

'I'm sorry, Sean,' she said, as they stepped out at the ground floor.

'Don't worry about me,' he said. 'You've waited your whole life to meet your dad. You've barely had a year with him. I've had . . .'

He stopped himself from saying any more. It was a pact he'd made with himself. Whatever he thought of Jack, he didn't want it to sour Chloe's relationship.

'It's been amazing, Sean, having a dad.' She smiled up at him and he saw the same look on her face as when he'd first told her, in this very hospital, that the DNA test proved they were half-siblings. She wasn't bitter about what had happened in her life, just delighted that it was all getting better. He admired her for that.

He ordered two coffees and carried them to the table where she was waiting.

'The doctor told me about Jack naming you as next of kin,' he said.

She looked up suddenly and a spot of colour appeared on her cheeks.

'I didn't ask him to change it.'

'It's all right,' Sean said. 'Really. As long as you don't feel it's a burden. I mean, I'm here, you can phone me whenever you want, it's just that from now on the hospital will phone you first.'

He was relieved to have said it, convincing himself in the process that he meant it. She nodded, as if nothing else needed to be said on the subject.

'How's Lizzie?' she said.

'Good. You know, busy.'

'Busy Lizzie,' she laughed. 'No, that's wrong. She's much more classy than a Busy Lizzie.'

'How do you mean?'

'It's a flower,' she said, 'a bedding plant. The council's fond of putting them on roundabouts.'

'No, that wouldn't suit Lizzie at all.'

'She's more natural, flowing. A delphinium, maybe.'

'If you say so.' He was glad they were off the subject of his dad. 'Is it busy up at Halsworth Grange?'

'It is in the garden. The visitor numbers are picking up, now the weather's better.'

'How's Bill?' Sean asked. He liked Chloe's boss, a large, old-fashioned Yorkshireman. He'd been good for her, taken her on and trained her up in the gardening team.

'He's all right,' she said. 'Yeah, he's good. How's things with your work?'

He thought about telling her about his application for CID and the interview, but he hesitated. The fewer people who knew, the better. Then if he'd failed, it wouldn't be so embarrassing.

'Okay, got the whole weekend off, which makes a change. What about you?' he said. 'Are you staying here for a bit, or have you got other plans?'

'I'll check Jack's got everything he needs, then I thought I might get a haircut,' she said, pulling her ponytail in front of her and flicking through the split ends. 'Just a trim.'

'Good idea. Treat yourself.'

He said goodbye and watched her walk back towards the lifts. Outside, beyond the smokers attached to their drip stands, the sun was shining and the sky was intensely blue. He looked back at the hospital and mentally wished his sister well. Then he turned and headed back into the centre of town.

He thought about going to the market and buying something nice for Lizzie. He could surprise her with a fridge full of fresh vegetables and a pair of steaks. He might even look up a recipe and have a go at some cooking. It was ages since they'd had a meal together.

He could smell tomatoes and garlic when he opened the door.

'Something smells nice,' he said.

'I made pasta,' Lizzie said. 'There's some left in a pan in the kitchen, but it'll be cold by now. Where have you been?'

'Buying something for lunch,' he said.

'I've just told you, I made something. I'm going to have to go in a minute.'

'Go where?' he said, putting the bag down on the kitchen worktop.

He stood in the door of the living room and watched her, sitting on the sofa, jabbing at the keyboard of her laptop.

'Autopsy. Lucky to get anyone in to do it on a Saturday.'

'Is the boss going to be there?' He wondered if DI Khan would say anything to Lizzie about the application to CID.

'I expect so. He's the SIO. Unless he sends DS Knowles.'

'That'll be nice.'

'What's your problem with Knowles?' She was looking at him now, a tight frown line, like an exclamation mark between her eyebrows.

Sean shrugged. 'Nothing, just a joke Gav made.'

'Go on.'

'Forget it.'

Somehow telling her that Ivan Knowles was known as Ivor Biggun didn't seem very funny now.

'He's a bloody good detective,' she said, 'which is more than—'

She stopped herself, but the rest of the sentence hung in the air between them.

'Damn you,' he said, quietly, and immediately wished he hadn't.

He retreated to the kitchen. He should tell her about the interview. He should tell her about being at the hospital with Jack and Chloe. But he didn't. He took out a frying pan and peeled off one of the steaks he'd bought on the way home. When the fat was hot, he dropped it in and listened to the sizzle of the flesh searing. He looked at the other steak, soft and red against the butcher's plastic bag. An image of the man in the school flashed through his mind, his face a mangled mess of soft, bloodied meat.

He heard her go through to the bedroom and the sound of the wardrobe door opening and slamming shut. He turned the steak over and opened the bag of salad. The second steak lay in the plastic bag on the worktop. He was thinking about putting it in the bin. Lizzie came back into the kitchen and he changed his mind. He dropped the second steak into the frying pan. He wasn't going to waste it out of spite. He could manage both of them.

'I'm off, then,' she said. 'I'll let you know how it goes.'

Olive branch, he thought. Should he take it?

'Okay,' he said, and shifted the frying pan on the hob. 'What about the guy we picked up? Homsi? Anything on him?'

'A lot of blood on his T-shirt, but it looks like expiration, as if he was leaning over the victim after the injuries were inflicted, but while the victim was still alive. The blood on his hands may be from the floor. The tread pattern in his boots matches some of the marks on the floor, but there are other shoe smears, muddying the waters. Anyway, Khan's going to try and keep him in for as long as possible. Ivan interviewed him, and apparently he's saying he heard shouting and hid, then went to see if his friend was all right.'

'Why didn't he leave, like the others?'

'He told Ivan he had nowhere to go.'

'Gav thinks I should push for him to be charged with assaulting a police officer.'

'Did he, though?'

Sean shook his head. 'He missed, from less than a metre away. So he wasn't trying very hard.'

'Pleased to hear it,' she said.

'What about his trousers?'

'What about them?' she said.

'You were looking at the pattern of blood spatters, the killer

60

would have the victim's blood on their trousers. His looked clean.'

'Thanks, Sean,' she said. 'I do know how to do my job.'

'So?'

'So, nothing visible to the naked eye, but obviously all his clothes have been sent off for analysis.'

'Obviously,' he said and turned his attention to the steaks, to hide the feeling he'd been slapped down.

'Right,' she said, 'I'll see you later.'

He flipped the steaks onto a plate and put a handful of salad next to them. He should have put some chips in the oven, but it was too late now.

'Looks like I'm on the Atkins diet,' he said.

He looked at her, but she wasn't smiling.

'See you later,' he said. 'I'd better eat this before it goes cold.'

She turned and left the flat without saying goodbye. Sean took his food into the living room and sat down to watch the football. It was a European match, Poland–England, and he'd been looking forward to it, but tiredness overwhelmed him before he'd finished eating. He rested the plate on the floor and his head sank back against the settee. He heard the commentator's voice saying something about a foul, Pazdan guilty of a high boot on Walcott, and talk of a penalty, but he didn't hear the outcome.

CHAPTER EIGHT

Saturday afternoon

The market was busy. Chloe worked her way in from the edge to find the hairdressing stall, next to *Stan's Vinyl*. It hadn't been open long and she'd seen a piece about it in the local paper. The price was within her budget, so she hoped they could do a reasonable job. On the side where the counter would have been, the stall had been modified, its original shutters covered with three framed photos of glamorous hair models, two women and a man. The rest of the woodwork was painted gloss black. A door at one end opened onto a tiny two-chair, hairdressing salon. There was a girl in one of the chairs, twirling a long strand of hair round her finger, gazing into the mirror as she pinned it to the top of her head. Chloe waited until the girl noticed her.

'He won't be long,' she said, jumping up. 'He's just gone to get his lunch. Have a seat.'

Chloe sat down in the chair nearest the door.

'Got an appointment?' the girl said, flicking open a diary on the narrow shelf behind the chair.

'No. Do I need one?'

'Not really,' the girl giggled. 'But I'd better do it properly.' She assumed a voice: 'Let me see if I can fit you in, madam. What name is it, please?'

Chloe gave her name and the girl wrote it in the appointment book. Chloe looked around the cramped space. It was a hair salon in miniature, like being in a shed, or a child's playhouse. In front of her, on a shelf beneath the mirror, there was a stack of flyers.

Chasebridge Greyhound Stadium, Grand Re-opening. Two-for-one offer, burger and drink included.

She picked one up. The date was today. Jack would have liked this, but there was no chance of getting him out of hospital. She ran a finger over the picture of the greyhound on the cover, black and sleek, he was beautiful. She'd love a dog like that.

'D'you fancy it? A night at the dogs?' The girl was standing behind her.

Chloe shrugged. 'Maybe.'

'Here, take a couple, bring your mates. That's my family's place.'

'Lucky you,' Chloe said, 'having all those dogs around you. I love dogs.'

'I don't actually live there,' the girl said. Her smile vanished and Chloe wondered if she'd said something wrong.

Neither of them spoke for a minute, while the girl picked up a dustpan and brush and bent down to sweep up a pile of clippings.

'What was it you wanted doing?' she said.

63

'Just a cut and blow dry,' Chloe said.

'You've got nice hair,' the girl said, straightening up. 'It's very natural.'

She tipped the dustpan into the bin and wiped her hands on a paper towel.

Chloe wasn't sure what to say. Her hair always seemed lifeless to her. Straight and brown and uninteresting. She caught the girl peering thoughtfully at the back of her head. She was young, Chloe thought, no more than fourteen or fifteen. This must be her Saturday job. The girl's hair was curled and pinned on top of her head, as if to make her look older.

'I'd put a bit of colour in, if I were you,' the girl said. 'Highlights.'

'Another time,' said Chloe. She didn't want to say that she didn't have the money. 'A cut and blow will be fine today.'

'Good morning, good morning!' a voice called.

The mirror framed an image of a man with a leathery tan, standing in the doorway. He had very dark lashes, or was wearing eyeliner, Chloe couldn't decide which. He wore a tight V-neck jumper over a crisp white shirt and pinstriped trousers that clung to his hips and thighs.

'What can we do for you today?' he said. His smile appeared to fill the tiny space.

He listened to what Chloe wanted, and pursed his lips.

'I think we can do better than that, can't we? What about a bit of layering at the side and then we can work that into the fringe.'

He ran his hands through the hair on either side of her face. Lifting it and letting it drop.

'Just a trim,' she said. 'Two or three inches off the bottom. Not much. I need to be able to tie it back for work.'

'Well, if you're sure,' he said. 'It's a shame not to frame that face a bit more.'

'I'm sure,' she said.

He rested his hands on her shoulders for a moment longer than was comfortable. Behind him, reflected in the mirror, the girl stood watching.

He dampened Chloe's hair with a fine water spray and combed it through. His hands worked quickly with the scissors.

'Mel, darling,' he said to the girl, 'can you pop over to Gayle's and get me a bottle of water? I'm dying of thirst. There's a pound in the drawer. Do you want anything love?'

Chloe shook her head.

Once the girl had gone, the hairdresser started asking Chloe about herself. She told him she worked as a gardener and he picked up one of her hands to study it.

'What a shame,' he said. 'Such lovely skin.'

He lifted her hand and she thought for a moment that he was going to kiss it, but then the girl burst back into the cramped space holding a bottle of mineral water.

He finished cutting and let the girl blow dry Chloe's hair, while he watched. Then he stood behind the girl and reached round her, placing his hand over hers to guide her hand on the roller brush. The girl nodded.

'Like this?'

'That's better, we'll make a stylist of you yet.' The man smiled at her in the mirror.

Chloe looked at the curled ends of her hair and the way it

stood out from the top of her head, like a wig, she thought. She fought an urge to brush it back to normal. The girl, Mel, offered to put it up for her.

'Yeah, why not?' Chloe said, eventually. 'Yours looks nice.'

Mel beamed and filled her mouth with pins. When it was all done, Chloe looked like someone else, a girl from one of the hair magazines. Her hair was gathered up from the nape of her neck and curls fell by her face.

On the bus back to Chasebridge, Chloe took the two flyers out of her pocket and unfolded them. It would be lovely to go and watch the dog racing, but she had nobody to go with. There wasn't much point in a two-for-one offer, if there was only one of you.

The bus stopped opposite Asda and three people got on. An elderly man, a teenage girl and someone Chloe knew well. She watched as the woman fumbled for her bus pass and exchanged a joke with the driver. When she turned to make her way down the bus, Chloe gave her a little wave.

'Hiya, Maureen,' she said, almost too quietly, but Maureen had spotted her.

'Chloe, love,' Maureen grabbed the rail and swung into the seat beside her. 'Doesn't your hair look nice?'

Maureen was Sean's grandmother, but not Chloe's. She shared a dad with Sean, but their mothers were different, both dead now, and the one probably never even knowing the other existed. Despite not being a blood relative, Maureen had been trying to get her to call her Nan, but Chloe wouldn't. She tried with Mrs Casey at first, but Nan wasn't having that, so they agreed on Maureen as a compromise.

'What have you got there?' Maureen reached for one of

the flyers. 'Ooh, I love a night at the dogs. Two for one and a burger included, that's a good deal, isn't it? I heard they've done the place up. Shall we go?'

'I've never been. My mum always preferred the horses. What's it like?'

'It's a right laugh, great atmosphere. Less crowded than the horses.'

'Oh, good.' Chloe chewed her lip. 'I don't like big crowds.'

'Right then, it's a date. You can show off that fancy new hairdo.'

Chloe thought about how easy that was, suddenly to go from feeling alone, to the two of them making plans for the evening.

'And we can see if Lizzie and Sean want to come too,' Maureen said.

Chloe wasn't sure it would be Lizzie Morrison's scene, but she didn't say anything to Maureen, who was gathering up her shopping bags and ringing the bell.

The bus arrived at Winston Grove and they got off.

'I'll phone Sean,' Maureen said. 'See you later.'

Chloe waved goodbye and watched her cross the road by the shops, in the direction of her semi on Clement Grove. Chloe turned up Darwin Road towards the Eagle Mount flats. The sky behind them was bright blue and the sun glinted off the windows. Things didn't seem so bad when the sun was out. She caught her reflection in the library window and smiled at her new hairstyle.

CHAPTER NINE

Saturday

Sarah was in the kitchen. Despite having the door to the car park propped open with a fire extinguisher, it was hot in there. She was beginning to regret the rush of getting up and skipping her shower. Lou was doing the accounts at one of the cafe tables, from where she could keep an eye on Sarah and the Polish girl, Agnes, through the hatch. She sat with a tea towel on the table beside her to throw over the accounting books whenever she was interrupted. Lou O'Connor was a good boss, kind enough when the mood took her, but there was something steely about her, under her soft frame. Her husband, Derek, was a wiry little man with dyed black hair, plastered thinly across his narrow head. Jack Spratt and his wife, Sarah had heard one of the trainers call them. Not to their face, of course, they wouldn't dare.

At exactly midday, Derek burst into the cafe.

'Where are those lazy-arsed bastards when I need them?' He yelled. 'Joe and Tommy, where are they? I can't get any lights turned on in the new kennels. I've had the guy from the National Grid out, and he won't turn us on while there're cables in an open trench.'

'What about the Chuckle Brothers, I can't remember their names,' Lou said. 'But the two you've had on-site all month?'

'Didn't bloody turn up,' Derek said. 'I knew I shouldn't have paid them till it was all over, but they were bleating on about having debts to pay. Bloody typical. They'll be off on some other job, no doubt. If I find out who's employed them, I'll ring their bloody necks.'

'What's this got to do with Joe and Tommy?' Lou said.

'I need a bit of muscle,' he said. 'You don't expect me to do it, do you?'

Agnes looked towards the hatch, as if she was about to speak, but Sarah reached out and held her arm. She would be the one to help out, it was more appropriate. She might not be family, but she lived on-site, while Agnes just came in on race days, and while Sarah might be an outsider, Agnes was an actual foreigner.

She went through into the cafe and cleared her throat.

'They're in the yard,' she said. 'Joe said something about doing a repair on the lure mechanism.'

Derek swung round, as if he'd forgotten he employed two people in the kitchen, but his face softened when he saw her.

'Ah, Sarah, love,' he said. 'What would we do without you? Eh, Lou, how did we ever manage before this one turned up?'

Lou didn't answer. The truth was that Sarah took far more of Lou's workload than Derek realised. It was Lou who couldn't manage without her. Derek slid past her with a pat on the shoulder and a wink.

'Good lass,' he said, like she was one of his greyhounds, and scurried through the kitchen and out of the back door into the car park.

'Why did you say that?' Agnes whispered. 'About the lure? It's not true. Mechanical hare is not broken. Tommy was testing on the track, just maybe half an hour ago. It's working fine.'

'Mind you own business,' Sarah hissed. She didn't care about the truth. It wasn't important.

She and Agnes got on with their work in silence.

Forty minutes later, Lou finished her painfully slow writing in the two sets of accounting ledgers. She closed the books, gathered them to her chest, and carried them back into the kitchen.

'That's done for another month,' she said, with a sigh.

Sarah watched her go into the storeroom at the back of the kitchen and open the old safe with a heavy key, from a bunch she kept in her pocket.

'I could show you how to do it on the computer,' Sarah said. 'On a spreadsheet. It would save you loads of time.'

'No thanks,' Lou said. 'I don't want to get hacked by some snotty-nosed kid and have all my secrets let out on the Internet, for everyone to see.'

'Fair enough.' She stifled a laugh at Lou's ignorance.

Sarah waited for Lou to go upstairs to the bar, before entering the storeroom, which also housed the washing machine and dryer. She opened the washing machine and scooped the clothes into a clean plastic bin liner, then shoved the tea towels and bar towels into the dryer.

'Back in a minute,' she said to Agnes, 'and if Lou asks, tell her my period started. I've gone back to my caravan to get a tampon.'

Agnes looked disgusted, but Sarah didn't care. She stepped out of the back door and set off across the car park. The heat of the day was a shock and her feet kicked up miniature dust-storms in the ruined tarmac.

'Oi!' Joe Heron was shouting at her from the building site, but she pretended not to have heard. 'You silly bitch! Come over here, I want a word with you!'

She broke into a run, but hadn't reckoned on her rubber clogs, fake Crocs she'd got on a market stall. She stumbled in one of the potholes and fell forward, trying not to drop the bag of wet clothes. Although he had the whole width of the car park to cover, Joe Heron had long legs and was as fit as the dogs on the track. She'd barely picked herself up and checked the palms of her hands for grit, when he was on her.

'Don't you dare ignore me,' he spat.

'I'm not. I just need to get these clothes hung up to dry.'

'What's in there?' he said. 'Let's have a look.'

He snatched the bag out of her hands and pulled out a dark-grey hoodie.

'Doing our Tommy's washing now, are you? You could have done mine.'

'Just did him a favour, that's all.'

'Oh, yeah? In return for what?'

'Nothing!'

'You been leading my little brother on, have you? He might talk like a child, but he's all man between his legs.'

He shoved the bag at her groin and she grabbed it, trying to deflect the blow.

'I've got to go.' She stepped to one side to get past him, but he gripped her wrist.

'Why did you send Uncle Derek after us?' he said. 'You lost it or something?'

71

She shook her head. 'He needs your help. I thought it would be a good idea to keep him on side.'

'Don't tell me what to do.' He jerked her arm around and back, until the ball and socket in her shoulder screamed with pain. 'Don't ever tell me.'

A car engine made them both look up and they saw Derek's dark-green Jaguar pulling into the entrance. Joe dropped her arm. The pain in her shoulder had brought tears to her eyes, she blinked and let them fall as Derek looked her way.

'Just fill the trench in, Joe,' she hissed. 'Do what your Uncle Derek says, or I'll tell him about your other little business, and he won't like that.'

'What the fuck do you know?'

'Tommy tells me all sorts. He tells me how you charge those poor buggers rent next door, and if they don't pay, you smash up their things.'

'You know nothing.'

'I know you're also growing skunk in the old bus at the back of the yard. Imagine how your Uncle Derek would react if he knew about that.'

'You wouldn't dare,' he said.

'Wouldn't I?'

'You've got too much to lose.'

She looked at him for a moment, then a laugh bubbled up in her throat. 'You think so? I've got nothing to lose, Joe Heron, nothing at all.'

She turned away from him and hurried to her van, the bag clutched in both arms.

Five minutes later she'd hung the clothes on a rope, slung along the back of the van, away from view. There was a knock on the door. She was expecting Joe, an apology perhaps, or even a continuation of the argument, but whoever it was didn't try to force the door open. They waited.

She opened the door and there was Derek with a dog. It looked larger and heavier than a greyhound, but with the same sleek nose and sharp eyes.

'You all right, pet?' Derek asked. 'Only I didn't like what I saw back there.'

Sarah rubbed her arm and winced. 'I'll be okay.'

'Stay away from that lad,' Derek said. 'Don't tell my Lou I said this, but he's a wrong 'un. Too much like his dad. Bad breeding. Once they get the fight in them, you can't get it out. I'd hate to see you get hurt. We, Lou and me, we'd hate to lose you.'

'Thank you,' she said quietly. 'I'll be okay, although there is one thing I need some help with.'

'Your wish is my command,' he said, and swept the flat cap off his greased-down hair with a flourish.

'My door doesn't lock properly. I get a bit nervous at night.'

Derek looked at the loose strike plate. 'I'll get a screwdriver and some strong glue. That should do it.'

'If that's all it needs, I'm sure I can do it myself,' she said.

'Sure, you're a dab hand at most things,' Derek's eyes twinkled as he smiled at her. 'Pop up to the house tomorrow, when things are quieter, and I'll dig out what you need.'

'What shall I do tonight?'

The dog was looking at her, head cocked to one side.

'He likes you,' Derek said. 'I just got him off a fellow in The Royal Oak, in lieu of a debt he owes me. How about he stays here, with you? Be a guard dog.'

'What's his name?'

'Wolf. He's a bull lurcher. Three-parts sight-hound, one-part pit-bull. He's got a loud voice, and a good set of teeth, but he's kind. Just keep him muzzled around the other dogs.'

She looked at the dog and smiled. 'He's perfect, Mr O'Connor. Thank you.'

Before the punters arrived for the evening races, Tommy had planned a little party in the cafe. He brought the girl into the kitchen to meet Sarah.

'This is my sister, Melissa,' he said proudly.

She was pretty, her hair shot through with highlights and pinned up. Someone had done a good job. Too much make-up for a girl of her age, Sarah thought, but then she caught herself; she'd been just the same, wanting to be noticed. How things changed.

'I'm Sarah,' she said. 'Your hair's nice.'

'Did it myself. I'm learning to be a hairdresser,' the girl said. 'I've got a part-time job.'

'Yeah,' Tommy said, grinning proudly. 'She's doing ever so well.'

Sarah bit down on the urge to sneer. She'd been sweeping up cuttings and shampooing old ladies since she was fourteen. Not any more, though. She was no longer part of that world.

'That's nice,' she said, and hoped it sounded sincere. 'Do you work somewhere local?'

'In town. *Hair Today*, it's a new little salon on the market,' Melissa said, tossing her head as if to show off just how wonderful it was. 'Shall we see if Aunty Lou's coming, Tommy?'

Sarah was glad she wasn't expected to respond, because she was on the verge of losing her carefully controlled expression of disinterest. Of all the places the girl could be working, it had to be that one. Silly bitch. How dare she walk in here and drag up a tidal wave of unwanted memories, just when Sarah was trying to live a quiet life? Sarah blinked and shook away the feeling that she'd just done very badly at the quiet life experiment.

She picked up a broom and swept the kitchen floor until her arms ached. Then she stood and watched through the hatch as Joe and Derek arrived. They said to come on through, but she had too much to do. Besides, she didn't need any reminders of happy family reunions. Agnes was upstairs, setting up the bar and it gave Sarah a glimmer of satisfaction to note that she hadn't been invited.

When Lou came into the cafe, she looked from Melissa to Tommy's grinning face and back again, then she glanced at Joe, who'd cleaned himself up and was looking almost respectable, but she said nothing. Lou O'Connor didn't give much away, but Sarah was fairly sure she didn't like surprises.

'Look who's here, Aunty Lou!' Tommy bubbled with happiness. 'It's our kid.'

Sarah shut the hatch then. She didn't need to see any more. There were breadcakes to slice for the burgers and another pile of onions still to chop. She ran the kitchen knife back and forth on the wall-mounted sharpener and tested it on the flesh of her upper arm. At its touch, her skin opened in a hairline fissure and a thread of blood came to the surface. Finally, she felt something.

CHAPTER TEN

Saturday evening

Despite having lived on the estate as a child, Chloe had never been to the greyhound stadium.

'I didn't imagine it would look like this,' she said, taking in the wide expanse of the car park, gradually filling up with cars and minibuses.

Maureen stood next to her, catching her breath. They'd walked from her house, along the Horse Road, a track overgrown with thistles and ragwort, loved by dog-walkers and glue-sniffers, which led from behind the shops on Winston Grove.

'Aye, well,' she said. 'It's come on a bit since I first came here.'

There was a concrete mixer in one corner, and a new building beyond it, making it look as if the 'Grand Re-opening' had come too soon. To the left of the car park, there was a high corrugated iron fence, enclosing what looked like a scrapyard. They'd passed a gate to the yard on the Horse Road, but when you looked at it from the car park, it seemed that the scrapyard and the greyhound stadium were part of the same business.

The main building was newly painted in white with

CHASEBRIDGE STADIUM picked out in black lettering. A string of bunting hung over the turnstiles.

'Well, it was all different years ago,' Maureen said. 'Just a flapping track for the diehards. None of this two-for-one and meals-included malarkey.'

Chloe wrapped her arms around herself and wished she'd brought a coat. It had been beautiful earlier and she could still feel the glow of the sun on her face, but by six-thirty the air was cooling. She followed Maureen across the car park with a shiver.

They waited by the turnstiles and watched the cars pulling in and lining up to park. After a few minutes, Chloe spotted Lizzie's dark-blue Mazda hatchback. Sean and Lizzie got out, deep in conversation, until Maureen waved madly.

'Coo-ee!' she called, shrilly, and Lizzie's face snapped into a polite smile as she waved back.

Maureen led the way to the entrance. Chloe followed her. As she pushed hard against the cold metal of the turnstile, the feeling of being closed in gripped her for a moment and she caught her breath. She thought she heard a metal gate clanging shut, a key turning, but she shook the memory away. Maureen placed the flyers on the counter and said something to a young man behind a glass window. Chloe focused on Maureen's fingers, counting out their entrance money, and wished she would hurry up, so they could get out of this pen and into the open again.

The young man waved them through, and Chloe took a deep breath, as they filed out onto a tarmac path that ran along the side of the greyhound track, towards the main stadium building, a Union flag waving from its roof. Someone bumped into her from the side.

'Sorry!'

She looked round. It was the girl from the hairdresser's. Mel, the man had called her.

'Hello,' Chloe said.

'It's just you stopped,' Mel said, giggling, 'and I didn't!'

Mel teetered on high heels, and Chloe could smell alcohol on her. She was too young for that, Chloe thought. She'd never been much of a drinker herself, even at Mel's age.

'You've kept your hair up, then!' Mel said.

'Yes,' Chloe said. 'I fancied a kip this afternoon, but I had to make do with sitting bolt upright on the settee, trying not to mess it up.'

The girl laughed.

'Thank you for fixing it up for me,' Chloe said.

'That's all right. It suits you,' Mel said. 'Are you okay? You look cold.'

'Freezing,' Chloe said. 'I thought it would be warmer than this.'

'I'm boiling,' Mel laughed. 'You can borrow my jacket if you want.'

It was like a miniature biker jacket, a pattern of a heart shot through with an arrow picked out in studs on the back. It was pretty.

'It's okay,' Chloe said. 'No, I couldn't.'

'Go on, take it. I'll come find you if I want it back, and if you can't find me, leave it with the girl in the cafe.'

Before Chloe could protest any more, Mel had thrown the little leather jacket across her shoulders. It was warm from the girl's skin and Chloe pushed her arms into the sleeves, grateful to be protected from the cooling evening air.

'See you later,' Mel said and tottered off with a little wave.

Chloe wondered about her. She was so trusting, keen to make friends when they'd only just met. It reminded her of some of the girls she'd known in prison. She thought about what Mel had said earlier that day. This was her family's place, but she didn't live with them. It occurred to Chloe that the girl might be in care. She had that look about her. Tough and vulnerable at the same time, and older than her years.

Maureen was waiting for Chloe by the main entrance, a set of double doors leading to a staircase. On one side of the doors was the cafe and on the opposite side was a room full of men standing on little platforms, with signs next to them, covered in names and numbers. It was like the bookies' stands at the horse racing, but more cramped. For a moment she felt the grip of claustrophobia and a memory of being a small child, knee-high in a crowd of dark-trousered men, the air full of cigarette smoke, losing her mother's hand in the noise and the crush.

'All right, pet?' Maureen was there, her hand on Chloe's arm. 'You look like you've seen a ghost.'

'I'm okay,' she said. 'Just, you know, all these people.'

'Say no more,' Maureen said. 'Why don't you stay outside? Find yourself a place to stand along the rail, you'll get the best view of the race. I'll bring you out a drink and something to eat.'

'Thanks.'

Chloe wanted to say something else, but she was stuck for words. That was the good thing about Maureen, you never needed to explain anything to her. She understood how you felt.

Chloe turned away from the building towards the track. It wasn't a big place. She knew there were greyhound stadiums where there were seats and stands all the way round, and thousands of people crammed in to watch the racing. She'd seen it on the television. But here there was only room for a couple of hundred to stand by the rail and on the flimsy-looking stands in front of the building. Tonight there were no more than about twenty or thirty people milling around outside, but it was still early. She looked up and saw a long window on the first floor of the stadium. It was lit with coloured disco lights. There was Mel again, waving down at her, a drink in her hand. Chloe waved back as a voice on the loudspeakers announced the first race.

She stood close to the rail and watched as men and women in white coats began to lead the dogs out. They talked to them and pulled their leads close. The dogs sensed the excitement and circled their handlers. Each dog had a number on its coat and Chloe wondered which one she would follow. There was a dark-grey dog, not quite black, being led across the grass by a woman in a headscarf. She heard the announcer say the dog's name: 'Susi's Holiday, number six.' *That's the one*, she thought. *She can be my winner*.

Someone nudged her arm.

'Here, I've got you a can of Fanta,' Maureen said, 'and a cheeseburger, is that okay?'

'Thanks,' Chloe said, 'how much do I owe you?'

'It's all included, remember?' Maureen said. 'The voucher covers the food and one drink.'

Chloe was both pleased and relieved. She'd spent more

money than she should have done today. First there were the things Jack needed in hospital, then she'd paid for the haircut. It wasn't expensive, but still, she didn't have much left. The dogs were being led to the traps and she watched them go past. Each one was so perfect, but she was happy with her choice, a dark-grey dog with long limbs and fine-boned head. The dog looked round and Chloe felt it had seen her, their gaze locking together for a moment, until the handler led it away.

She leant against the rail, barely conscious of Maureen standing next to her, and kept her eyes fixed on the black and white striped jacket of number six, as the dogs hurtled out of the traps and round the track in a blur. In seconds, they'd almost completed the circuit. She felt the sand fly up, peppering her cheek, as the dogs rushed over the finish line. It was over so quickly.

'The four dog! Mr Liviiandi!' Maureen said, clapping her hands. 'I put a pound on him. We can stretch to another drink after I collect my winnings. Are you coming up to the bar before the next race?'

Chloe shook her head. She still had a half-eaten burger and she intended to make the can of Fanta last as long as she could.

'I'm all right,' she said. 'I want to watch the dogs going back to the kennels.'

She walked along the rail. Most of the punters were moving towards the building to collect their winnings from the bookies, or upstairs to the bar to drown their sorrows. The handlers had put the dogs back on their leads and were leading them into a low shed beyond the stands. Susi's Holiday nudged her handler and the woman stroked her head and murmured to her.

Chloe had reached a gate with a sign that read: TRAINERS

ONLY. She put her can down on the flat top of the gatepost and craned round to see into the shed. It was then she sensed that someone had come to stand next to her. There were very few spectators at this end of the track, so she wondered why anyone would need to stand so close. She didn't look round, trying to not miss a last glimpse of her beautiful dog.

'All right?' a man's voice said.

She turned to see a tall young man with curly black hair and blue eyes, who stepped back when he saw her face.

'Eh? I thought you were someone else,' he said. He reached out and held her arm, rubbing his thumb over the leather of the jacket. 'Where did you get this?'

'It belongs to my friend,' she said, hoping that knowing the girl for less than a day qualified to count her as a friend. 'She lent it me. I'm going to give it back.'

'Just make sure you do,' he said.

He squeezed her arm tightly until she pulled it away and he walked off, leaving her clutching her drink, wondering what the hell had just happened.

Lizzie dabbed tomato ketchup from the corner of her mouth with a paper serviette.

'I hate to think what was in that burger,' she said. 'Horse?'

Sean thought the cafe food was all right, but he didn't say anything.

'Right, then,' Lizzie had a false cheeriness in her voice. 'That was delicious. Shall we go back upstairs and get a drink? First round's on me.'

They met Maureen coming in through the main front doors.

'What will you have, Maureen?' Lizzie said.

The announcer named the runners for another race.

'Don't worry, love, I can get my own. I backed a winner.' Maureen headed for the stairs. 'And I want to get another bet on.'

'I'll catch her up,' Sean said.

'I'll be there in a minute,' Lizzie said. 'I need a pee.'

At the foot of the wide staircase his nan stood still, looking lost, as a crowd of people poured down both sides of the central bannister. Sean was quickly at her side and took her arm. The group was noisy and dressed for a night out.

'Look at those heels!' Maureen said, too loudly.

A girl with her hair piled up in loose curls shot her a look, before reaching for the bannister and steadying herself on towering spikes. The shoes were at Sean's eye level. They were joined by a pair of men's loafers, patent black, with a crocodile skin pattern. The owner of the shoes was a head shorter than the black-haired girl and forty years older. He hooked his arm in hers and said something that Sean couldn't hear but it made her laugh. Sean and Maureen stepped aside as they passed.

Maureen took a seat by the viewing window, a glass of white wine on the shelf in front of her.

'It's my lucky night,' she said. 'I'm five pounds up and we've only just started.'

The pattern of placing bets, following each race intently, then making her way back to the betting office, was keeping Nan entertained, but after four races, he sensed that Lizzie was getting bored.

Before the next race he suggested they go outside.

'We could keep Chloe company.'

'Will you be all right, Maureen?' Lizzie said.

'Of course I will, you two go on. If you've not been before, you should see it close up.'

They went downstairs into the cool dark air. The floodlights bathed the grass in such a virulent light it made the grass look fake.

'It's better out here,' Lizzie said. 'There's more atmosphere. Look at that dog, he's huge. And that one's really sweet, the little black one with the white nose.'

Sean was watching the punters, not the dogs. This was where the real money changed hands. The serious gamblers ignored the Tote office upstairs, they even shunned the bookies' room downstairs, where a few old-timers still wore the traditional pork-pie hats. Deals mumbled outdoors were made for handfuls of grubby banknotes in the shadows around the track. A young man caught Sean's eye, dragged hard on a cigarette and started ambling towards him. Sean looked away fast. He'd given off the wrong signal.

He spotted Chloe, standing by the rail, just beyond the finish line, and walked over to her.

'Great view you've got here,' Sean said.

She nodded and moved along to let him and Lizzie in. There were families here, with children who looked like they should be in bed, couples and workmates. Even a hen-do, in matching printed T-shirts. It seemed like a nice enough crowd, but Chloe hugged her jacket close to her and kept looking around uneasily.

The dogs were out of the traps and rushing past them. On the far side of the track they passed a stand of tall, dark conifers and Sean realised what was on the other side of those trees. They marked the boundary to Chasebridge Community High School. Beyond the trees the school site would be swathed in incident tape, waiting for daylight and another day of combing through the classrooms and grounds for evidence. Lizzie had told him she'd delegated to Janet Wheeler so she could have a day off tomorrow. Her first in two weeks. The autopsy hadn't given them more than they could see with the naked eye, and unless the toxicology tests said different, the victim appeared to have been attacked in his sleep, arms in his sleeping bag, unable to defend himself.

'Look!' Lizzie cried. 'That one's broken away.'

The crowd had seen it and a roar went up, a mixture of excitement and disappointment. A dog had left the track and was running right across the grass in the centre. He rejoined the track ahead of the mechanical hare. The crowd held its breath. A white-coated dog handler was running towards the animal and someone was shouting.

'Stop the hare!'

But it was too late. The lure hit the dog's foreleg and threw him, yelping, into the air.

'No race! No race!' the voice came over the tannoy. 'Race abandoned. The race will not be rerun. All bets will be refunded. Please clear your dogs from the track.'

Chloe was gripping the rail, shaking her head.

'Poor thing,' she said. 'Why did he do that?'

'Probably thought it was quicker,' Lizzie said.

Chloe looked at her, tears in her eyes. 'It's not a joke.'

'Sorry, no, you're right. Maybe he was distracted by something.'

An older man, beyond Chloe, turned round. His flat cap

was pulled down hard over tufts of grey hair, sprouting over his ears.

'Something in the hedge,' he said. 'Rabbits or a fox, I reckon. Bloody shame. That's his career over.'

'What will happen to him?' Chloe asked.

He shrugged. 'Might be kinder to put him down. But the vet'll try to save the leg. Then, if he's lucky, he'll be off to the rescue charity.'

'Hey, don't be upset,' Sean said. 'Do you want to come upstairs, Chloe? Get something to drink.'

'In a minute,' she said.

She moved away, towards the end of the rail and the gate to the trainers' area. He noticed she was still wearing the jacket the girl had lent her when they first arrived. It was the same girl in the high heels, who'd passed them on the stairs. He wondered how Chloe knew her. His sister didn't have many friends, just those she worked with at Halsworth Grange, and this girl didn't look like a gardener.

Near the trainers' area Sean noticed a group of people clustered round a room marked Veterinary Office. A bright, fluorescent light was on inside. A man was taking off a tweed jacket and replacing it with a pale-green apron. He rolled up his sleeves and turned expectantly to the open door.

The injured dog was being carried across the grass in a sling, his head lolling to one side and his eyes wild with pain. It was almost unbearable to watch, but Chloe couldn't help it. Someone opened the little gate and the procession passed in front of her. He was a reddish-fawn colour, like a deer. His saliva frothed into his muzzle.

'Oh my God!' Mel was standing beside her. 'It's Whisper.'

Chloe turned and saw the younger girl's face wet with tears.

'The vet's going to try to save his leg,' Chloe said, ignoring the other part of what flat-cap man had said. 'He's going to be okay.'

'He's so beautiful!' Mel said. 'He's one of Derek's dogs, did you know?'

'Derek?'

'My uncle. Derek O'Connor. He took me to look at him before the race. Indian Whisper is his full name, said he was going to be a winner one day. I thought he was just so beautiful.'

They turned and followed the group towards the door of the vet's office. Then the door closed and they were left outside.

'I'm going up to the bar,' Chloe said. 'My brother's getting me a drink. Do you want to come?'

Mel shook her head. 'I'll stay here, see what happens. I'll come and tell you if there's any news.'

'Thanks,' Chloe said, and then they were hugging and Chloe wondered again about how easily the girl attached herself to a new person, although Chloe didn't mind, she liked her.

Sean stood at the bar. Most of the other punters had come inside and sat clustered around tables, looking up at screens, or gathered at the viewing window. Since the dog's accident, the mood had changed. Disgruntled punters queued up at the betting office window to get their refunds. The jostling at the bar felt more urgent, less good-natured.

A group of young men had pulled three tables together.

87

They were dressed in tight-fitting T-shirts and short-sleeved shirts, all designer brands. A lads' night out. The number of empties on the three tables suggested they'd already had a few. Sean felt his response officer instincts kicking in. He kept them in his peripheral vision while he placed his order with the barmaid, a slim girl with dyed red hair and a Polish accent.

As he was carrying a tray of four drinks over to the window, Cokes for him and Chloe, white wine for Nan and Lizzie, he noticed the red-haired girl approach the three tables and the group of lads. She began to clear their glasses.

All of a sudden someone shouted: 'I was fucking drinking that!'

'Okay,' she said. Conversations stopped and there was just the background tinkling of a chart song playing without enough bass. 'No problem.'

The man who'd spoken stood up. 'Who says it's not a problem? You filthy Polish bitch. You don't get to come over here and speak to me like that!'

Sean put his tray down and reached into his back pocket for his police badge. 'Steady,' Lizzie said. 'There's six of them, and you're not at work.'

'I'm not standing by and having that little racist think he can speak to her like that,' Sean said. 'Look at this lot. Nobody else is going to back her up.'

He crossed the floor and the group started getting to their feet. The girl was backing off, but the young man had picked up the almost empty pint glass and swung it at her. The last inch of liquid sloshed over the side, but it didn't catch her.

As Sean held his badge up and was about to speak, two figures appeared, at a run, from behind the bar. One was tall and muscular, with dark curly hair and blue eyes, the other was fatter, with a soft face, but enough like the other man for Sean to assume they were brothers.

'Put your badge away, copper,' the taller one said. 'We've got this.'

They took the racist guy under his arms and lifted him away from the table. His feet didn't touch the ground as they carried him towards the fire exit. The fat brother aimed a high kick at the security bar and the door opened out into the night. They appeared to be at the top of a metal staircase. Sean hoped to God they weren't going to throw the man down the fire escape, but as he moved towards the door, it slammed shut in his face. He turned back and in the hush, realised he was being watched from every table, and the looks weren't friendly.

Sean put his badge in his pocket and approached the barmaid, to see if she was all right. She was stacking glasses on her tray, eyes down, as if nothing had happened. She lifted the tray and in passing, whispered, 'Better if you leave, I think. The management is not a friend of the police.'

Lizzie insisted on driving Chloe and Maureen home. Although it wasn't far, the lift would mean they could avoid the cut-throughs and back alleys of the estate. Maureen was annoyed because they'd missed the last race, but Lizzie was adamant that they should go. There was no point in making a scene. Chloe had been more than happy to go home, she didn't look as if she'd enjoyed the evening very much.

They dropped Maureen first, then turned up Darwin Road towards the high-rise blocks. Sean felt strange leaving his half-sister at the door of Eagle Mount One, his childhood home. He would never get used to it.

'Oh, shit!' she said, as she stepped out of the car. 'I never gave Mel her jacket back.'

'Who's Mel?' Sean said.

'The girl who gave me the flyers. Her family own the track.'

'You could take it back tomorrow,' he said.

'She doesn't live there,' she said. 'I've got college on Monday, so I'll go and find her after that. She works on the market on Saturdays, so maybe she's there after school too. I'd rather not go back to the track. Not on my own, anyway.'

'That's sensible,' he said. 'It's not the sort of place you want to spend too much time hanging around.'

'Thanks, Sean,' she gave him an ironic smile. 'Maybe you need to start telling your grandmother how to suck eggs, too!'

'Sorry.'

'No, I mean it. Maureen thinks it's wonderful. She loves a flutter, and now the place has been done up, you'll have a job keeping her away.'

'But it's not your cup of tea? Maybe you noticed things she doesn't. She can be a bit naïve.'

'It's not that.' She shook her head, as if she was about to say something else, then changed her mind, and turned to go inside.

'Well, have a good day tomorrow,' he said, 'whatever you get up to.'

'I think I'll go and see Jack,' she said.

'Right,' he said. 'Thank you.'

'You don't have to thank me,' she said. 'He's my dad too.'

He watched Chloe cross the lobby to the lift, then walked back to the car.

Lizzie switched on the stereo. It was her usual playlist, too folky for Sean's taste, but he liked this Vance Joy number, 'Riptide'. It had a line about being afraid of dentists that made him smile.

'Home James, and don't spare the horses,' Lizzie said.

'You what?'

'Something my dad always says. I think it was a music hall song that he learnt from his father.'

'Aye, well, home's about right. I'm shattered.'

'Me too. I'm glad I've got a day off tomorrow,' she said. 'I might be able to think straight by Monday. There's something I can't quite put my finger on about that school murder.'

'Oh?'

'No, I mean I have to stop thinking about it, then maybe I'll have a light bulb moment when I'm not expecting it.'

He watched the estate and the ring road go by, as she drove them back towards the centre of town. The encounter at the track had left him feeling uneasy. Perhaps he should have pursued the men down the fire escape. He wondered what DI Khan would have done. If it had been a scenario on the CID interview, how would he have answered the question? He shook away the feeling that he should have done more. Lizzie was singing along to the song, and he joined in, badly and loud, to silence the thoughts in his head.

CHAPTER ELEVEN

Sunday morning

Sean had been dreaming about a bus stop and a man in a yellow coat, who said his name was Happiness. There were several people under the canopy of the bus stop, and the rain was coming down hard. There was nothing else there, no street, no shops, just rain. The people were grey, and only the yellow coat stood out.

Then he was awake, blinking in the bright sunshine that poured into the bedroom. The dream began to fade and he couldn't recall any details, except the name and the coat. If he'd been in his old bedroom, at his nan's house, he'd have shared his dream with her, over a full English breakfast, and she'd have enjoyed trying to interpret it. He stretched and looked at his watch. Nine-thirty. Nan would be awake by now. He could ring her, but he didn't want to disturb Lizzie.

He watched Lizzie's shoulder rise and fall with her breathing. When they got home from the dog track, they'd made love for the first time in a week. He'd been aching for her, terrified that it would all be over too soon. Then he'd kissed her slowly and she kissed him back, her fingers feeling their way across his shoulders.

They'd fallen asleep soon after, still wrapped round each

other. At some point in the night, they'd rolled apart and now she lay with her back to him, breathing softly.

He checked his phone and saw a text from his nan.

THANK LIZZIE FOR THE LIFT. LOVELY NITE OUT. LETS DO IT AGAIN.

Maybe not, he thought. He put his phone back on the bedside cabinet and closed his eyes again. He let the sound of Lizzie's breathing lull him back to sleep.

When they woke, they made breakfast together, although by now it was nearly two in the afternoon. It felt like it used to, when he first moved in, just being together in a comfortable way, fitting neatly into this little kitchen at the top of the house, where the light was always brighter than in the square below.

The smell of bacon cooking made his stomach growl. In the living room he pulled the little table out from against the wall and opened out the drop-down side. They hardly ever ate at the table, but Sunday brunch was a ritual. Lizzie had been out for the newspaper, the big, thick national with the magazine, which rarely mentioned Doncaster, unless it was a scandal.

'Nothing in about our school murder?' he said.

She was reading the travel pages and looked at him wearily.

'Leave it, Sean,' she said. 'I'm trying to enjoy a day off. I've only just got the smell of that place off my skin.'

'Sorry,' he said, adding a shot of tomato ketchup to his bacon sandwich. 'I just wondered if you'd had your light bulb moment.'

'No, I haven't.'

'Fair enough,' he said.

He took a bite of his sandwich and chewed hard. Then poured himself another glass of orange juice. He hadn't been going to tell her yet, because he wanted to know the outcome before he jinxed it, but he couldn't keep it to himself any longer.

'I applied for CID.'

She looked up from the paper. 'Really? When?'

'Three weeks ago.'

'Three weeks? But what about the forms? I would have helped you fill them in.'

'I know you would. But I wanted to do it on my own. Don't look so worried, I got Sandy Schofield in the admin office to check my spelling.'

'Oh. When will you hear?'

'I had a panel interview last week.'

'That's great,' she was smiling. 'Well done!'

'Nothing's decided yet, don't get too excited.'

'Of course.' She slid her arm around his waist and squeezed him gently. 'I'm proud of you for doing it, even if you have been a bit secretive.'

Sean had worked hard to overcome his dyslexia. He'd gone back to college and taken the English and Maths he'd needed to become a police constable, but it was still a struggle sometimes, and he'd been terrified of misreading a question in the application, or making a stupid spelling mistake. He knew they would be looking for reasons to disqualify people, and he had to prove he was as good as anyone else. His old friend Sandy had been kind and gentle with him. She'd just corrected the spellings, but not interfered with what he wanted to say in his personal statement.

'What next?' Lizzie said.

'Just waiting for a letter.'

'Oh!' Her hand flew to her mouth. 'I think it came yesterday. There was a letter for you and a bank statement and a catalogue. I'm sorry. I just put them in the kitchen drawer when I was clearing up.'

He stood up too fast and his knee nudged the flap of the table, sending his plate crashing into the orange juice carton. Lizzie caught it just in time.

'Steady!' she said.

'Why do you have to be so tidy?' he said. 'I only have to put something down for a minute and you put it away. How was I supposed to know the post was in the drawer?'

She frowned, and he wished he hadn't been so easily riled, but fear was twisting his guts and a clammy sweat broke out on his neck. He was in the kitchen and yanking open the drawer. There was the catalogue, a bank statement and, underneath, a white envelope addressed to Sean P Denton. His fingers shook. Finally he managed to rip the envelope open and pulled out a letter, scanning it for the key words: *pleased . . . accept . . . traineeship.*

Lizzie was silent in the other room. He went back to her, a smile splitting his face.

'I'm in,' he said. 'Meeting with DI Khan on Monday morning to talk about the next steps.'

'Oh, Sean!' her eyes shone. 'I'm so bloody proud of you. I can't believe you went and did all this without telling me.'

'So, now I've been a good boy,' Sean said, putting his arm round her and pulling her close to him, 'and one day soon I'll be a real detective in CID, are you going to tell me what you think happened with our school victim?'

She pulled away. He couldn't tell if she was amused or angry.

'You don't give up, do you?'

He shook his head. 'Tenacious, my last appraisal said. That's good, right?'

'Tenacious. From the Latin, *tenere*, to hold on to something. Yes, that's about right. But you need to go carefully.'

'What do you mean?'

'You know,' she said, 'going beyond your pay grade. You've got a reputation for stepping over the line.'

She folded the paper over and put it down.

'Well,' he said. 'What about my attacker? Surely I'm entitled to know about him.'

Finally she smiled.

'Okay, you win,' she said. 'You know the man who tried to bottle you, Elyas Homsi, had blood on his skin and on his T-shirt, which matched the same blood type as the victim? Well, we're still waiting for the full DNA report, but it's likely that it is the victim's blood. But Homsi didn't have the right blood spatter on his trousers. So I don't think he's the killer, I think he got there after the attack, but while the victim was dying. The other odd thing is that we haven't found the victim's shoes. You might assume he had them next to him where he slept.'

'Maybe they're still in those piles of clothes and bedding, covered in blood.'

'We'll have to wait and see. There's bagloads of stuff to work through. But he really is a Syrian refugee. The letter he was carrying confirmed he'd got through the first stage of hearings and was just waiting for the next part of the process.'

'Who was the letter from?'

'The Refugee and Migrants Advice place in York. I guess they were acting for him.'

'RAMA?' he said.

'Yes,' she said. 'The organisation who worked with us on the Su Mai case.'

He nodded. It took him back to his first case. Not yet twenty-one, a rookie police community support officer, dealing with the murder of an unknown woman.

'What about the victim?' he said.

'Homsi says he was called Abbas. He's from Northern Iraq and, he said, his friend.'

'So who killed Abbas?'

'He doesn't know, or isn't saying.'

'Did Abbas have any ID on him?'

'No.'

'So how do we even know that's his real name?'

'I think I've told you enough,' she shook her head. 'When you start as a trainee detective, you'll have to pretend you heard nothing from me.'

She got up and went into the kitchen. It would be great if he could keep working on this case. In the response unit he'd become tired of attending incidents, dealing with the immediate situation and then handing everything over to CID, sometimes never even knowing the outcome. Soon he'd be on the other side, seeing the process through to the end and seeing justice done.

He heard Lizzie open the fridge.

'Have you been drinking my wine?'

He joined her in the kitchen and they stood close again, the chilled air from the fridge washing over them.

'That bottle of Italian white?' he said. 'We took it to your parents' house last Sunday.'

He drove, she drank, that was the deal when they went to see Mr and Mrs Morrison.

'Isn't it a bit early for wine?' he said. 'We've only just had breakfast.'

'It's the afternoon and I need to relax.'

'Here,' he reached into the cupboard and took down a tiny bottle of Prosecco. 'I bought you this the other night and forgot about it. I'll make you a Buck's Fizz.'

He gave her a squeeze and she leant back against him.

'Thank you,' she said. 'But we should share it. To celebrate.'

'You have it,' he said. 'I fancy a cup of tea.'

They curled up together on the settee and soon fell asleep again. When he woke, it was nearly four o'clock. It was a mistake to sleep so much in the day. He would spend the next few nights fighting insomnia. He decided to let her sleep, lifted his numb arm carefully from behind her shoulders and tiptoed into the bedroom.

He wondered about the two men in the school. Homsi had asked them: *What has happened to my friend?* But were they really friends? Perhaps they were just people who coexisted in the same hellhole of a squat. Something tugged at the back of his mind. He picked up his phone and scrolled through his address book to see if he still had the number. There it was: RAMA, the Refugee and Migrant Advice Centre in York. He'd liked Karen Friedman, the woman who worked there. He'd helped her to solve the mystery of her missing brother. No point in ringing on a Sunday, he'd do it tomorrow. After his meeting with Khan.

'Sean?' Lizzie's sleepy voice came from the living room. 'What are you doing?'

'Nothing,' he said and put his phone in his pocket.

CHAPTER TWELVE

Sunday morning

'Sarah?'

Someone is calling her. Lou's voice. That bloody lock still isn't fixed. She'll have to dodge sleazy Derek, up at the house, to get the gear to mend it. She can hear the older woman pulling herself up the steps of the static caravan, wheezing.

'I wish the doors weren't so bloody narrow in these things.'

Sarah stands at the foot of her bed, checking herself in the mirror, which runs above the headboard. She pulls her clean T-shirt down over her jeans. Apart from the shadows under her eyes, she looks okay.

'I'll be right out!' she calls.

'Hello,' Lou says. 'Hello, Wolf, there's a good boy.'

She's forgotten about the dog. He didn't bark when Lou came in. Some kind of a guard dog he's turned out to be.

She comes through to the kitchen.

'You got it looking nice,' Lou says. 'It's important in a small home.'

'Thanks,' she says.

'When I was a child, we lived in a proper trailer, a caravan, you'd call it. It was beautiful inside. White lace at the windows and Grandma's china lined up on the shelf. My brother Levi cried his eyes out when we had to leave. I'll never forget the hatchet-faced policewoman, standing there, watching while we got into the social worker's car.'

Wolf nuzzles against Lou's hand, sniffing cautiously.

'Late night, was it?' Lou says. 'You look tired.'

'I was over at Joe and Tommy's.'

''Nuff said. Come on, there's a cafe and a bar area that won't clean themselves and I haven't even looked at the toilets yet. I'll get the kettle on.'

She turns to go.

'Hang on, I'm coming.'

Sarah puts her feet into her fake Crocs. The dog pricks up his ears and watches her.

'Sorry, Wolf, you'll have to wait.'

As they leave the yard, Sarah notices the door of Joe and Tommy's static opening a crack. Someone is watching.

'Is that you, Joseph?' Lou calls. 'Fancy getting up of a Sunday morning and putting a bit of work in, like the rest of us?'

The door closes again.

'Joe keeping an eye on his latest conquest, is he?' Lou says.

Sarah says nothing, just keeps her eyes on the uneven surface of the yard and follows Lou into the car park.

'I don't want you getting mixed up with that nephew of mine,' Lou says, over her shoulder. 'It won't last. It never does. And when your heart's broken, you won't want to stay, and that would be a shame. You're a hard worker and no trouble.'

Sarah hopes she isn't expected to reply.

Once inside the stadium building, she goes straight to the cleaning cupboard.

'I'll do the Gents first,' she says.

'You're keen.'

'It's the worst job. Gets it over with. Then I'll get a brew and catch my breath.'

'Fair enough.'

When she's finished, Sarah stands back and looks around the Gents' toilets. The cistern handles gleam. The smell of lemon-scented disinfectant dominates the undertones of stale urine. Two lavatory pans, two urinals, and their glazed tile surrounds all shine white. She has missed nothing. Where there was a reddish-brown mark to the right of the urinals, she's rubbed so hard she's begun to take the paint off. She runs the tap in the sink and rinses her cloth, squeezing it and soaking it in turn, until the water runs clear.

Her fury at what Joe and Tommy did in here last night is beginning to subside. There was no point in showing Joe how angry she was, he'd just match it with even more aggression, but last night, she let Tommy know that she was very disappointed in him. Drawing attention to himself by beating up a punter was a stupid move. She could see he'd got confused, carried away with his role as a knight in shining armour, but it was only the Polish girl, and nothing actually happened to her. Still, she thinks, standing back and checking the wall for any remaining spatters of blood, better to be safe than sorry, just in case anyone goes to the police.

She was wary of the boys at first, but then she realised they were wary of her. She wasn't from their world, stumbled into it by accident, and stayed. She was different when she arrived, still fretting about her make-up, and whether her tan was even, or what shoes she was going to wear. But she soon stopped caring. She began to fade into the background. Just a cleaner. Most people ignored her, as if she didn't speak English. Well, that was fine. Just fine. It suited her. She couldn't carry on the life her parents had mapped out for her. That plan had been snatched from her, torn up and trampled into the dirt. Her parents missed her, even when she was still with them. They missed the person she was supposed to be. They missed her so much, she became invisible to them. She's better off here, invisible, but in control and without them nagging her.

She's still looking at herself in the mirror when the air cracks with a sudden noise. A shot, it must be. She watches her mouth open in shock. She's surprised she didn't scream. *You have nothing to be afraid of*, she tells herself. She opens the door slowly, peering down the corridor. The light spills in through the front windows. She sees two rabbits running away, their tails flashing white, and one long brown shape, unmoving on the grass.

She walks into the cafe area, where Lou is shutting the window. A double-barrelled shotgun lies on the table.

'Where did you learn to do that?' Sarah says, trying to control her voice, not wanting Lou to see it's rattled her.

'At my daddy's knee, where else?' Lou laughs. 'We can't have rabbits all over the track. The dogs would lose the scent of the hare, like that poor bugger last night.'

Sarah doesn't reply.

'Here, drink your tea. You can't be sentimental about animals in this game.'

Sarah drinks the lukewarm tea quickly and goes upstairs

to the bar. She starts wiping down the stools, sticky where the punters sit close to the window, sloshing drinks out of their glasses in their excitement at winning or losing. She watches as Joe Heron comes out from underneath the stand and crosses the neatly raked sand, leaving a pattern of footprints behind him. He picks up the dead rabbit by its back legs and turns towards the building. He sees her and swings the rabbit higher, grinning. She shudders, picks up a bottle of window cleaner, and sprays the glass, misting the view of Joe in fine droplets.

'Sarah?'

She drops the cloth, startled. It's Tommy, standing directly behind her. She didn't hear his feet on the carpet.

'God, your voice sounds just like Joe's. What's up?'

Tommy is chewing his lip. 'What you said about him, it was true, wasn't it?'

She looks at him for a moment.

'Yes, it was all true.'

'That's all right, then,' Tommy says quietly. 'I just needed to be sure.'

'We mustn't talk about it, do you understand?' Sarah says.

'I know.'

He bends down to pick up the cloth she's dropped and hands it to her.

'Thank you,' she says.

He turns to go and she watches him. She will need to watch them both. One is a fool, but the other is an unknown quantity, and that's more dangerous.

CHAPTER THIRTEEN

Sunday

The peace of their relaxing Sunday afternoon was shattered by the phone ringing. Hardly anyone used the landline, except double-glazing salesmen and Lizzie's mother.

'Hello?' she picked it up cautiously.

Sean watched her expression register that it was indeed her mother, and not someone chancing it with a special offer on UV light-resistant secondary-fit panels.

'Tonight?' she said. 'I don't know.'

He couldn't make out the words, but he could hear Mrs Morrison's tone well enough.

'Look, I'm sorry, Mum, it's been a really busy—' But she didn't get to finish. She listened a little longer, then sighed. 'All right, we'll be there at seven.'

'Dinner?'

She nodded.

'But we went last week.' Once a fortnight was barely tolerable. If it was going to turn into a weekly occasion, he was going to have to study Zen mind control to get through it.

'My brother's home,' she said. 'With his new wife.'

'Wife?'

'Yes, that's what she said. He thought it would be a nice surprise. They phoned from Heathrow yesterday, apparently. She's Thai.'

Sean sat back on the settee and considered this information. Lizzie's mother struggled with him coming, as she put it, 'from the wrong side of the tracks', so he could only imagine how she was going to react to her beloved son returning home with a Thai bride.

'I'll make us some coffee,' he said. 'Come on. We can do this! We've got an hour and a half to get our shit together.'

In the kitchen he filled the kettle, reached the mugs down from the cupboard, and opened the fridge for the milk. He didn't hear his own phone ring, just Lizzie calling from the living room.

'It's Chloe, for you,' she said, bringing the phone through to the kitchen.

'Hiya. You okay?'

'Yeah,' Chloe said. 'I'm at the hospital.'

He felt a knot of anxiety in his chest.

'Dad needs some more clean pyjamas. Is there any chance you could drop some in?'

The knot relaxed. Sean looked at his watch. If he skipped the coffee, he could just about make it.

'Okay, I've got my key.'

A key his father didn't know about, so he hoped the old man wasn't feeling too sharp today, or he might get rumbled.

He handed a mug of coffee to Lizzie. 'I'll take the moped, it's easier for nipping in and out of the estate, then I'll be back here in plenty of time to drive you out to your mum and dad's.'

'Families,' she sighed. 'Who'd have them?'

* * *

105

Sean let himself into Jack's flat. He felt like an intruder. Glancing into his father's room, he saw Jack's bed was made. Since Chloe had moved in, the rooms had been decorated and, although she'd had no money for new carpets, she'd done her best to clean up the old ones. He'd helped her one weekend, during one of Jack's earlier hospital stays. They'd hired a steam cleaner from the DIY superstore on the ring road, to give him a surprise when he came home.

Before Chloe became part of Jack's life, Sean had tried to clean the flat on his own. It was a time when Jack was trying to prove he could stay sober and Sean had a notion of rebuilding bridges between them. This was when Khan involved him in the case on the Chasebridge estate that led him right back to his own doorstep, and put Jack back on the booze. After that, he never felt comfortable when his father was in residence. Even now Jack was sober, he still didn't trust him. Sean had been fooled by him too many times before.

Chloe's room had been his childhood bedroom, until he was twelve and moved to his nan's. She'd given it a coat of paint, a pinkish off-white that made it seem lighter than he remembered. After he left, it had become a dumping ground. Jack was forever picking up a bargain TV, or an old piece of furniture he was convinced was a genuine antique. There'd been a whole crate of mismatched fire irons and horse brasses that he said he was going to sell one day. Sean assumed they were stolen. Chloe put them all on eBay and got a few hundred pounds from vintage collectors. Jack was delighted, said it proved he'd had an eye for antiques all along.

Sean opened the chest of drawers in Jack's room. The clothes were neatly folded and he found the pyjamas in the third drawer down. He took three pairs and put them in a holdall that was in the bottom of Jack's wardrobe. He threw the bag over his shoulder, locked the flat and went back down to where he'd parked his moped.

As he kicked it off the stand, he had an idea. Instead of turning right, back onto the dual carriageway into town, he turned left along Darwin Road and cut through a narrow side street in the direction of Chasebridge Community High School. He wasn't sure why, or what he was looking for, but it wouldn't hurt just to have a look.

A fresh lock had been fixed to the loose fencing, securing it to its neighbouring panel, and police tape stretched across the whole length of the fence. Maybe the building had given up everything it was going to, and the answers lay outside. There was a man walking towards him from the direction of Springfield Gardens. Although he didn't have the dog this time, Sean recognised him as the concerned resident of Friday night. Davies, Sean recalled, John Davies. The other man broke into a jog and raised his arm in a wave. Under his helmet, Sean couldn't hear his voice, but his mouth shaped a clear: 'Oi!'

Sean turned the engine off and took his helmet off.

'Oh, it's you,' Davies said, coming to a standstill a few feet away. 'What's going on here, then? We've had no end of your lot coming and going.'

'I'm not at liberty to say, sir,' Sean said. He felt like pointing out that he wasn't on duty.

'You know the other night?' Davies said.

'Friday?'

'Yeah, there was someone else, I forgot to mention it because I didn't connect it at first.'

'Go on,' Sean said.

'When I was coming home – I work late on a Friday – I nearly drove over a guy, running across the end of Springfield Gardens. I had to swerve to miss him. I parked the car, went indoors to get the dog – she'd not been out all day, so I couldn't hang about – and it was when I came round the corner with her, that I saw all those people milling about.'

'And they weren't milling about when you saw the person crossing the road?'

He shook his head. 'Don't think so, but on the other hand, I was too busy trying not to run that one down. He's a flipping nutter.'

'You've seen him before?'

'Yes,' Davies said. 'You must know him. Tall guy. Stars tattooed on both cheeks and crescent moon on his bald head. He wears a shell suit like it's 1985 and runs about the place as if he's on something.'

Sean suppressed a smile. The man he was describing usually was on something. He was known as Longfeller, on account of him being six foot seven and stick-thin. He was a drug user, well known to the police for a string of offences, from burglary to possession with intent to supply.

'Didn't you give this information to the officers doing house-to-house?'

Davies shook his head. 'Haven't seen anyone. They might have tried the doorbell, but I disconnect it when I need to sleep in.'

'Can you do me a favour, Mr Davies?' Sean said. 'And ring 101? Ask to be put through to someone in CID at Doncaster Central, and tell them what you've just told me.'

'Can't you tell them?' he said.

'It would be better coming from you, sir, direct to the detective on duty.'

Sean hoped the 'sir' would be enough to flatter Davies into taking action himself. Sean didn't want to have to explain to anyone why he was snooping round the crime scene on his day off, but he would need to check tomorrow if a call had been logged. He doubted that Longfeller would have any more to do with the murder than Mary, they were two of a kind, more harm to themselves than anyone else, but it was worth logging, just in case he'd seen something.

'Right, then, I'll do that,' Davies said. 'It's a damn shame they don't pull the place down, it's just a bloody magnet—'

'Much appreciated,' Sean cut him off.

He put his helmet back on, before John Davies could launch into another diatribe about refugees and junkies, and set off, past Springfield Gardens and back to the dual carriageway.

Jack was sitting up in bed when he arrived at the hospital. Chloe slipped out and left them together.

'She's ironed them lovely,' Jack said, stroking the striped cotton pyjamas with his thumb. 'She's a hard worker, that lass. Gets it from her old man. When I was her age, I was down the pit.'

Sean had heard it several times before and didn't correct his dad by pointing out that both Chloe and he were now older than Jack had been when he stopped work, his injury on the picket line putting paid to manual labour, and his alcohol addiction putting paid to any other kind of work.

He wanted to tell him about passing his interview for CID, but he couldn't find the words. Jack would never be comfortable with his son as a police officer. It used to make Sean ashamed, but he'd come to terms with it. The world had changed and the old industries had gone, taking the options for men like his father with them. The policeman who'd shattered his father's hand probably retired years ago on a full pension, and even if things were different now, Jack would never get justice and he would never be happy about Sean's job. There was no point in wishing it were different. A silence grew between them, and after a while, Sean was relieved to see Chloe come back onto the ward, a packet of Jack's favourite biscuits in her hand. He said his goodbyes and went back home to Regent Square.

When Sean arrived at the flat, there was no sign of Lizzie. He checked his watch. Shit. It was much later than he realised. The Morrisons would be sitting down to Sunday dinner, candles lit, wine poured and the undercurrent of a row ready to bubble up through the polished surface of their lives. He walked into the bedroom. Lizzie had made the bed, smoothing the white linen duvet cover as if it was new out of the packet. Their flat was a world away from his dad's place – and his nan's, come to think of it. All the work he'd done on her house seemed a bit tacky in comparison to Lizzie's way of doing things. Everything here was white, or muted tones of beige or grey. There was no lime green statement wall or huge red poppies, embossed with gold on the wallpaper. He and Nan had thought it was cheerful when he put it up in the front room at Clement Grove. He wasn't so sure now.

He flopped back on the bed, feeling the thick down duvet fluff up around him, like a nest. He'd ring Lizzie, to see if it was still worth setting out. He'd need to fill up with petrol to get as far as the village where Mr and Mrs Morrison lived. Maybe he was too late already. Perhaps, he thought, if he left it a little longer, then he could avoid going altogether. He closed his eyes and let his mind wander. Longfeller's distinctive face came to mind, with the two blue stars on his cheeks. Sean had arrested him twice in the last eighteen months, but neither time had resulted in a custodial sentence. He was a lost soul, strung out on a lifestyle choice that had begun more than twenty years ago, when the rave scene was still big. It was a wonder he was still alive.

He rolled over and selected Lizzie's number on his phone.

'Sorry, love, I got held up,' he said, but she cut him off.

'Don't be, it's my fault . . . well, not entirely. My dad phoned, said it was urgent. Mum was shut in her bedroom crying, saying Tim's ruined her life. Tim stormed down to the pub, calling my mother a Nazi. Dad was left sitting on his own with Pakpao, who doesn't speak much English, and who was also crying by this time. He was completely at a loss as to what he should do. I thought I'd better just come.'

'Jeez. What a welcome for Pakpao. Shall I jump on the ped and join you?'

'Don't worry. Have a quiet night in. You want to be on form for your meeting with Khan tomorrow. Like I say, I'm sorry, we should be celebrating.'

'I'll treat myself to a takeaway,' he said, trying hard to disguise the relief he felt.

The chippy round the corner was shut on Sundays, so he walked further towards the centre of town, heading for a takeaway that did great kebabs. He took note of the characters hanging around the quiet streets, but saw nobody he recognised. He remembered Gav saying he'd spoken to a couple with a supermarket trolley, but he couldn't see anybody pushing one around now. The door-to-door teams were going to have their work cut out with a bunch of witnesses who had no front door to call their own.

He got his kebab and jogged back to the flat, making sure it would still be hot. He was a bit short of breath when he got to the top of the stairs. That would have to change. More time in the gym was called for, if he was going to keep his fitness levels up in CID. He knew a lad who'd done so much surveillance, sitting, waiting, and eating, that he'd gained three stone and given himself a blood clot.

Sean flopped his meal out of the greasy paper and onto a plate. Fewer takeaways too, he thought, but not now. This could be the last kebab, he smiled to himself. Tomorrow my body becomes a temple. Tomorrow. A wave of anxiety threatened to spoil his appetite. What would Khan say in their meeting? How soon would there be a vacancy for him to start as a trainee detective? And where? He hadn't really thought about that, but he realised it was possible he might have to move to another area.

Just get some food down you, he thought to himself, *get some kip, and worry about all this in the morning.*

He took his plate over to the settee and turned on the TV.

'Here's to the last kebab!' he said, and took a big bite of bread, meat and salad. The chilli sauce set his mouth alight.

CHAPTER FOURTEEN

Monday morning

Sarah presses herself into the tiny shower cubicle, the moulded plastic squeaking under her feet, and lets the lukewarm water trickle over her. She picks the scab on her arm where she tested the kitchen knife and lets the blood dilute in a pinkish trickle. The dog's whining outside the door. It needs taking out. It's her day off, so she has nothing better to do. At least it will get her out of this stifling caravan.

She pulls on her T-shirt and shorts. Perhaps she'll sunbathe a little out on the track.

She holds the lead tightly coiled in her hand and Wolf trots by her side sniffing the air. He's not been out much since he arrived, just to do his business in the undergrowth at the edge of the yard. She's never had a dog, she's not even sure she likes them, but she has to admit he is handsome. His short black coat shimmers in the sunlight and he turns to look up at her, as if he knows he's being admired. He pulls across the car park, towards the new kennels and she lets him lead her, loosening the leash to give him more freedom.

The earth is still uneven and waiting for turf where the trench

113

ran in front of the kennel block. Wolf sniffs at the earth and she pulls him up with the lead. She can hear something inside the building. Wolf hears it too. A high-pitched whine, repeated over and over. Then she hears a male voice, speaking softly. Joe or Tommy, she can't tell which. Keeping Wolf close, she pushes open the door. Inside it's cool. There is a smell of fresh concrete and freshly planed wood. Each kennel is like a small stable, opening off a whitewashed passage. She walks towards the sound, Wolf's paws clicking lightly on the concrete floor.

At the last kennel, the top half of the door is open and she looks in. A fawn-coloured greyhound is lying on a dog bed, padded out with blankets. The dog's foreleg is wrapped in a splint and bandage. He wears a plastic cone. It's the dog that got hurt on Saturday night. Beside it, on the ground, Joe Heron is stroking his back. He doesn't look round and she's sure he doesn't know she's there.

She watches as Joe opens the cone and takes it off. The dog nudges the splint and whines louder. Joe strokes its head. He has something in his other hand. It looks like a small electric drill. He brings it up and presses it between the dog's eyes. She realises too late and can't turn away in time. He pulls the trigger and the dog spasms. There is blood pouring from a hole in its forehead.

Joe turns round.

'Enjoyed that, did you?' he says. He has tears in his eyes.

She pulls Wolf close and walks away down the passage and back out into the light.

CHAPTER FIFTEEN

Monday morning

The sun poured through the window behind DI Khan's desk and Sean had to tilt his head to avoid being dazzled.

'Each year plenty of constables apply,' Khan said, 'but very few are selected. Normally, even with a successful application, there can be a wait before the candidate is placed.'

Sean tried to stay focused. He didn't want to miss anything, but Khan's voice washed over him, leaving certain words and phrases behind in the shallows. The DI was smiling at him, or at least Sean thought he was, it was hard to tell with the sun in his eyes.

'But,' Khan said, pausing to take a mouthful of coffee.

Sean dreaded what lay behind the word 'but'. Maybe he'd misread the letter, or it had been a mistake and was meant for someone else instead of him.

Khan smiled and continued speaking: 'I'm pleased to say that you shone at interview and your record, especially on secondment to Major Crimes last year, demonstrates that you're more than ready.' There it was, the words in the letter were confirmed. 'You'll be assigned to an experienced detective, who will be your tutor. Someone for you to shadow, as you build your portfolio of key competencies. And then, of course, there will be the courses you need to attend, and the exams.'

Sean's stomach tightened at the word 'exams'. He was prepared to work as hard as he could, but nothing filled him with as much fear as the thought of sitting in an exam room, the words in his head stubbornly refusing to arrange themselves in any sensible order on the paper. His face must have given him away.

'Don't worry,' Khan said, 'you'll be fine. I passed them, so that means anyone can.' He smiled, but Sean didn't think it was funny. DI Sam Nasir Khan had a brain the size of a planet. 'Now, do you have any questions?'

'What about location, sir? Will I need to move away?'

'The thing is,' Khan picked something out of his fingernail with a paper clip as he spoke. 'With all the cutbacks we've been experiencing, we're short in Major Crimes here, especially with a murder case open. I've checked with the divisional commander and he's given me the go-ahead. If it wouldn't be too unadventurous for you, I'd like to keep you here.'

'Yes,' Sean stammered. 'I'd like that.'

'And it's an investigation that is not getting any less complicated, so I'm proposing that you start as soon as possible. I'll give your sergeant the rest of today to make sure you don't leave any loose ends on the response team, but I'd like you to come to the briefing at ten, then I can introduce you to the person I've lined up for you to work with.'

Sean suddenly thought about Gav, and how he would manage with a new partner. They worked well together, and Gav had taken Sean under his wing from the beginning, guiding him on the journey from PCSO to constable.

Khan cleared his throat, waiting for an answer.

'Yes, sir.'

'Good. Someone from HR will be in touch to sort out the necessaries.'

Khan was distracted by an incoming message on his phone and Sean took that as a sign that the interview was over. He stood up.

'Thank you, sir,' he said, and offered his hand for Khan's crushing handshake.

Sean's dry mouth was unable to make any sensible sound, so he turned on his heel and left the room. He almost ran down the stairs, gravity and speed threatening to throw him off his feet, but he didn't care. He flicked the exit switch and pushed open the glass doors into the car park. The fresh air hit his throat like a gulp of cool water and he wanted to shout out to the four walls of the police yard: *I'm a detective!*

He couldn't wait to tell Lizzie that Khan wanted him on his team. He decided to go and buy her a bunch of flowers, then he'd come back to the station and check whether the dog-walker, John Davies, had phoned in his sighting of Longfeller crossing Springfield Gardens on Friday night.

He came round the corner of the building, wondering if he should get Lizzie delphiniums, the flowers Chloe had said she resembled. He wasn't sure he knew what delphiniums looked like, but he could always ask. He nearly collided with a woman coming towards him.

'Sorry,' she said, grabbing his elbow to steady herself.

It was DC Tina Smales who worked in the sex crimes

unit. At only five foot tall, she came up to Sean's chest.

'I wasn't looking where I was going.'

'My fault,' Sean said, 'I was miles away.'

'You look happy,' she said.

'I am,' he said.

He wanted to tell her, but thought it was only fair to let Gav know first. If he heard from someone else, Sean wouldn't hear the last of it.

'Well,' she said. 'I'll see you later. We're on at twelve, aren't we?'

'Are we?' he said, his mind blank. He struggled to recall what it was he was supposed to be doing with DC Smales at midday.

'We're in court. The Velasquez case?'

'Of course!'

What an idiot. He'd been so preoccupied with his interview and his meeting with Khan, not to mention his father being hospitalised and the small matter of the murder in the school, he hadn't even looked at his calendar for today.

'I'd better check my notes,' he said. 'Don't want to get caught out. Thank goodness I saw you!'

His heart was racing. It was like a near miss in a high-speed chase. If he didn't turn up to court, it would jeopardise everything he'd just achieved. The Velasquez case. It was coming back to him. He'd been the arresting officer. DC Smales had dealt with the victim. It looked like date rape. The blood tests showed signs of an opiate, but the girl had no history of drug use.

'He's been on remand, hasn't he?' he said.

'Yes,' she said. 'Four months. The judge didn't grant bail, even though it was a first offence.'

He checked the time.

'Right,' he said. 'I've got to run. Need to be in a briefing at ten, then get my notes together. I'll see you in court.'

'Good job you came to work in your dress uniform!'

'Yeah, it was, wasn't it?'

He wondered if she'd rumbled him.

Sean looked around the ops room. The briefing was due to begin in three minutes. He tried to decide where to sit. From now on, everything he did would be monitored. Every minute would feel like a test. There was an empty seat on the back row. He took it, and realised he was sitting next to DS Rick Houghton, who worked in the drugs squad. They were old friends and often played pool together in the pub. Rick nudged him and whispered a greeting. There was no time to reply. DI Sam Nasir Khan was speaking.

'Chasebridge Community school, still no murder weapon,' Khan indicated a large whiteboard, covered in diagrams and photos from the crime scene. 'Blood patterns on Homsi's sweatshirt and face suggest expiration, so we know he was close to the victim during or after the attack, at least while our vic was still breathing. However, there was nothing on his trousers, which, if he was standing behind the victim when the blow was struck, you would expect. You can see from the CSI mapping that blood has travelled backwards and hit the floor, here. The gap, here, is where the assailant was positioned. His reaction to the two officers who found him' – Khan broke off and scanned the room – 'Denton, ah, there you are. Sean's joining us, as of today, as trainee DC. So, Sean, his reaction?'

There was a murmur as he got to his feet, a few approving nods from those who knew him.

'First thing he said was "sorry, sorry",' Sean said. 'But he had just tried to bottle me. He looked scared, so it's possible he thought PC Wentworth and myself were the attackers coming back.'

Khan nodded. 'And yet he says he didn't see the attackers, but he did mention some men who've been coming in and demanding money from the residents. Homsi tells us his friend is called Abbas. He doesn't know very much more about him, except he comes from Northern Iraq. They've been living in the school for a month. He was a bit vague about where they were before that, but they've made their way from a seaport, where they were in the back of a lorry. He doesn't know the name, but it sounds further afield than Hull or Grimsby.'

'How much longer can we keep him?' someone asked from the front row.

The accent was unusual for South Yorkshire. Sean peered round the person in front of him and saw it belonged to DS Ivan Knowles, the new boy up from London. He had an urge to tell Rick about Gav's nicknames for him, but decided he'd better behave himself.

'We can't charge him with anything,' Khan said. 'So we'll have to let him go today. Let's hope we can get him to an address where we can keep tabs on him. Meanwhile we've got no witnesses, or maybe several. An unknown number of rough sleepers, who could be anywhere in the town. We need to track down Mary, who we've identified as Mary Dobbs. She led DC Denton to the murder site and she's on the PNC for theft, soliciting and possession. She's local, so I don't think she'll have gone far. DS Knowles, have we got much from the door-to-doors?'

'We covered the local area at the weekend,' Ivan Knowles said, 'but got nothing useful. A call came in last night, though, about a sighting of someone called Longfeller.'

'Michael Bartram,' Rick said. 'Check his record if you've got a spare day or two. It's long enough. He's one of our regulars.'

So John Davies, the dog-walker, came good. Sean was glad to hear it.

'Keep your eyes out for him. Rick, talk to your regular informers and have a look in the usual places for Longfeller. We need to find the others who were there. Ask on the streets and at St Bernadette's,' Khan said. 'Try the Salvation Army drop-in, or anywhere rough sleepers are likely to be in the daytime. I need you all out there gathering as much intel as you can.'

Sean wondered where Mary was, and whether she could have told him more if she'd been able to speak to him again and hadn't been so afraid of John Davies' dog.

'Any questions?'

There was a shifting of weight along the rows of chairs, but no hands were raised.

'Right,' Khan tugged at his beard. 'Let's get to it.'

As they stood up and started to move towards the door, Rick put a hand on Sean's shoulder.

'Nice one, Sean lad. But you're a sly dog not to say a word about applying. Are we going to drink to your success later on?'

'Aye. I reckon we should. Catch you later?'

The urgency of telling Gav was becoming more acute. Now everyone in CID knew, it wouldn't take long to reach the rest of the station.

He looked for Gav in the writing-up room, where the uniforms were based, but he wasn't there. He collected his notes for the court hearing, and checked his watch. He still had time to buy some flowers for Lizzie. He left the police station and headed down towards Hall Gate and into Silver Street. He stared into the florist's window.

'Delphiniums,' he said, under his breath.

CHAPTER SIXTEEN

Monday

The bus was unbearably hot. Every window was open, but that did nothing to improve the atmosphere inside. Chloe had Mel's jacket in a plastic bag on the seat next to her. Even touching the bag made her fingers sweat. That morning she'd sat through a dreary lecture on planting patterns, part of her day-release course in garden design. This afternoon was meant to be study time, but it was the only chance she would have to go to the market before the following Saturday. She didn't want the girl to think she'd just walked off with the jacket. She also wanted to know if there was any news of the dog that had broken its leg on Saturday night, Indian Whisper. It was a beautiful name for a beautiful creature.

She got off at Silver Street and cut through to the marketplace, narrowly avoiding a collision with a man on a mobility scooter, who was heading straight for the door of the Red Lion. It was wrong to judge, she knew, but it looked like the last place he needed to be, all twenty stone of him.

She kept walking, dodging the shoppers and outdoor stalls until she came to the market hall, where she wove her way along the aisles until she came to *Hair Today*. It was closed, a heavy padlock on the door. She felt her energy dissipate. A stitch in her side, which she'd ignored as she walked up here, took her breath away and she doubled over, reaching for the locked door, her hand on the black painted plywood.

'You all right?' a voice said.

A young woman, carrying a box of lettuces, was looking at her.

'Yes, just out of breath.' She pushed herself up to standing. 'I was hoping to catch the girl that works here.'

'He doesn't usually open on a Monday,' the young woman said. 'And you won't see her on a weekday, she's just Saturdays. Or at least she should be. She's still at school.'

'Do you know her?'

'Oh, yes, I know her. She gave me this.' The young woman turned and lifted up her hair. On the side of her neck was a blistered patch of skin, still healing. Chloe winced.

'If you want my advice, I'd steer clear of her.'

The young woman hoisted her box of lettuces higher and walked towards the door to the adjoining food hall. Chloe watched her go. The mark on the woman's neck looked like a burn. She'd seen the result of women fighting plenty of times, but she couldn't be sure if that was a friction burn, or caused by a flame. She swung the bag back and forth, trying to decide what to do. After a couple of minutes, she followed the lettuce woman between the stalls and into the food hall.

At the first fruit and veg stall she came to, a large Turkish man and his equally large wife bustled behind the counter. She walked on. In the next aisle she found Edwards & Sons, Greengrocer. A man in his fifties was weighing out potatoes. He looked like lettuce girl, just older and greyer, the same pinkish tone to the skin and the same thin mouth. As she approached, the girl appeared in front of the counter, arranging the lettuces from the box onto the display.

'Excuse me,' Chloe said. 'But I really need to find Mel. I need to give her this jacket back.'

The man looked up from the potatoes and the girl turned round and stopped what she was doing.

'What's this about?' he said.

'Your daughter said she knew this girl, Mel, who works at the hairdresser's.'

'Melissa, yes, we know her.'

'I need to get this jacket back to her, that's all. Can you tell me where she lives?'

'Ah,' he said. 'I'm afraid I can't do that. When she moved on from our home, well, it's data protection, you see.'

Chloe wondered if Mr Edwards realised he'd already given away more than he should have. So Mel had lived with them and now didn't, and she didn't live with her own family. Chloe's hunch was right, she *was* in care.

'Where did you get the jacket?' the girl said.

Chloe decided to tell a white lie. 'She lent it me after I got my hair cut.'

'You can leave it here and I can give it her next time she's at work.'

Chloe thought about the offer and turned it down. She didn't trust the girl, although her old man looked harmless enough. She slung the bag over her shoulder and set off, through the next market hall, until she came to the Exchange Building, with its beautiful glass atrium. There was a cafe on the mezzanine level and she decided to get a coffee. She found a table looking over the balustrade to the craft stalls below. There were some beautiful stained glass ornaments laid out on a red velvet throw. She'd love to get something like that to brighten up the flat for when Jack got home. She was just wondering if they were expensive, when she noticed someone approaching the table. It was the greengrocer's daughter.

'Here,' she said, thrusting a paper bag at her, on which an address was scrawled in spidery writing. 'Don't tell anyone you got it from me. We had enough trouble when her brothers showed up. But if you are her friend, then I don't see why you shouldn't know where she is.'

'Thanks.'

'You seem pretty normal, and that's what she needs, a good influence in her life. She used to be okay, quite sweet really, but she changed when they got back in contact, for the worse.'

Normal. That made Chloe smile. If only the young woman knew the life she'd led.

'I'll bear that in mind,' she said.

'Right,' the girl said. 'I'd better go. He thinks I've gone for a pee.'

Chloe looked at the address. She didn't recognise the name of the road, although the postcode suggested it was close to the town centre. She wished she had a smartphone, which would instantly work out her route, but she only had a cheap, old-fashioned burner. She finished her coffee and decided to go to the library, where they would have an *A to Z*. She might even spend a couple of hours on the college work she was supposed to be doing. If Melissa was at school, there was no rush to deliver the jacket.

As she came out into Silver Street, she saw Sean leaving the florist's shop. She waved at him and he waved a bunch of flowers.

'Delphiniums!' he shouted.

She caught up with him. 'You seem very pleased with yourself!' she said.

'I remembered the name. Flowers for Lizzie.'

'Is it a special occasion?'

'I couldn't tell you yesterday, at the hospital, because I didn't think Dad would want to hear it, but I've passed the interview to become a trainee detective.'

'That's brilliant!' She wanted to throw her arms round him, but the bunch of flowers and the smart formal uniform he was wearing held her back. 'Have you told your nan?'

'Oh, God, no. I must do that. I haven't even told Gav yet.'

'He'll be pleased for you.'

'Aye, in the long run, but Khan wants me to move teams immediately, so that leaves Gav in the lurch. Look, I'd better run, I'm in court in fifteen minutes.'

'See you later. And I'm really proud of you!'

After he'd set off down the street at a sprint, she realised she could have asked him to look up Mel's address on his phone. Never mind. It would be cooler in the library. She couldn't wait to get out of the heat.

At four o'clock, Chloe was standing outside a large red-brick house with black and white timbering above the front door. It must have been quite a smart house when it was built, but now it looked shabby. All the other houses at this end of the street were divided into flats, but this building had just one front-door bell and a camera built into a speaker unit.

'Hello,' Chloe said. 'I've come to see Melissa, my name's Chloe.'

The speaker unit crackled with static and the latch on the door clicked off. She pushed the door open and found herself standing in a large hall. The floor was covered in thick lino, like a hospital corridor, but elsewhere someone had made an effort to make it look less like an institution, and more like a home. A framed picture of a pair of Shetland ponies, grazing in a field, hung above a chest of drawers. On top of the chest a bunch of flowers had been arranged in a pretty blue and white vase. Chloe went closer and rubbed one of the petals between her fingers. It was fabric, and the vase, when she tapped it with her fingernail, gave off the 'plink' of plastic.

A young man appeared from a room to the left of the front door.

'Hiya!' he said. 'Chloe, is it?'

'Yeah.'

'Hang on. I'll give Melissa a shout. You're from school, are you? Nice for her to get a visitor.'

He took off up the stairs two at a time. Chloe wondered how good his eyesight was, or maybe it was the lack of natural light in the hall, but she hadn't been school age for at least ten years.

She heard muffled voices and then a squeal of pleasure. Suddenly Mel was running down the stairs in bare feet. She was wearing a skimpy yellow sundress.

'I brought your jacket back,' Chloe said, offering the

bag. 'I'm sorry, we had to leave in a bit of a hurry.'

Mel's eyes flicked back up the stairs and she put her finger to her lips. Chloe nodded. The young man came down the stairs behind Mel.

'Why don't you get your friend an orange squash or something? There's some ice in the freezer.'

'I'm fine with water,' Chloe said, 'but the ice would be fantastic. I'm melting!'

They took their drinks out into a garden strewn with plastic toys. A yellow and red toddler car was lying on its side in the dry grass and someone had abandoned what looked like a mud-pie-making enterprise in one of the flower beds. Chloe shuddered at the damage that had been done to the shrubs that clung on around the edge.

'I hope you don't mind me asking,' Chloe said, 'but how old are you?'

'Fifteen,' Mel said. 'I know I look older.'

Right now, she looked much younger, but on Saturday night, in heels and make-up, she could have passed for twenty-one.

'How did you know where I lived?' Mel said.

Chloe wasn't sure she should let on. 'Just worked it out. Asked a few questions.'

Mel shrugged, as if it wasn't important to her.

'How's the dog, Indian Whisper?' Chloe said.

'He's going to be okay. Uncle Derek sent me a text on Sunday. They've got him all tucked up in the new kennel. The first resident! He's got his leg in a splint, but he should make a full recovery.'

'I'm pleased to hear it,' Chloe said.

'He won't race again,' Mel looked serious, 'so he'll have to be rehomed.'

'I wish I could have a dog.'

'Maybe you could?' Mel's eyes lit up. 'You could adopt him!'

'I'm not sure. I live in a flat and my dad's really poorly. I'm not sure it would work.'

'What are you doing Tuesday night?'

'Me?'

'Yeah,' Mel said. 'We could go and see him. There's a charity race meet, first Tuesday of the month. That's tomorrow. Just a few people turn up with rehomed rescue dogs, gives them a chance to run again. Uncle Derek was telling me all about it. We could go and see Whisper, then watch the races.'

Mel's face had a new energy, flushed with excitement. Chloe tried to think of a reason why she shouldn't agree to go, but she couldn't. Other than hospital visiting, her evenings were empty, and Sean might go and see Jack, if she asked him.

'All right,' Chloe said. 'I live over that way. After work I get the train into town and then the bus home, so I could call for you here and we could get the bus together.'

'Can I see where you live?'

Chloe laughed. 'If you like, but it's nothing special! I'll need to get changed and we can have a cuppa before we go out.'

'Or something stronger!' Mel winked.

'Maybe,' Chloe said. 'There's just one thing.'

'What?'

'We need to get our story straight with your key worker, or whatever he is. He seems to think I'm from your school. I'm twenty-eight, Mel. I think you should know that. I don't want to get you into any trouble.'

If the girl was surprised, she didn't show it.

'It's cool. I'll tell him I met you on the market, at my Saturday job. It's not even a lie. And it doesn't bother me that you're old. You're like a big sister. I've never had a sister.'

Me neither, thought Chloe, unsure of the new responsibility she had unwittingly taken on.

CHAPTER SEVENTEEN

Monday

Sean took the bunch of flowers to Lizzie's office, but she wasn't there. He didn't want to leave them, so he put them in his locker, the base of the stems standing in one of his running shoes. He figured it would be cooler in there.

He'd arranged to meet DC Smales on the steps of the police station. She arrived looking hot and tired, her olive skin flushed pink.

'You okay? Tough morning?'

'Just been to talk to a rape victim in the hospital. I want her transferred over to the Sexual Assault Referral Suite in Rotherham, but she's refusing to go.'

'How come?' Sean said.

'The suspect's her husband and the witness is their fourteen-year-old daughter. We're charging him with GBH as well. She's in a bad state.'

'He sounds like a nice piece of work,' he said.

He was going to say something else but just then a familiar figure came through the glass doors and hesitated on the top step.

'Mr Homsi?' Sean said.

The man didn't appear to notice he was being addressed, so Sean went up to him.

'All right, mate?'

Homsi looked startled. 'You are policeman in the school? I am sorry.'

'Don't worry. I realise you were frightened back there.'

Homsi nodded. Sean noticed that he was wearing a pair of ill-fitting shoes, some grey tracksuit trousers and a Leeds United shirt. The custody sergeant kept a store of spares for people who couldn't go back out in their own clothes. Homsi's clothes were probably in the lab, along with several bags of evidence from the school.

'Where will you go?' Sean asked.

'I have address,' Homsi said and showed Sean a slip of paper with the address of St Bernadette's night shelter. 'But it is temporary.'

'You might see some familiar faces there,' Sean said.

'I don't understand.'

'From the school. I think St Bernadette's have taken some of the others who haven't got anywhere else to go.'

Homsi frowned. 'I don't like these people. They don't like me. It's not safe where they are.'

'The staff will keep an eye out,' Sean said. 'And then you could get back in touch with RAMA, they might be able to help you find something more permanent.'

Homsi looked confused.

'The agency in York?' Sean said. 'The letter you had, it was from RAMA. The people who are working on your case.'

'I don't have it.' Homsi said. 'Can you get my letter back? It's the only proof I can stay here.'

'Ah, I see,' Sean said. 'You'll get it back eventually, but it's probably still being held as evidence. Hang on, I can give you the number of the woman who works there, Karen Friedman. She might be able to get you a duplicate.'

He got his phone out, found the number, and wrote it on a bus ticket he found in his pocket.

'Tell her Sean Denton says hi,' he smiled at Homsi, 'if she remembers me.'

'Come on, Sean,' Tina said. 'We need to go, or the judge will be rapping our knuckles.'

'Best of luck, Mr Homsi,' Sean said.

Homsi nodded, shoved the bus ticket in his pocket, and walked down the steps with his shoulders hunched.

'How do you think the Velasquez case is going to go?' Tina asked him, as they walked the few hundred yards to the Crown Court building.

'If the victim's plausible, we might get a conviction,' Sean said. 'The lad admitted to having sex with her, just denied coercion.'

'What do you reckon to him?'

'Xavier Velasquez? Twenty-one. Born in Madrid, but lived here since he was a child. Dad runs a bakery, where Xavier worked until his arrest. No previous convictions.'

'You've done your homework! But I meant, what did you make of him as a person?'

'To be honest, I was surprised he was remanded to custody at the pretrial hearing, but I suppose there was a risk of him nipping off to Spain. He seemed like a regular guy, probably drinks too much on a night out. Date rape's not a spur of the moment action, though, is it? He would have planned it. But

I wonder why? He's a nice-looking lad. I can't see why he'd need to drug someone.'

'It's not only the ugly blokes who get off on a power trip.'

'I didn't mean—'

'Don't forget you're on the side of the prosecution, Denton.'

'Yes, ma'am.'

She opened the door to the court foyer and they were immediately greeted by the cool relief of air conditioning. Tina turned to him and spoke quietly.

'I interviewed her, Sean, the victim. Her name, incidentally, is Bethany Winters. I took her to Rotherham so she could be looked after in a properly equipped rape suite. I sat and held her hand. She was in pieces. The doctor who examined her said that intercourse had been violent. She had opiates in her bloodstream and no memory of anything after the defendant asked her to dance.'

'Okay,' Sean said. 'I'll keep my answers factual. I just have to confirm his statement from when we arrested him.'

'Exactly,' Tina said. 'Right, let's see if we can find the court clerk and work out when we're on.'

The foyer was full of people milling about. A couple who could easily have been the parents of the defendant were standing to one side. He was dark-haired and portly. She was slim and her hair was coloured with tawny-blonde highlights. They were dressed in their best clothes, uncomfortable in this heatwave.

The doors to the courtroom opened and the lawyers and public from the previous case poured out. The couple stepped back against the wall, lost in the throng. A woman ran out crying and Sean guessed someone had been sent down.

Tina came back and confirmed their case was up next.

'The prosecution barrister is a bit edgy,' she said. 'Bethany Winters hasn't turned up yet.'

'When did you last speak to her?' Sean said.

'I rang her on her mobile on Friday. She said she'd be here.'

A grey-haired woman in a gown approached them. Sean recognised her from a few cases he'd worked on. She was called Elaine Farmer, a barrister who worked for the Crown Prosecution Service. She was a fearsome interrogator.

'I've asked the court clerk to ring her,' she said to Tina, 'but he's getting no reply. Have we got a landline number?'

Sean noticed the well-dressed couple looking over in their direction.

'I think they're the defendant's parents,' he said quietly. 'Are there any other witnesses here for Velasquez?'

'The defence is calling two friends who were with him,' Elaine Farmer said. 'I'm not sure what evidence they've got, but it can't be more than hearsay. We had a girl who claimed to be with Bethany on the night, and who was willing to testify that she doesn't drink, but she's out of town. Moved to Devon, inconveniently.'

'Shelley Martin,' Tina said. 'I'm not sure how much use she would have been, she was a bit of a drip, to be honest. Look, I've got Bethany's parents' number. She lives at home, so they'll know if she's on her way.'

She moved away towards the front door, to avoid being overheard.

The Velasquez parents and the others who had been hanging around the foyer began to file into the courtroom. Sean recognised a journalist he'd seen here a few times. A short guy in an ill-fitting suit, he'd grown a mangy beard since the last time Sean had set eyes on him. It didn't suit him.

'Well?' he said to Tina, who'd finished her call. Her face was drawn.

'No reply,' she said. 'Just rings off the hook, not even an answer machine.'

'When did you last see her?' Elaine Farmer said.

Tina shook her head. 'Face-to-face? Not since she was discharged from the referral suite in Rotherham. She wouldn't engage. Kept cancelling appointments. She was the same with Witness Care Service, but whenever I spoke to her on the phone, she said everything was fine. I think she's just bottled it, to be honest.'

'Right!' Elaine Farmer's voice bounced off the marble floor as she snapped into action. 'We'll just have to get an adjournment, then.'

She swept through the doors into the court, followed by Sean and Tina, who stood in the aisle. Elaine approached the bench and spoke in hushed tones to the judge. The defendant was already in the dock. He was thinner than Sean remembered, but four months on remand could do that to a young man. His dark hair was cut short and he had a bruise healing under one eye. He kept his eyes down, aware perhaps that his mother was desperately trying to make eye contact with him, a pained smile tightening the lipstick across her mouth. No doubt she wanted to offer him silent encouragement, but the effect was grotesque.

The judge sat up and cleared his throat.

'In the absence of the key prosecution witness,' he announced, 'the case is adjourned until further notice.'

The defence barrister immediately requested bail for his client, which was granted. Sean and Tina stepped aside as the young man left the dock. His mother ran forward and took him in her arms. He allowed himself to be hugged and kissed. When she finally let him go, Sean saw that he was crying, his hand over his face to disguise it. His barrister ushered him out, speaking quickly and urgently, no doubt trying to explain that this didn't mean he was out of the woods yet, but it would certainly work in his favour when the trial was rescheduled.

'That was a nice waste of time,' Elaine Farmer said tightly.

'I am sorry, ma'am,' Tina said. 'If she'd given any indication that she wasn't going to attend court, I would have alerted the CPP.'

'It's not your fault,' she said, in a way that wasn't entirely convincing. 'But I'd be grateful if you could get to the bottom of what's going on before the next hearing, otherwise I'm afraid we'll just have to drop it.'

'Yes, ma'am.'

Elaine Farmer swept past them and in her wake came the short, bearded journalist.

'Any comment for the press about why she didn't show up?' he whined.

'No,' Sean and Tina spoke together.

They turned and walked away from him, through the foyer and the double glass doors, back into the heat of the afternoon. Halfway between the court building and the police station, Tina stopped to check there was no one in earshot, before letting off a barrage of expletives. Sean couldn't help himself. He burst out laughing. This five foot nothing of a detective constable, a sexual offences trained officer, no less, had a vocabulary like a sailor.

When she'd finished, she smiled sweetly at him as if nothing had happened.

'That's better,' she said. 'Now let's go back to work.'

Sean wasn't sure what going back to work entailed for him. He wasn't due to check in with DS Knowles until the morning, so technically, he was still part of the response team. He decided to head to the writing-up room to update the files with the no-show at court.

The room was busy, everyone's eyes fixed on their computer screens. Nobody seemed to notice him come in. He sat at a desk and logged on. He slowly typed the words into the correct boxes on the Velasquez case files, confirming that he had attended court and what the outcome had been. Suddenly, he realised that the room had gone quiet. Sean looked up and was greeted with a burst of applause. Everyone was looking at him. Then a joker from the other end of the room called out: 'Good riddance, you bastard, we never liked you!' There was laughter all round, and a promise of a drink later. So they knew, they all knew.

At knocking-off time, Sean was in the locker room. Doors were being thrown open on their hinges, each clattering against the next locker. The raised voices of the day shift swapped banter with the night shift. It all sounded oddly distant, like he was trying to capture something for the last time. He opened his own locker and a sickly sweet smell hit him. The delphiniums for Lizzie. He'd forgotten all about them. They'd wilted in the cone of paper and drooped sadly in the corner of the grey metal locker. He pulled them out.

'Those for me, sunshine?' Gav said from just behind him. 'Oh dear, looks like they've got brewer's droop.'

'Looks terminal,' another voice called. 'Unless you try giving them mouth to mouth.'

Sean dropped them in the nearest bin.

'Do you fancy a swift pint, Gav? I expect you've heard, I mean, I wanted to tell you myself, but I've passed the interview for CID. I'm going to be a detective.'

'Good lad!' Gav said, giving him a hearty slap on the back. 'And no, I hadn't heard, been down the canal all afternoon with some poor fellow who had his porthole kicked in by a bunch of yobs. I'll give Sheila a ring on the way down, tell her I'll be late.'

'Not too late,' Sean said. He'd need his wits about him tomorrow, but Gav hadn't heard him.

CHAPTER EIGHTEEN

Tuesday morning

Sarah wakes from the recurring dream of being held down, but now it has developed a new element. Lou appears with the shotgun and presses it between the eyes of the man who's attacking her. He doesn't let go when the gun goes off, but leans down on her shoulders, his face mangled and bloody.

She forces herself awake, and throws the duvet off her legs. Sweat pools between her breasts. She checks her watch. She needs to get moving if she wants a shower.

There's a noise in the kitchen. She listens. It sounds as if there's someone else in the caravan. That can't be right. She went up to the house, at Derek's suggestion, and borrowed the right-sized screwdriver and some strong glue. The latch is working now and the door's locked. Having Derek pat her on the backside is a small price to pay for her own security. Fortunately Lou was there, so he didn't try anything else. She wonders if he would. She saw him with Lou's niece on Saturday, arm in arm like she was his new bit on the side, and the girl's only a child. They're all the same. Her mother was right about that, at least.

There it is again. Who on earth is moving around in her kitchen? She creeps out of bed and opens the bedroom door a crack. A pair of dark eyes is looking up at her.

'Wolf!'

She can't believe she's forgotten about him, that the dream still has so much power over her. He wags his tail slowly.

'Are you hungry? Or do you need to go out for a pee first?'

He just wags his tail again. She can see it's going to take some time to learn Dog. She decides to take him out as soon as she's had a wash. The plastic cubicle creaks as she closes the door and turns on the weedy shower. She'll have to be quick about it. The gas canister is running low.

'We know what you're doing!' Joe's voice sings from outside in the yard. 'We can see you!'

'No, you can't!' she shouts. 'So you can get lost!'

'Leave her alone, Joe.'

Tommy sounds so serious, it makes her smile. Her knight in shining armour.

'Leave her alone!' Joe taunts him with a lisping imitation. 'Why? Are you fucking her?'

There's the sound of a scuffle and a muffled cry from Tommy. Jesus. They're a pair of animals.

She gets out of the shower and goes into the bedroom, turning the radio up to drown out the sound of the Idiot Brothers. When she's dressed, she clips Wolf's lead on and leads him into the scrapyard. He sniffs around the roots of the plants that grow at the base of the fence, finds a place he likes, and lifts his long back leg.

From the edge of the stadium car park Sarah watches a van turning in to the main entrance. The sun is coming up

142

behind it and Sarah has to shield her eyes to see what it is. The bread van. Agnes's bicycle is propped up against the back wall of the stadium. Good, she can put the buns away. Sarah is sick of doing everything.

She watches the van pull up to the kitchen door. A figure gets down from the cab and comes round the back to open the double doors. It isn't the usual delivery driver. This one is slimmer and younger-looking. He takes a tray of breadcakes from the van and goes to the kitchen door. A chill creeps up Sarah's spine. The way he walks those few steps, the way he carries the tray, there is no mistaking him.

She winds the dog's lead tightly round her hand and keeps him close as she crosses the car park. She slips around the van until she's next to the open door to the kitchen, her back flat against the wall. Agnes is speaking, counting the breadcakes. Any minute now he will come out for another tray. He mustn't see her. She backs along the wall until she reaches the turnstiles. She pushes against the metal bar, but it's locked, so she tucks herself in, hidden from view. Wolf begins to whine softly. She strokes his head and whispers to him.

'Shh! Don't worry.'

Behind her there's a sudden noise of metal on metal. She turns to see Tommy with a key, unlocking the mechanism that keeps the turnstiles from moving.

'There's someone there,' she mouths.

'What's the matter?'

'There's a man in the kitchen with Agnes. I know him. He's going to hurt her.'

Tommy looks at her for a moment, then pushes his way through the turnstile like a bull through a gate. He passes her

without looking back. She peers from her hiding place to see
the bread delivery boy coming out of the kitchen. He looks
at Tommy, a smile on his face that is immediately replaced
by one of shock, as Tommy barrels into him. She steps back
again, leans against the turnstile and gathers the dog close to
her. It was not easy keeping his feet clear of the turning metal,
but soon they're inside the narrow payment kiosk.

'Come on, Wolf.'

The dog shifts uneasily until they're on the trackside.
They skirt the building and she presses her face up against
the window of the cafe.

'Agnes!' she shouts, hammering on the glass. 'Agnes!'

CHAPTER NINETEEN

Tuesday morning

PCSO Carly Jayson was standing on the pavement outside the derelict Chasebridge Community High School watching DS Knowles step out of his black Mondeo. Sean followed him from the passenger side.

'All right, Sean, how's your head this morning?' Carly said.

'Not bad,' he smiled.

'Late night?' Knowles said.

'No, sir,' Sean said. 'Just went for a quick pint after work, to celebrate getting onto the Major Crimes Team.'

'Well I hope it won't impair your judgement,' Knowles said.

'It won't.'

'Sorry I couldn't make it,' Carly said. 'I had a migraine threatening. Need to nip them in the bud when they start. My sick leave sheet's looking bad enough as it is.'

'Well, we'd love to chat,' Sean said quietly, 'but we've got detective stuff to do.'

'Get on with you!' she said, laughing.

Knowles took no notice. It was as if Carly didn't exist.

They entered the car park and made their way to the

side entrance of the school. Knowles looked around him.

'What's on the other side of those trees?'

He was pointing across the stretch of unmown turf, where a single rusty goalpost was stranded in the last remnant of the sports field. Beyond it a ragged hedge grew into the lower branches of a row of overgrown conifers.

'The dog track. Chasebridge Greyhound Stadium, to give it its proper title,' Sean said.

'What do you notice?' Knowles said.

Sean followed his gaze. At first, he couldn't make out anything significant. Grass that hadn't been cut, the goalpost, the hedge, and tall, bushy trees. He glanced back across the pitch again. And then he saw it. A path through the grass and thistles, leading towards the edge of the field, where it bordered the greyhound stadium. It was not much more than a parting of the ways, like an animal track in the woods.

'Someone, or something,' Sean said, 'has made a regular journey between this corner of the building over to that hedge.'

'And what are you going to do about it?'

'Follow the path and see where they were going?'

'Off you go then, eyes open,' Knowles said. 'I'm going to see what the state of play is inside.'

Sean set off, treading carefully, watching the ground before each footfall. He put his gloves on and moved slowly, scanning the grass in front of him. Something caught his eye, light brown against the green stem of a tuft of long grass. It could just be a stone. He bent down, parting the grass with his fingers. It was a cigarette end. He picked it up carefully between his finger and thumb, thinking of Lizzie and the precision of her job. This butt might be nothing, but on the other hand, it could

146

belong to the suspect, running away from the scene.

The rest of the path was reasonably clear. At the hedge it continued along to a corner, where a new stretch of fencing had been built. This marked the rear of the properties in Springfield Gardens. The path stopped. Sean bent down, and there, more suited to a fox than a person, he found a hole at the end of the hedge leading to the dog track. He could see the rails, and beyond them a scoreboard, advertising dog food. He straightened up. They should get a CSI down here, check for fabric threads or hairs caught in the hedge. This could have been the suspect's exit route.

He wondered if the stadium CCTV cameras reached this far. He'd spotted a rudimentary system on Saturday. There was definitely a camera in the bar and one aimed at the track itself. There were probably others.

He hurried back to the school building and saw that something was going on inside. The flash of a camera lit up the line of frosted windows that marked the toilets, to the left of the entrance door. Several officers were gathered around the door itself. Two white-suited figures emerged, carrying a clear plastic bag, in which he could see a soft white object. As the bag turned in the CSI's hand, he saw a distorted face, with black-rimmed eyes, a crushed nose and shrivelled mouth. It seemed to be staring at him.

'What the hell is that?' he said.

'A rubber Halloween mask,' Lizzie said, lifting the bag higher to show him. 'The Grim Reaper, I think.'

'Bloody hell!' he said. 'I thought it was a human face.'

'It was neatly stashed in the panelling behind one of the toilets,' said DI Khan, from behind his own hygiene mask. 'It might be something left from when the school was still open, some kid's

Halloween prank, but the way the panel had been dislodged looked recent. Let's hope there are some skin cells inside.'

Khan lifted his own face mask and took a long breath of air.

'That's better. You wonder how anyone can live like that. Ah, Denton, can you get us a bag for these forensics suits, and some antibacterial gel from the glovebox of my car?'

Sean took the keys from Khan's gloved hand, trying not to touch too much of their surface.

'Yes, guv. And can I get an envelope for this? Found it on the field.'

He opened his other hand and showed Khan and Lizzie the cigarette end. She raised her eyebrows.

'There must be thousands of cigarette butts around here,' she said.

'I don't want to think of the cost of getting them all tested,' Khan said, shaking his head.

'It was near the corner of the field,' Sean said. 'Might be nothing, but there's a way through to the greyhound stadium, and we may be able to get CCTV footage from that side.'

'Very well,' Khan said. 'Bag it and label it. But be quick, these coveralls stink of shit.'

When Sean came back from Khan's car, DS Knowles was waiting for him, a thin smile playing at the corners of his mouth.

'There you are,' he said, eyeing Khan's keys and the small bottle of antibacterial gel. 'Find anything on your walk across the field?'

'I did, as it happens,' Sean said. 'Cigarette end. I've bagged it and logged it. I also found a hole in the hedge, leading to the dog track.'

He held a large bag open for DI Khan to dispose of his forensic suit, mask and gloves. The bag would also be logged and sent to the lab, along with the Grim Reaper mask. Khan was rubbing antibacterial gel over his hands, his face still twisted in disgust. Knowles watched the whole ritual with detached amusement.

'Come on, Denton,' he said, 'you better show me this hedge.' When they were out of earshot he added: 'I'm not being funny, but you're meant to be a trainee detective, not a trainee butler.'

Sean shrugged. 'I don't mind. I was just helping him out.'

'But you're supposed to be shadowing me, not playing nursemaid to the SIO.'

'I think I preferred trainee butler to nursemaid. Don't nursemaids breastfeed other women's babies?'

As soon as he said it, he thought he'd overstepped the mark. Knowles was an unknown quantity and the sense of humour Gav had developed in him over the last two years was probably way out of line here.

'So,' Knowles sucked his cheeks in and spoke in that cut-glass accent he had. 'Are you saying you wouldn't let the DI suck your tit?'

'Get lost!'

But to Sean's relief, Knowles was laughing. Sean joined in, thankful that the tension was broken. Maybe Lizzie was right about Ivan Knowles, and it was going to be okay.

They made their way back across the field, keeping their eyes down, in case they noticed else anything of interest. In the corner, where the hedge grew ragged and gave way to the hole, they crouched down. The hedge framed a view of the track, deserted now, except for a pair of seagulls.

CHAPTER TWENTY

Tuesday

DI Khan listened to the theory that someone could have entered or left the school site via the hedge. He glanced at the trees and ran his fingers through his beard.

'Good work, Knowles,' he said. 'You and Denton should pay a visit to the greyhound stadium.'

Sean noticed that he got no credit for the discovery, but he could see how keen his new partner was to impress, like the girls in school who always shot their hand up to answer the question, so they could get moved up a set. Chasebridge Community High School had not been without its ambitious students. A girl in Sean's year had got a place at Oxford University, the first in the school's history. She was a bit of an oddball, Sean remembered, but the name-calling was soon forgotten when she got a double-page spread in the local paper. His nan talked of nothing else for weeks.

'Are you coming, Denton?'

He hadn't realised Knowles was speaking to him. He snapped out of the past and followed him to the car.

'Which way, Tonto?' Knowles said.

'You what?'

'Did you never watch *The Lone Ranger*?'

'Oh, yeah,' Sean said. 'So now I'm your native guide?'

'I think it's a promotion from nursemaid.'

Sean forced a smile, but he wasn't feeling it.

They drove up Disraeli Road towards the dual carriageway.

'Second right at the roundabout, sir.'

As they drew up to the give-way line, Knowles hesitated.

'What's going on there?' he said.

A hundred yards to the left of the roundabout, where the dual carriageway ran behind the Eagle Mount tower blocks, a van had been parked at a crooked angle, half up on the grass verge. The back doors were open and a group of people were collecting loaves of bread. One woman had an orange plastic tray loaded up with breadcakes.

'Food parcels?'

'Maybe a mobile shop,' Sean said. 'But it's a stupid place to park.'

Knowles drove onto the roundabout and Sean craned his neck round to see what was going on with the van.

'I think we should call it in,' he said. He didn't add that in his previous role they would have immediately parked up and had a word with whoever was running their business on the roadside. It was unsafe and almost certainly illegal.

'It's not a priority, is it?' Knowles said. 'You get a car sent out to something like that, and that's one less vehicle able to attend a serious crime. We live in straitened times, Denton.'

'Fair enough.' He wasn't in uniform now. He would have to get used to things being different.

Knowles took the second exit onto a road that snaked

away from the dual carriageway. The homes built along the right-hand side of this road were detached houses with an unbroken view of the smooth grassy mound of Chasebridge Country Park. Scattered with trees, it was hard to imagine that this was the site of the old coal mine. The hill had been the slag heap, and at its base, a lake had been formed from water pumped up from underground.

'It changes quickly, doesn't it?' Knowles said. 'I wasn't expecting to be out in the leafy suburbs so quickly.'

'Aye, well. Don't hold your breath. It doesn't last. Next right, down that road.'

They turned into a narrow lane with overhanging birch trees, their summer leaves shimmering green. Ahead of them the corrugated iron fence that surrounded the greyhound stadium was rusty and patched. They drove under the vinyl banner hanging across the gate posts and into the empty car park.

Knowles whistled through his teeth. 'See what you mean. We're back in the Wild West now, Tonto.'

Sean said nothing.

DS Knowles parked the car and they got out. The heat came up to meet them from the broken tarmac. A door in the back wall of the stadium was propped open with a mop and bucket.

'Do you know this place well?' Knowles asked.

'I was here on Saturday, as it happens.'

'So quite the regular!'

'I wouldn't say that. Just something my nan fancied doing. They were having a special re-opening event.'

'So you brought your old granny along, nice.'

'And my sister, and Lizzie, my girlfriend. It was two for one.'

Knowles peered at him against the glare of the sun.

'Oh!' he said, as the penny dropped. 'I see. I didn't realise. You're the one who goes out with the forensic manager, Lizzie Morrison.'

Sean clenched his jaw, trying not to react to the surprise in Ivan's voice. And what did he mean by 'the one'? Had he been asking questions about Lizzie and been told she lived with a dyslexic PC, four years her junior, from the wrong side of the tracks? What larks, Knowles must be thinking, to find himself landed with this specimen of the working class.

Before Sean could think of any suitable reply, a crescendo of raised voices erupted from beyond the open door and a young woman came rushing out, pulling an apron off over her head. She threw the apron back into the doorway.

'You can keep your bloody job,' she screamed in accented English at someone inside. 'I get another one, somewhere I don't have to take bloody abuse. May you rot in hell. All of you.'

She turned as if to stride across the car park and faltered when she saw Sean and Ivan Knowles. It was the girl from Saturday night who'd been clearing the glasses.

'You!' she said to Sean. 'So now they call police on me for nothing!'

Sean was about to deny it, when Ivan put his hand out, as if to caution him from giving anything away.

'My name is DS Knowles, this is my colleague, DC Denton.' He hesitated over the word 'colleague' with the trace of a smile. 'We're here to speak to anyone who can help us with our enquiries about an incident next door in the old Chasebridge School building on Friday night.'

'Friday? I don't work here Friday. I am at home in my house in Hexthorpe on Friday, watching TV. I watch *Gogglebox*, it is very funny. I only work here Saturday and Sunday, Tuesday and Wednesday. Get place ready for races and clear up after races. But not any more. I'm leaving.'

She took a breath and looked from Knowles to Sean and back again.

'So they didn't call you?' she said.

'No,' Sean said. 'They didn't.'

She came closer to him and lowered her voice. 'I'm surprised you don't want to know about Saturday. You were here then. I remember you, flashing your badge around. I think you should ask some questions about Saturday.'

Sean looked to Knowles for direction, but the DS was wandering towards the kitchen. He knocked on the open door and went in.

'Is there something you want to tell me about Saturday?' Sean said.

'Not me,' she said and nodded towards the building. 'I can't tell you. You must ask them and those thugs they call their nephews.'

'Is there any way we can contact you,' he said, 'if we have any further questions?'

'My name is Agnieswska Wo niak,' she said in an urgent whisper, 'but they call me Agnes because they are not clever enough to say name in Polish. I live 142 Selby Avenue, Hexthorpe. You not going to write this down?'

'I'll remember,' he said. '142 Selby Avenue.' He pulled his notebook out of his pocket. 'But you can write your name down for me, if you like. I want to make sure it's spelt correctly.'

If she had been about to take the notebook, a glance towards the kitchen door caused her to change her mind. She backed away, shaking her head.

'No,' she said. 'They can't know you get anything from me. I say more than enough already.'

She turned and began to walk quickly away from him, across the car park and towards the lane. Sean followed Knowles into the kitchen.

Another young woman with spiky blonde hair, dark at the roots, was washing up at the sink. She ignored Sean, turning away to place the steel tray she was washing on a rack. He headed in the direction of the voices, through an open door, which led into the cafe.

CHAPTER TWENTY-ONE

Tuesday

When the two detectives are settled in the cafe with Lou, Sarah goes to the door to check that Agnes has really gone. She's just in time to see her walk out through the main entrance and set off up the lane. It's been surprisingly easy to get rid of her. Unfortunate, but essential. There was money missing from Saturday's takings. The plastic bags of coins and notes in the safe didn't add up to the total on the till, so it was clear someone had taken something. And as it's Sarah who helps Lou read the information from the new tills, and downloads it for her in a way she can understand and write up in her old-fashioned accounting book, and as it was Sarah who noticed the error, then she can't possibly be the thief. Anyway, she's practically family now, whereas Agnes is just another foreigner. It wasn't difficult to make the case against Agnes.

'I'm sorry if that young lady was abusive to you,' Lou is saying, 'it's not easy managing staff sometimes, you know. Hard to tell who you can trust.'

One of the detectives says something that Sarah can't

quite hear, so she moves closer to the hatch.

'We have CCTV all around the grounds,' Lou says, 'so I'm sure we can help. What's happened?'

'There was a serious incident in the old school, which resulted in a man losing his life. I'm sorry we can't tell you any more at this stage.'

It sounds like the tall one. He's got a posh voice. He's asking about the staff, and do they have their own security.

'We're a family business, my nephews help out with most things. On a race night we have part-time staff on the gates and there's a couple of girls who help with the catering. We don't need a lot of security. It's not like horse racing, Officer, it's more of a family crowd.'

Sarah holds her breath, hoping Lou won't go into too much detail about the 'couple of girls'.

'Excuse me a moment, Officers.' Lou pushes the hatch open a few inches. 'Sarah?'

Sarah looks over Lou's shoulder at the two men sitting at a table by the window. One of them is staring out over the track, while the other seems to be taking a mental measurement of the room.

'What's going on?' she says quietly.

'Nothing for you to worry about,' Lou says. 'Something happened in the school on Friday night. I'm relieved to say it's nothing to do with us, so just this once, I don't mind helping the police. I've even offered them a cup of tea. Can you do the honours?'

Sarah turns away to get two mugs out of the cupboard. Lou slides the hatch open a little wider.

'How does the CCTV work?' she whispers to Sarah, her ample back blocking the view of the police officers. 'It's all digital, but I haven't a clue how to give them the pictures.'

Sarah puts the mugs down.

'What do they need to see?'

'Anything that shows the edge of the track where the hedge and the trees are. They say there's a gap in the hedge that someone could have crawled through. Well, that's news to me, but then I never go that side, so I wouldn't have noticed. They want any footage of the area from Friday night.'

'Derek will need to give me a password,' Sarah says. 'And we'll have to copy the files onto a memory stick.'

'I don't want Derek to know, not yet. He'll go mental with the boys, they're supposed to keep the grounds secure. I'd rather leave him to his golf, if we can. Is there any other way?'

'Well, it'll have a hard drive,' Sarah says. 'I've seen these systems before. We could give them the whole DVR, but the cameras will be off until we get it back.'

'What's that? A DVR?'

'Digital video recorder. It'll be a box connected to Derek's computer. It has a hard drive and the files are transferred from there to the computer itself.'

'You seem to know a lot about it,' Lou says and Sarah feels as if she's being scrutinised for longer than is comfortable.

'I'm a bit of a geek, that's all, same with the computerised tills,' she smiles. 'I just like all that stuff.'

Lou turns to the officers.

'It's on a DVR,' Lou says brightly. 'You can have it for four hours, but we've got a charity race meeting tonight. We'll need it back.'

Sarah doesn't hear their reply, but Lou is unclipping the keys from her belt and handing them over.

'Let yourself into Derek's office, and don't touch anything you shouldn't. I'll keep them talking.'

As she turns back to the two officers, Lou gives them a big smile and the older one smiles back. The younger one is looking through the hatch. Sarah backs into the shadows, drops the keys into her pocket, and leaves through the door to the car park. She sprints round to the fire escape, goes upstairs and through the bar to Derek's office.

The office is lined with wooden panelling and still smells of polish from the last time Sarah cleaned it. Derek was working at his desk that day and she watched him tapping in a password. She didn't catch it all at first, but later, when he'd finished checking all the footage from the previous night and left the room while she did the hoovering, she stood behind the desk, the vacuum cleaner still running, and tried out what she thought she'd seen. It didn't work at first, so she looked around her for clues. She was sure it was the name of a greyhound and a date. Suddenly the framed photograph to the right of the desk gave her the answer she was looking for.

Today the room is still and undisturbed. A shaft of sunlight warms the wood of the desk. Sarah fingers the keys, and checks her watch. She has minutes, at most.

When she's finished, she disconnects the DVR. As she crosses the thick carpet of the office, she fingers Lou's bunch of keys and chooses the newest key, a shiny Yale, slides it around the ring, and slips it into her back pocket. She opens the door to the landing to find the younger detective standing there.

'Sorry,' he says. 'Did I startle you?'

She holds out the DVR and gives him what she hopes is a shy smile.

'Camera six is the one you want to look at.'

CHAPTER TWENTY-TWO

Tuesday

In the viewing room the Force's technical CCTV specialist, Mark Headingham, copied the files from the DVR to his computer. He then disconnected the DVR and returned it to the evidence bag.

'That can go back to its owners now,' he said.

'No rush,' DS Knowles said. 'We've got a couple of hours. Let's sit back and enjoy the show.'

Sean sat behind Mark, and watched him select the folder marked CAM6. It appeared to be on the corner of the building, quite high up, and showed one half of the race track, the tall conifers and the hedge along the boundary. At the bottom of the screen, in the right-hand corner, there was a white horizontal pole that Sean recognised as a section of the rail, where they'd stood among a small crowd on Saturday night. On Friday the place looked deserted. Mark fast-forwarded until the time code showed 17:00 hours. Nothing happened for several minutes, until a cat moved away from the hedge, hesitated, and then went back the way it had come.

'Fascinating,' Knowles said, yawning.

The minutes ticked by.

'There,' Sean said finally. 'Who's that?'

Mark froze the picture, then nudged the image forwards in small jumps, frame by frame. A figure had come into view from somewhere to the right of the screen, beyond the trainers' enclosure. He was running, stumbling slightly. Then a second figure appeared, as if from the stadium building. He crossed the track towards the first, his hand raised in greeting.

'The second one's Homsi,' Sean said.

'And I think the first is our victim, Abbas.'

On the screen, Homsi caught up with Abbas, and they continued to the far corner of the track. At one point, Abbas stopped and gestured back towards the stadium. Mark zoomed in, but the image was too blurred to make out what was happening. When they reached the hedge, they ducked down and disappeared.

Mark Headingham juddered the image backwards again and wrote down the time code. He passed a piece of paper towards Sean and asked him to sign, to show who'd been part of the viewing, in case they had to give evidence in court. He then handed the form to Ivan Knowles.

'Is that it?' Sean said.

'Well that's the answer, isn't it?' Knowles said. 'The path was used as an access route by these two.'

'But why?'

'It looks like Abbas is wearing a vest. The same vest he had on when we found him. He's wearing boots. I think he's been at work on the stadium site. Homsi too.'

'Yes, there's a new building over on this side, where he's come from. When we were there on Saturday, I noticed that the ground in front of the building was unfinished, like it was waiting for gravel or tarmac or something.'

'So why didn't Homsi mention it?' Knowles said.

'Maybe he can't work here legally. I'm not sure what status that letter actually gives him, but I can find out.'

'It explains why the path through the playing field was only lightly worn down. Two people, just going back and forth once a day. That would do it.'

'Abbas looked distressed,' Sean said. 'Can we look at it again?'

Mark rewound the images back and they watched again as Abbas ran, stopped at his friend's waved greeting, then gesticulated towards the stadium buildings. As Homsi reached him, he seemed to guide his friend towards the hedge, a hand on his shoulder.

'We shouldn't have let Homsi go,' Knowles said. 'I'm starting to wonder what else he chose not to mention.'

'We could contact St Bernadette's,' Sean said. 'See if he showed up there.'

'Okay,' Knowles said. 'You go and do that. And if you see Khan, tell him what we've got. I'll watch a bit more. I want to see if that cat comes back, he was good.'

'Did you notice where the other cameras were placed?' Mark Headingham asked Sean, as he headed for the door. 'Then we could see where he came from.'

'There was one central to the track and one over the car park,' Sean said.

'Which leaves three more,' Mark said. He paused the video and minimised the image, before opening CAM1.

It showed a narrow counter, a concrete floor and walls of plywood, covered in posters, advertising special offers.

'What's this?' Knowles said.

'We're inside the payment kiosk.' Sean recognised it from his visit on Saturday. 'Am I all right to go and make that call?'

'Sure,' Knowles said. 'I'll have to do my best without your specialist expertise.'

Sean noted the sarcasm and wondered if it was meant to be banter, or if Knowles thought he was being a smart-arse. As he closed the door, Mark Headingham restarted the video.

Sean hesitated in the doorway of the ops room. Every desk was taken and there was a buzz of activity. DC Tina Smales looked up and gave him a smile.

'Everything okay?'

'Just need to perch somewhere to make a phone call about Elyas Homsi, the guy we found in the school.'

'Be my guest,' she said, getting up. 'I hot-desk as it is, but you should be okay for ten minutes. I'm not expecting to be turfed off in a hurry. Fancy a coffee?'

'I'd prefer a cold drink.' He reached in his pocket for some coins. 'Can of Pepsi would be great.'

He rang St Bernadette's and listened to a woman on the other end give him the usual spiel about client confidentiality.

'I do understand,' he said, 'but confidentiality doesn't apply when a serious crime has been committed. We just want to know if Homsi reached the hostel.'

There was a pause. She took an overly dramatic breath before she spoke again.

'He didn't. At least, we have no one of that name here. We've been full since early Saturday, so we've been turning people away. I'd know if someone new had arrived.'

'One of my colleagues phoned ahead to arrange a bed for him. We didn't want him back out on the streets.'

'Well,' the woman sounded dismissive, 'if they did ring, they spoke to the wrong person.'

'Thanks for your help.'

He put the phone down and swore under his breath.

'Feeling the strain already?'

It was DI Khan, who had materialised right next to him. Sean stood up awkwardly.

'Sir,' his mouth was dry. 'It's Homsi. We've got footage of him and Abbas leaving the dog track and heading for the school grounds on Friday, shortly after 17:00 hours. Knowles is just watching the rest of the footage to see if we can see what they were doing there before that.'

'Excellent. Until we get the forensic reports back, that's the best lead we've got. Let's go and have a word with him.'

'Homsi didn't arrive at the hostel.'

'Ah,' Khan's frown deepened.

'Would it be useful for me to phone RAMA, in York? The letter he had was from them. They might have some ideas about any known associates or places he's stayed before.'

Sean withheld the information that he'd also given Homsi the number for RAMA. It had been a spur of the moment decision, to help the poor guy out, and may have been against the rules.

'Mm, go ahead.' Khan walked over to the whiteboard and circled Homsi's name in red. 'But first I need you to call through to dispatch. We need all units looking for Homsi. He clearly omitted to tell us vital information.'

'Because he was working on the track illegally.'

'We'll see,' Khan said. 'But he was at the scene, last person to see the victim alive, blood on his clothing. I think he's just moved back up to prime suspect.'

He underlined the name and made a full stop with so much anger that the red marker pen flew out of his hand and across the room. The room fell silent.

Sean picked up the phone on the desk that Tina shared with several other officers and rang through to dispatch. As he listened to the internal ringtone, he rearranged a procession of shock-haired Gonks on the desk.

After a while, Tina came back and put a cold can of Pepsi in front of him. He'd finished passing on the message to dispatch and was now waiting for someone to pick up the phone at RAMA. He listened to eight rings before the answer machine kicked in.

'Hi, it's PC, I mean, DC Sean Denton here at Doncaster Police. Can you give me a call back on the following number please?'

Tina was writing him a note on a yellow Post-it.

XAVIER VELASQUEZ IS MISSING.

He ended the call, knocking the Gonks over in his hurry.

'What do you mean?'

'First day back at work and he didn't come back from his morning delivery. It's a family business. His dad's been trying to get hold of him all afternoon. Half an hour ago, the dad gave up, and phoned it in as a misper. Lisa-Marie took the call and remembered it was our case.'

'What's the family business?'

'It's a bakery. Sunhill Bakery.'

CHAPTER TWENTY-THREE

Tuesday evening

Chloe and Melissa walked up through the Chasebridge estate to Eagle Mount One.

'Is this where you've always lived?'

'Not exactly.'

'You're like me, I bet. Moved around a bit.'

'Something like that.'

Chloe pushed open the door into the hall and headed for the stairs.

'Can we take the lift? My feet are killing me.'

Melissa had come to the door of the children's home in a pair of killer heels, tight white shorts and a vest top. Chloe had pointed out they would have to do a fair bit of walking, but Melissa was undeterred.

'Okay,' Chloe said, as they stood in the lobby of the tower block. 'But it's only one floor and you'll need to hold your breath. The lift stinks.'

The metal box clunked slowly up to the first floor and Chloe felt a sense of relief as the doors opened. They crossed the landing and she let them into Jack's flat. It was strange not to call out a greeting and hear him reply. It reminded her that she needed to text Sean to see if he could make visiting time.

'Nice place,' Melissa said. 'I wish I could have my own flat.'

'It's not mine. It's my dad's. Here's the kitchen. Why don't you make us both a cuppa while I get changed?'

She glanced out of the kitchen window towards the dual carriageway. There was a line of police cars on the verge, but she couldn't see what they were doing, the other blocks were in the way. She sighed. There was always trouble on this estate.

She decided to put on jeans, even though it was still warm, and take a jacket. She didn't want to get caught out if they stayed late. She pulled on her trainers.

'Are you sure you don't want to borrow some shoes that are a bit more practical?'

'I'll be all right. I've made you a cup of tea.'

They drank their tea in the sitting room, watching a quiz show that Melissa chose. She insisted on washing up the mugs and Chloe stood back, noticing how the other girl enjoyed playing house. It was like watching herself not so long ago, when she was still institutionalised, desperate for any experience that felt like it belonged to the outside world.

As they passed the newsagent on Winston Grove, Melissa announced she wanted an ice cream. Chloe smiled at how quickly she went from adult to child.

'Come on, then.'

They went in. Chloe bought them both a Cornetto.

Back outside on the pavement, she peeled the paper away

and bit into the teeth-chilling centre. It gave her a tiny buzz of energy. Sugar going straight to her brain.

'Come on, then,' she said to Melissa. 'Let's go and see these dogs.'

They walked past the health centre and turned up the Horse Road, retracing the route she'd taken with Maureen on Saturday. Soon their ice creams were almost gone. Melissa licked the last remnants of chocolate from her wrapper, screwed it up and threw it in the long grass at the side of the track. Chloe held her tongue, folded her own wrapper into a tight square and shoved it in her pocket.

The track seemed much longer when she had to keep waiting for Melissa, who was struggling on the rough ground in her heels, but finally they reached the locked gates of the scrapyard.

'See that,' Melissa pointed to the sign above the gate. 'That's my dad, Levi Heron.'

'Does he live here too?'

The girl shook her head. 'He's in prison.'

'Oh'.

'Are you shocked?'

'Hardly.'

Chloe didn't want to be drawn into this kind of conversation so she went ahead, squeezing round the side of the five-bar gate at the end of the track. They joined the pavement for a few yards, then turned into the stadium car park. On Saturday it was full of vehicles, and there'd been a steady stream of people funnelling through the turnstiles. Today, a shimmer of heat hung over the ground. It was empty and silent, apart from the song of a persistent bird somewhere nearby.

Chloe walked under the sagging banner, which still carried the announcement of Saturday's grand re-opening. Instinctively, she stayed close to the fence that divided the scrapyard from the car park. There was shade here, and she felt more comfortable away from the direct view of anyone coming out of the main building. She turned round to see Melissa hobbling in behind her.

'It looks dead,' Chloe said.

'We're early. The racing doesn't start for another hour.'

'It gives me the creeps.'

Chloe followed the fence to where it ended and the scrapyard opened up on her left. Suddenly something darted out of the yard and came straight at her, tongue lolling, mouth open, a mouth full of jagged white teeth. Inches away, it gathered its back legs and rose up, front legs level with her shoulders.

She screamed and stepped back into the corrugated iron fence.

'Wolf!' a female voice called.

The dog dropped down, glanced back to where it had come from, then turned to Chloe again, tail wagging, gathering himself as if to jump once more. She could see now that he was just trying to play, but she was shaking.

A young woman appeared from the scrapyard. She had dyed blonde hair, cropped and spiky, and she held a lead and collar in her hand.

'Come here, Wolf!'

She looked at Chloe and Melissa.

'Oh,' she said, and seemed to forget about the dog. 'What are *you* doing here?'

The *you* was directed at Melissa.

'Do Lou and Derek know you're here?' She grabbed the dog's neck and managed to get its collar back on.

'We came to watch the rescue dogs race. Are you going to let him run?'

'What?' The girl looked at Melissa as if she was mad. 'Look, you need to go home and take your friend with you. Go on. Before Lou and Derek find out. I heard them saying they were having second thoughts about you coming to live with them anyway, because you're a bit of a handful, aren't you? So what are they going to think if they know you've come here on your own?'

'You don't know what you're talking about.'

'I do, Melissa Heron. I do know, because I listen. Now it's your turn to listen. Get out before I tell your social worker myself.'

Melissa didn't answer. Chloe watched a flicker of sadness pass across her face, then it was gone, and in its place a look of grim determination settled across her clenched jaw.

'Come on, Chloe,' she said. 'She doesn't get to tell me what to do.'

She teetered off towards the stadium building in her heels. As Chloe made to follow her, the other woman grabbed her arm.

'What were you doing skulking round the fence like that?'

Chloe just shook her head. 'Nothing.'

'Get her out of here, if you're her friend. And stay away from the yard, or I won't call the dog off next time.'

Chloe turned and went after Melissa.

'Who the hell is she?'

171

'Just some girl who works for my aunt and uncle. She's nobody.'

'What's she so worked up about?'

Melissa turned to face her. 'She's right, in a way. I'm not supposed to be here. I'm still on supervised visits. That means Aunty Lou visits me but there has to be someone else there, like a social worker or one of the staff from the home. It's because my dad's got a criminal record and I've got a history of running away.'

'So you shouldn't have been here on Saturday night either?'

Melissa shook her head. 'I'm supposed to be coming on a proper visit soon, with the social worker, but it keeps getting cancelled.'

Chloe chewed her bottom lip. She didn't like the situation she'd got herself into. It had trouble written all over it.

'If anybody asks,' she said, 'I don't know any of this. I just came to watch the dog racing and as soon it's over, I'm putting you in a taxi back into town, and I'm going home.'

'Don't be pissed off with me, Chloe.'

But Chloe wasn't listening. She was walking towards the new building.

'Is this the kennels, then?'

'Yeah,' Melissa said, staggering slightly to catch her up. 'Shall we see if Indian Whisper's there?'

In front of the new single-storey block, someone was rolling out turf on their hands and knees. Chloe watched for a moment, itching to suggest he should have the rolls closer together, but she was wary of speaking to anyone here after the young woman's outburst.

'Hiya, Tommy!' Melissa called.

The man looked up. He was plump, with an easy smile. He looked familiar and Chloe wondered if she'd seen him on Saturday.

'Hi, Melissa! Who's your friend?'

'This is Chloe.'

He stood up and rubbed the soil off his hands on the back of his trousers. He held out a hand for Chloe to shake. She took it, and remembered where she'd seen him, dragging the drunken customer out of the bar towards the fire escape. His hands were muscular and he gripped hers tight before he dropped it, as if he didn't know his own strength.

'We came to see Whisper,' Melissa said.

'Whisper?' he spoke slowly.

'Yes, Derek's dog that hurt his leg. Indian Whisper. Is he in the kennels?'

Tommy shook his head.

'Joe shot him.'

Melissa gasped.

'He shot him with a bolt gun and buried him in the field on the other side of the Horse Road.'

Melissa's eyes filled with tears. Tommy shuffled from one foot to another, at a loss as to what he should do. Chloe took Melissa in her arms and held her close.

'There, there,' she whispered into Melissa's hair, as the girl sobbed into her shoulder. 'Perhaps there wasn't any choice. If it was a bad break, he would have suffered too much and it might never have got better.'

She didn't believe what she was saying but Tommy nodded, relieved she'd come to his rescue.

'Maybe we should go,' she said. 'I'll take you back home.'

'Yeah,' Melissa said, between sobs. 'I don't want to stay here. How could he do that?'

She let Chloe guide her, one arm over her shoulder, across the car park towards the road.

As they reached the gates, a battered red pick-up drove in and stopped level with them. The window opened.

'Hey, little sister.' A man who looked like a slimmer and more muscular version of Tommy, smiled out from under a baseball cap.

This time Chloe had no trouble recognising him. He'd spoken to her at the rail on Saturday night, mistaken her for Melissa, then threatened her. He'd been the first to grab the drunken punter too. While Tommy's features were soft and gentle, this brother was all cheekbones and chiselled chin. To some he might be handsome, but to her he simply looked cruel.

Melissa glared at him.

'How could you, Joe?'

'What have I done?'

'That poor dog, you killed him!'

'Hey, hey.' He held his hands up as she approached the car window. 'He was really badly hurt. What kind of a life was he going to have, in pain and waiting forever in a dogs' home for someone to take pity on him? It was a mercy killing.'

'You had no right!'

'Life's tough sometimes, Melissa. That's just the way it is.'

Melissa pushed past the pickup and headed for the road. She stumbled on a loose stone and twisted her ankle with a yelp. When she lifted her right shoe, the heel was hanging loose. Joe backed up until he was level with her.

Chloe followed and reached out to steady Melissa.

'At least let me take you home,' Joe said, his voice softer this time. 'It doesn't look like you're going to get much further on those shoes.'

Chloe felt as if she had become invisible, as Melissa, tears streaming down her cheeks, shrugged her off and got into the car. Joe looked up at Chloe as if he'd only just noticed her.

'Do I know you?'

She shook her head.

'Whatever you think you've seen or heard here, forget it,' he said. 'Not your circus, not your monkeys.'

She watched them drive away, then she turned towards the Horse Road. She glanced back into the car park, half-expecting to see the spiky-haired girl, but there was no one there.

CHAPTER TWENTY-FOUR

Tuesday

Sean looked at his phone and read a text from Chloe. Would it be all right if he popped over to the hospital to see Jack? She couldn't make it this evening. Sean sighed. It wasn't really all right. DI Khan had stormed into the ops room and reallocated half the team to help search for Xavier Velasquez in the woodland beyond the Chasebridge bypass. The theory was that he'd ditched the van, intending to take his own life. He'd been on suicide watch while he was on remand. But Sean wasn't so sure. He'd seen him in his mother's arms as he left the court. His family supported him; his dad had given him his old job back straight away. Sean raised his hand and asked if it could be a hijacking gone wrong, but that had caused laughter amongst his colleagues and a few comments about the sorry state of things if Chasebridge residents had resorted to hijacking bread vans.

Sean and DS Knowles were part of a reduced team on the school murder case.

Abbas was already slipping as a priority as manpower dwindled. Just a rough sleeper, a refugee at that, with no family to demand justice on his behalf. He'd been overtaken by a suspected rapist from a respectable family.

'Give yourself an hour, then update me,' Ivan Knowles said. 'Cover the town centre as systematically as you can and speak to anyone you recognise. And remember, Mary Dobbs is the priority. I need to sit through a few more thrilling episodes of the race track CCTV show.'

Sean criss-crossed the centre of town, talking to *Big Issue* sellers and buskers, even an old man reading the paper in the library, but nobody knew anything. Finally he made his way towards the market. Some of the food stalls on the outdoor market were already closing and there were rich pickings for anyone who wasn't too proud to pick up a few discarded oranges or cabbages.

He checked his watch. Only forty-five minutes of hospital visiting time left. He was ready to give up, and slip away to see Jack, when he spotted a couple who might be able to help him. An older man, red-faced and filthy, was pushing a supermarket trolley between the rapidly emptying stalls. There was a woman with him, younger, with lank brown hair tied in a ponytail. One of the stall holders chucked an orange into the trolley as they passed, but mostly they were ignored. Sean rang PC Gav Wentworth on his mobile.

'All right, mate?' Gav answered straight away.

'That couple you met on Friday night, leaving the Chasebridge estate with a supermarket trolley, was he older, red in the face and her, straight brown hair, possibly pulled back in a ponytail?'

'Aye,' Gav said. 'And the trolley was from Sainsbury's, if that helps.'

'Bingo,' Sean said. 'Thanks. It does.'

He was parallel with the couple. A long table, piled with men's hats, stood between them. He rounded the end of it and blocked their path.

'Can I have a word?'

'What for?' said the man, trying to steer around Sean.

The orange Sainsbury's logo on the front was chipped and muddied, but still legible.

'You spoke to my colleague on Friday night. PC Wentworth? Do you remember?' Sean said, showing his warrant card. 'I'm wondering if you can help us piece together what happened that evening.'

The woman let out a hard, humourless laugh.

'How the fuck am I supposed to know what I was doing on Friday? I can't bloody remember what I was doing last night. Neither can he. Fuck off, copper. We've got our shopping to do.'

The reek of spirits on her breath confirmed that she was probably telling the truth.

'Where are you sleeping?' Sean said.

'Mind your own business.'

'And before that?'

'Funny,' she said.

'Was it the old Chasebridge School? Do remember being there?'

She looked wary now, but the old guy was nodding slowly.

'Aye.'

'Why did you leave? Can you remember?'

'There was a bit of trouble.' He nodded slowly again, as if searching in his damaged memory for some detail. 'Bad lads, I reckon, fighting.'

'Do you remember anything about them, anything unusual?'

'I didn't see nothing,' the woman said quickly.

'So why did you leave?'

'Because he said, didn't you Jonno? You said we had to go.'

'Jonno makes the decisions, does he?' Sean said, and she just shrugged.

The old man smiled, and Sean saw he only had three blackened teeth, two up and one down, hanging in his soft gums. He looked ancient, but Sean knew better. The drinking had aged him, just like it had with his dad. At least his dad still had a roof over his head. He'd never thought he'd say it, but Jack had been lucky; there was always someone worse off. The nagging guilt about his father lying alone in the hospital came back to him. There was still time, as soon as he finished here.

'I didn't see any faces,' Jonno said slowly, 'because they had masks, like Halloween.'

'They? How many people?'

'There's two of them. There's always two of them.'

'So they've been before?'

The woman was becoming agitated and began to move the trolley away. 'We're not grasses. Leave us alone.'

'Do you know someone called Mary Dobbs? She was in the school. I'd like to talk to her. If I can find her, I won't need to bother you with any more questions.'

The woman looked at Sean for a moment, pupils wide and struggling to focus.

'Of course I know who she is, she's my fucking sister.'

'Okay,' Sean said and waited.

The woman lost the staring match that was going on between them, and broke her gaze.

'She's at The Limes,' she said. 'Don't cause her no bother, she's getting help there.'

'Thank you,' Sean said. 'Can I get either of you a cup of tea to say thank you?'

She laughed the hard laugh again. 'I won't be bought, copper! Not for all the tea in China, neither will Jonno.'

Jonno smiled his soft smile, the jagged teeth like bins in the mouth of a dank alley.

He watched them go and wondered where they would spend the night. It was going to be another warm one, so they might prefer to be out in the open, or in a doorway. He shuddered at how vulnerable that would make them.

He put in a call to Knowles and arranged to meet him at The Limes. It was a project off Nether Hall Road, set up to help women sex workers. Knowles said to give him an hour and, yes, it was all right to visit his dad in the meantime, if he was quick. That suited Sean – 'quick' was as much as either of them could tolerate.

In the hospital shop Sean looked across the shelves and picked out a motor racing magazine. Watching the Grand Prix on TV was one of the few times he and his dad were close. Perhaps Jack would remember it too, one of those long summer days when Sean was a little boy, with the curtains shut to keep the light out, his mum at one end of the settee and his dad at the other, Sean in the middle, eating a bag of crisps. It blurred into another memory, messier, sadder, after his mum was dead. Another Grand Prix, his dad asleep and missing the race, a bottle beside him on the floor, the air bitter with whisky fumes.

He took the magazine to the till. The photograph on the cover showed a shiny red Mercedes on a blurred background. Sean queued up behind an elderly woman with a walking frame, legs wrapped in bandages. He wished they could get a move on, he didn't have long before he was supposed to be at The Limes.

On the ward, Jack was sitting up in bed. His hair had been combed neatly over his scalp with a side parting that made him look like a businessman. Sean couldn't help smiling at the irony. Jack smiled back. When he spoke, his voice was slow and slurred.

'Hey up, lad, what have you got for me?'

'Car magazine,' Sean offered it to him.

Jack lifted an arm slowly, as if every movement required conscious thought.

'Ta.' He ran the thumb of his twisted hand over the cover. 'She's a beauty, isn't she? What speed do you reckon she could go?'

'A hundred and eighty, tops, I should think.'

Sean sat carefully on the side of the bed.

Jack looked slowly up from the picture to his son.

'What about you?' he said.

Sean waited.

'What about you?' Jack repeated, concentrating on every word, as if he was learning a new language. 'Have they let you drive any fast cars in that job you do?'

Sean considered telling him the truth about the clapped-out old squad cars on the response unit, but he decided to reward

Jack's rare show of interest with something more juicy.

'When I did a stint in traffic, we topped a hundred and thirty on the motorway, blues and twos going all the way.'

Jack wheezed half a laugh. 'Cops and robbers!'

'Something like that. A sixteen-year-old with no licence who broke into a house and took the keys for a BMW parked on the drive.'

'I bet he had the time of his life.' The wheeze broke into a cackle.

'The owner wasn't very pleased.'

'Bet he wasn't.' Jack shook his head, his mouth slackening in to a soft grin. 'Almost feel sorry for him myself.'

'The lad only stopped when he hit a fence, coming off the slip road. Lucky to be alive.'

'Aye,' Jack nodded thoughtfully. 'You only live once.'

He was looking at the car on the magazine cover and his eyes filled with tears. Sean looked away. His father cleared his throat.

'Is Chloe coming today?' Jack said. 'I thought she was, but I haven't seen her.'

Sean glanced out of the window. The vapour trail of a jet plane smudged a line across the sky.

'Something came up.'

'Bless her,' Jack said. 'She's a miracle, that one. When I think of all the lost years, though, the years I never knew her, it's a bloody crime! That's what it is!'

'All right, Dad, don't get worked up.' Sean could see how quickly Jack's mood changed.

'They stole her from me!'

'You're getting mixed up, Dad . . .'

'Don't you tell me, you bloody bastard!' Jack lurched forward and the magazine slipped to the floor. A nursing assistant came hurrying into the bay.

'What's all this about, Mr Denton? We don't want you getting overexcited.'

'Fuck off, I don't want any fucking darkies touching me!'

Sean groaned. 'I'm so sorry.'

'Don't be,' she said tightly. 'They often get like this. I'm used to it.'

That doesn't make it all right, he thought. He could predict what was coming next. Jack was unstoppable. The immigrants had taken all the jobs, the police were all bastards, Sean's mother was a whore. Chloe's mum, who in truth Jack could hardly remember, was a bitch for keeping their daughter a secret from him.

'Now, Mr Denton.' The nursing assistant stood over Jack, arms folded, while he paused for breath. 'What are you going to have for your lunch tomorrow? You haven't filled your card in.'

Jack responded with a combination of a shrug and a snarl, but she'd successfully distracted him. Sean decided this would be a good time to slip away. He picked the racing car magazine up from the floor and put it on the bed.

'I've got to go, Dad.'

There was a grunt in response.

'I'll call in tomorrow.'

As he walked away he wondered why he'd offered, but he recalled one of the nurses telling him something that had stuck with him. It was harder, she said, when you'd had a bad relationship with a parent, and you knew they were dying, because you felt you were running out of time to put things right. He would try to get there more often, he really would.

He was on the corridor with all the art. Landscape after landscape, like little rectangles of other worlds. There was one he hadn't noticed before, darker than all the others; a house painted black, on a dark purple background, but in the window a yellow light was shining. He found himself drawn to that glowing square of light. His father had no friends and no other family. Everyone was dead, or had given up on him long ago. It was just him and Chloe. He was like that abandoned house with the light still shining in one window.

'Hiya!' a voice said, right beside him. 'You look like you're miles away!'

It was Tina Smales.

'I was,' Sean said, giving the darkened house a last glance.

'Are you going to buy one?' Tina said.

'Buy one?'

'Yes, there's a notice. They're having a sale in aid of the hospital at the end of the month. Then they'll put some new ones up.'

Sean felt a strange tug of sadness that the pictures would be gone. He'd never thought of buying something like this. He wondered what Lizzie would say, but he suspected the dark house might not fit her idea of interior decoration.

'Maybe,' he said. 'What are you up to?'

'Just come to see my domestic violence victim.'

He looked back at the dark house, but now the light from the window was just yellow paint on top of purple paint.

'By the way,' Tina said. 'You know I've been trying to get hold of Bethany Winters? Well I got sick of listening to the phone ringing out, so I contacted BT, who said that number had been reassigned.'

'So?'

'So, I think I'm going to pay her a visit. You free tomorrow? You could come along.'

'Yes, I'd like that. If Knowles is okay with it. It must be a tough call to come forward in a case like that. I don't blame her for bottling it at the last minute.'

'It happens, sadly.'

'You know, I've been thinking I might specialise.'

'In sexual crimes?'

'Maybe, or children. Child protection, something like that.'

She raised her eyebrows. 'Now that really is tough.'

'Tough's my middle name,' he said. 'It's not actually. It's Paul.'

She laughed. It was a pretty laugh. He wasn't sure why he'd noticed that, and tried to shake off the lingering feeling of disloyalty it left him with.

'I'll be off, then,' he said. 'Hopefully I'll see you tomorrow.'

She gave him a little wave and walked away.

CHAPTER TWENTY-FIVE

Tuesday

Sean spotted DS Ivan Knowles' car outside The Limes. The Mondeo looked too new for this street and not pimped up enough to belong to a dealer. As he waited to cross the road, a van slowed down, indicating to overtake the parked car. *Very law-abiding*, Sean thought, *he's not fooled either*.

He knocked on the window. Knowles opened the door and got out.

'Here we are again,' he said.

'Yes, sir.'

'My eyes are still trying to readjust to the real world. I've been staring at a screen for too long.'

'Anything interesting?'

Knowles shook his head. 'Nothing. Nothing at all.'

The Limes was a modern building with windows set in various sizes of coloured, boxed frames. A top architect had designed it and Sean had been to the opening a few years ago, when he was first in uniform as a PCSO. Ivan Knowles rang the buzzer on the intercom and announced who they were. There was a long pause before the receptionist replied.

Something moved on the street. A car going a little too slowly. Sean turned to look. A battered red pickup, it accelerated as it passed. The hostel had to deal with unwanted visitors sometimes, the pimps of the women it was trying to help, who weren't too keen to lose them. It probably didn't help that it stood out like a multicoloured Lego castle in a sea of red-brick houses.

The door opened and a young woman in jeans and a long cotton shirt stood in the doorway.

'DS Ivan Knowles.' The DS held out his badge.

'Can I ask what this is about?'

'We need to talk to one of your residents, Mary Dobbs. She's not in any trouble.'

The young woman looked from Knowles to Sean, and her expression softened.

'PCSO Denton?'

'Detective Constable.'

'Do you remember me?' she said. 'Your grandma won the raffle at our opening garden party.'

Sean remembered the day very well. Nan had insisted on coming along, even though he told her he was working. She said it was a public event and he couldn't stop her. One of her friends was in the fundraising group, a lively woman called Marge, who'd lost her daughter to the streets and then to an overdose. The two women had managed to get themselves in all the photos. The following day, the front page of the *Doncaster Free Press* had featured Sean, sandwiched between Nan and Marge, holding the raffle prize, a furry toy tiger the size of a Great Dane.

'Come in,' the young woman said. 'I'm Debbie.'

In the foyer, on a wall of framed pictures of the Lord Mayor, and a number of local politicians, was the press photo of Sean.

'Hello, Tiger!' Knowles said, with a laugh.

'Mary's in the common room,' Debbie said, too polite to join in with the joke. 'We're doing card-making. She only got here yesterday, so go easy on her. I don't want her running off. We've been trying to engage with her for months.'

'You'd better do the talking, Denton,' Knowles said. 'I hear you developed quite a rapport with the lady.'

Debbie showed them into a room where the easy chairs had been pushed back against the walls to make room for a long table, covered with cards, scissors, ribbon and glue-sticks. Mary was sitting hunched over her work, methodically colouring a heart-shaped card with a red felt pen. A younger woman was snipping pieces of ribbon into tiny shreds. They were the only two attendees of the card-making class.

'Bit late for Valentine's, isn't it?' Sean said.

Mary looked up and gave him a lopsided smile. 'You think it's for you? No bloody chance.'

'This is my colleague, Ivan Knowles,' Sean decided dropping the job titles might be wise in this setting. 'Can we have a word?'

'Don't mind me,' the younger woman said. 'I need a tea break, anyhow.'

Sean and Knowles sat down.

'I'll be in the office,' Debbie said. She and the other woman left the room and the door closed softly behind them.

Mary looked warily at Knowles and turned to Sean.

'This about the other night?'

'Yes,' Sean said. 'You disappeared. And there were things we needed to ask you.'

'It were that dog. I'm afraid of dogs.'

'Just the dog?' Sean said.

Mary opened her mouth to say something, then thought better of it. She picked up her red felt pen and started to add more colour to the heart.

'When you left the school building,' Sean said, 'you found me at the petrol station.'

Mary nodded, but didn't look up.

'You led us to the crime scene,' he said, but she didn't react. 'You wouldn't tell me exactly what we would find, but did you know a man was dead?'

Nothing. The card was softening under layers of red ink. Finally the pen stopped moving.

'That's a shame,' she said. 'He was all right.'

'Who was?' Knowles said.

'The one that got hurt.'

'Can you tell us his name?'

She shook her head. 'Kept themselves to themselves.'

'But you saw who was attacked?'

Mary looked at him now and frowned.

'What did you see, Mary?'

She ran her tongue across her top lip, as if she could taste the memory of Friday night.

'I heard a lot of shouting and banging,' she said. 'Someone telling us to get out. They were going to burn the place down, he said. It was a right scramble and then we were outside.'

'Just one voice shouting?' Sean asked.

She nodded.

'And everyone else got out?' Ivan said.

Mary shrugged. 'There's different people there every night, hard to keep track. You don't sign in and out of a place like that.'

189

'But there wasn't a fire,' Sean said. 'Was there?'

'Maybe it went out?' Mary said.

'What about your sister,' Sean said. 'Was she living there too, with Jonno?'

'You don't want to believe anything she tells you,' Mary said. 'She's soft in the head. I had to give her a right kick to get her moving and he won't go anywhere without his bloody trolley.' She shook her head. 'He's got a good heart, though, that Jonno, or else he wouldn't put up with her.'

Knowles cleared his throat, as if to indicate that this wasn't getting them anywhere.

'Can you tell us the names of everyone you remember being there?'

Mary looked startled. 'I'm not naming names. You won't catch me grassing anyone up.'

'Not as suspects, Mary,' Sean said. 'Just to see if we can find anyone who saw what happened. You said the victim was a nice guy, so it seems odd that anyone would want to hurt him. The person who was shouting, did you recognise the voice, or had someone come into the building from outside?'

Mary shrugged. 'Must have done. I didn't see anyone, but they must have done. It happens. Sometimes it's kids, think it's a laugh to smash the place up or give some poor junkie a kicking. And then there's the two that come for the rent. Last time they took a load of piping from upstairs.'

She stopped and her mouth tightened, as if she should stop herself from saying any more. She fiddled with a bracelet, turning it round and round on her wrist. It was gold, engraved with a pattern of flowers. Sean watched her turning it and tried to picture her scrawny hand grabbing his sleeve at the petrol station. He was sure she hadn't been wearing that bracelet on Friday night.

Knowles took a statement pad out of his bag. 'I'm going to write down what you've told us so far, Mary. It will be a statement about what you've seen, as a witness. Then if you agree with what I've written, I'm going to ask you to sign it.'

'Oh no,' she said. She pushed her chair back and stood up. 'I'm not signing anything. I'm not getting dragged into court. I didn't see anything.'

'But you asked for help, Mary,' said Sean. 'On Friday night, you wanted me to come and see, to stop something from happening.'

'Well you didn't, did you?' She spat the words out. 'You were too bloody late and a good man's dead. There's no point now, is there?'

The door opened and Debbie came in.

'Is everything all right?' she said. 'Mary?'

'I'm not staying here!' Mary was shouting now. 'They'll be back, bothering me whenever they want to. I should never have spoken to him. Thought he was all right,' she was pointing at Sean, 'but I were wrong. He's just like all the rest.'

'Come on,' Knowles said quietly to Sean, 'let's go.'

'Thank you, Mary. You've helped us. It's really appreciated.'

She stared at the floor, her fists balled by her sides. Knowles was heading through the foyer towards the front door.

'Pretty bracelet you've got there,' Sean said.

She snapped her head up and looked him in the eye. 'What's that to you?'

'I'm pleased you managed to save it. It would have been sad to have left something like that behind when you had to leave the school. A lot of people didn't get to take their

191

possessions. If you know anyone who wants their things back, can you tell them to get in touch?'

'Didn't have it in the school.' She fingered the bracelet. 'It's new.'

'Well, it's very pretty.'

'It was a present from a friend.'

Sean looked at Debbie, but her face gave nothing away.

'It's not what you're thinking, copper. I'm retired from that game. No, my boyfriend Michael gave me this. It's to show I've turned over a new leaf.'

'That's lovely. Take care, Mary.'

He followed Knowles to the front door, but then something occurred to him. He went back to the room where Mary was sitting once again at the table, the red pen in her hand.

'Michael?' he said. 'Would that be Michael Bartram, known as Longfeller, by any chance?'

Mary gave him a crooked smile. 'Do you know him?'

'We've met,' he said, and left her to her colouring.

'Right,' Knowles said, as Sean got into the passenger seat, 'let's take the DVR back to the greyhound stadium and see if we can talk to the boss about what Abbas and Homsi were doing on his property at five o'clock on Friday.'

'So there was nothing else of interest on the video?' Sean said.

'No, it was all very uninteresting, and unnaturally empty. I know they didn't have a race on Friday, but I can't believe there was nobody there at all.'

CHAPTER TWENTY-SIX

Tuesday evening

The lengthening shadows cast strange shapes across the scrapyard. Sarah shivers. She unhooks Wolf's lead from the post outside her caravan and pulls her door shut, twisting her key carefully, feeling the repaired lock click into place.

'Come on, boy,' she says.

Wolf looks up at her expectantly.

She turns her back on rusting hulks of metal and glass, and leaves the yard for the stadium car park. She sometimes thinks about taking Wolf for a walk outside the stadium grounds, checking out the neighbouring streets, or even heading down the Horse Road, which Tommy says leads to some shops at the bottom end, but she's not quite ready for that.

The car park is empty, except for Derek's green Jaguar, parked close to the stadium building. The charity race is over and the handful of punters is long gone. She heads towards the back door of the kitchen and Wolf keeps pace with her, looking up at her occasionally, as if he's trying to sense her mood. His tail starts wagging as they come to the door. He's hoping to find kitchen scraps.

Inside, the kitchen is lit only by the red glow of the mains indicator switch for the cooker. In the walk-in store, the fridge and freezer lights shine green, like something out of a horror film. Sarah doesn't turn on the overhead bulb. She can see well enough. The disused chest freezer is pushed up against the back wall. She lifts the lid, checks its contents, and closes it softly.

Wolf whines.

'Shh, boy, it's all right. Stay quiet, and stay close, and nobody will know you came inside.'

Leaving the kitchen, they pass through the cafe and into the main entrance hall. Light spills into the corridor beyond the staircase. It's coming from the Gents' toilet. There's a smell of fresh paint. She listens to a metal step ladder being folded and the footsteps of the person who's carrying it towards the exit into the car park.

She pulls the dog close and lets herself out of the main doors onto the trackside, leaning on the release bar carefully, so it makes no sound. Wolf wags his tail with excitement, as if he can smell the adrenalin of all the races that have been run on this track.

She stays close to the building, under the overhang of the upper storey, where a light is on in the office. She doesn't have long before he'll be coming downstairs to lock up. She feels for the Yale key in her pocket and lets herself in to the vet's office. Once inside, the smell of antiseptic hits her. She pushes shut the door with her elbow, careful not to touch anything with her fingers. Wolf's tail is tucked firmly between his legs. For him this smell means nothing but pain. She doesn't turn the overhead bulb on, but takes advantage of the dusky light coming in through the windows. On Saturday she slipped in here among the crowd of onlookers when Indian Whisper broke his leg. She offered the vet a cup of tea while he worked, so she knows the layout.

When she's found what she's looking for, she creeps back outside. She hears another door close on the first floor, followed by the tap of Derek's shoes on the stairs. How is she going to explain what she's doing here?

Wolf pulls hard on the lead towards the track and she has an idea.

'Okay, boy,' she says, 'now's your chance.'

She slips his collar and he stands still for a moment, then, spotting something in the trees at the far side of the track, he's off. She gives him a moment before she runs after him, calling his name, waving her arms above her head.

The door behind her opens.

'Are you all right, lass? What's going on here?'

'It's Wolf,' she says, sounding on the verge of tears. 'I know I shouldn't have let him off, but now he won't come back.'

'You have to be careful. They see something, they go for it. That's what they're bred for.'

'Joe told me, but I didn't realise just how quickly he'd bolt. Thought it wouldn't hurt to let him have a bit of freedom.'

They cross the track together, Derek whistling for Wolf, and Sarah holding out the dog treats she keeps in the pocket of her jeans. Wolf will get bored or tired soon, and sure enough, as they approach the sandy track on the far side of the circuit, he comes walking towards them, tail wagging.

'Look at his gait,' Derek says. 'There's something off-centre about it. Like one of his back legs is stiff at the hip.'

'I see what you mean.'

She puts Wolf's collar and lead back on, and gives him the dog treat. They turn and walk back to the building.

'Thanks, Mr O'Connor, I don't know what I'd have done if you hadn't been here.'

'Aye, well,' Derek pats his moustache. 'I was looking at the plans for the building work to see what else needs finishing off. Looks like those two scumbags have left us in the lurch. I'd just paid them, and all. Bloody liberty. Just been ringing round a few folk to see if I can pull in some favours.'

'What about the boys?' she says. 'Haven't they been helping?'

Derek lets out a mirthless laugh. 'Did you see the mess Tommy's made of the turfing? He hasn't got the sense he was born with. And Joe's neither use nor ornament. Doesn't know the meaning of a hard day's work.'

She isn't sure if she should agree or not, she doesn't want to tread on family loyalties.

'You should have let him have a run tonight, in the charity race,' Derek nods at Wolf.

'I had to do the catering, didn't I?'

She doesn't want to tell him that she had no desire to meet the other owners of a bunch of retired greyhounds and lurchers. The fewer people she has to deal with, and their dogs, the better.

'Why wasn't that Polish lass working tonight?'

'Didn't Lou tell you?' Sarah wonders if Derek will take it badly that he hasn't been consulted, so she decides on a partial truth. 'She's quit.'

She promises Derek she'll race Wolf another time, when he's more settled.

'You're a good lass.'

Derek gives her a pat on the shoulder and she tries not to flinch.

She crosses the car park and notices a pair of headlights turning in. She ducks into the scrapyard, but finds a spot in the corrugated iron fence where the rust has worn a hole and watches the black Mondeo pull into the car park. It's the same car that was here earlier. Derek stands by his Jaguar and watches the two detectives get out. She's too far away to hear what's said, but she sees Derek shake his head and gesture to the new kennel block. Then he's leading the two men around that side of the building and they're looking up at the CCTV camera, which Derek had fitted to make sure the workmen didn't steal from the site.

Just then, a pair of hands grab her around the waist and she almost screams. She twists her head to see Tommy grinning at her. White paint flecks his T-shirt and face.

'Fuck's sake, Tommy!' she says. 'You'd better not have got paint on my top.'

'It's okay, it's all dry.'

'What were you painting?'

'Gents' toilets, where you cleaned it on Sunday morning. You took a layer of paint off and Derek had something to say about it. I told him it was Agnes who'd cleaned in there.'

'Well, I'm sorry about that, but someone had been bleeding all over the wall above the hand dryers.'

Tommy shrugged. 'Yeah. Well, it must have been his nose, I only gave him a little bump.'

'Was this the guy you dragged out of the bar?'

'Not saying.'

197

'We're lucky he hasn't been to the police – it's bad enough they're crawling all over the place as it is.'

'Do you want to know what I did to him?'

'No, not really.'

'I held him up against the wall with one hand, and pulled his trousers down with the other. I was trying to get his knob in the airblade, but Joey made me stop.'

'You're an idiot!'

'Don't say that.' His smile drops and his eyes take on a glassy look.

'I'm sorry.'

She reaches out and takes his big hand in hers. 'Friends?'

He looks away, playing for time, but the smile creeps back into the corner of his mouth.

'Friends,' he says.

'Good.'

'What are we going to do next, Sarah?'

She pulls the dog towards her and walks away from Tommy, across the yard.

'I need time to think. Is that okay?'

He shrugs. 'Whatever. I've got to rake the track again. Someone just let their dog run all over it! See you later.'

Sarah sits on the step of her static caravan and strokes Wolf's smooth head. His lead is looped around the pole hammered into the ground next to the steps. He leans against her leg. Any minute now, he will slide down to lie on the ground and fall asleep. She's never known an animal that sleeps so much. She wishes they could swap lives.

All around her the vehicles shine in the low evening sunlight, their colours deeper and richer than usual. A red single-decker bus sits on collapsed tyres, and beyond it a royal blue horsebox is flanked by a rusting yellow van. This evening the yard looks like a page from a child's storybook.

'Appearances can be deceptive,' Sarah says, but the dog doesn't stir.

CHAPTER TWENTY-SEVEN

Tuesday evening

Derek O'Connor's manner was polite, but there was an undercurrent of hostility. Sean thought it was Knowles' accent that was making the little man bristle, but perhaps it was simply the fact that they were police. He softened a little when DS Knowles reassured him that his main concern was for what had occurred in the school, and he had no worries about anything on the stadium side of the hedge. Sean thought about that man he'd seen, being dragged towards the fire exit on Saturday, and the shady characters taking bets at the trackside, and he wondered if Knowles was wise to make such a promise.

'We know how hard it is to get experienced tradesmen these days, Mr O'Connor,' Knowles was saying, 'so we're not here to judge if you've been paying cash in hand. I'm sure if you can help us, we can overlook any little issue like that.'

He didn't mention that he knew the two men were migrants, with no right to work here, whether they were paid cash, PAYE, or gold bullion.

They followed O'Connor around the side of the building.

The new block now had a line of wonky turf between it and the car park. The surface they were walking on was much newer than the rest of the car park and a metal fire escape spiralled up to their left.

'Is that the bar at the top of there?' Sean asked.

Derek O'Connor looked at him sharply. 'You seem to know your way around.'

'Just good at geography,' Sean smiled.

Attached to the roof, above the fire door, was a CCTV camera. Sean recognised the view.

'We understand that the two labourers, Abbas and Homsi, left the site at five. This is a still image from your own CCTV,' Knowles said, showing O'Connor a blurry photograph. 'Where were they before that?'

Derek touched his moustache. Sean wondered if he was about to lie.

'Abbas and Homsi? Is that what you call them? I never could get the hang of their names.' He looked at the picture. 'Aye, that's them. I called them Fred and Bert, and I paid the one who did all the talking. Bert, he was. He spoke the better English. It was about half four, quarter to five, the other one was still on the site, he said, just finishing off. I was up in the office. I owed them three hundred quid. Bert said they'd be back Saturday, but they never came. I had an open ditch with all the pipes and cables running through it and a race meet in the evening. Bloody nightmare. I should have trusted my instincts and not paid them until it was all finished.'

'So what made you change your mind?' Knowles said.

'He said they owed a debt, and if they didn't pay it on Friday night, they would have to disappear. Seemed the best way to keep them was to pay them. More fool me!'

'Did he say anything about who he owed the debt to?' Knowles said.

'No. None of my business. I got the feeling it was rent. But if you say they were living in that old school, that doesn't seem very likely.'

'And you didn't know that was where they were staying?'

'Not a clue.' He touched his moustache again. 'Just thought they were using it as a short cut.'

'Thank you, Mr O'Connor, you've been very helpful,' Knowles said.

'Is that it, then?'

'If it's no bother,' Sean said. 'We'd like to just walk round.'

'As my colleague says, we'll just get our bearings,' Knowles said, 'particularly over by the hedge where they were coming in and out from the school playing field.'

'Aye, well, if you must, but don't walk on the sand.'

They came round the end of the building and Sean waited until they were out of earshot before whispering to Knowles.

'Something doesn't add up. If Abbas was still on the site, why don't the images from the camera show that? It was just empty. The trench was like he said, with pipes and cables in the bottom. What else?'

'Hang on.'

Knowles turned back. He ran up the fire escape and Sean followed him. They stood at the top, looking down.

'There was a water bottle lying in the ditch,' Knowles said. 'It's easier to remember looking from this angle.'

'So maybe he knocked off early,' Sean said.

Knowles shook his head. 'Not three hours early. Not

unless they were working on a completely different part of the site, and O'Connor is lying. I've been over the tapes right back to midday, and that water bottle never moves.'

Back at the station, Tina Smales was moving the Gonks on the shared desk from right to left and back again. Sean watched from the door and cleared his throat.

'Gonk racing?' he said.

'Just trying to think,' she said. 'I've been through all the records of sexual assaults over the last six months to see if we've got anything similar to the Bethany Winters case.'

'And?'

'There's a cluster of potential date rapes, between three months and six weeks ago. Four victims tested negative for Rohypnol, but positive for opiates. The actual drug being used was something new, but with an opiate content, so we linked them, but hers was the only one that the CPP was taking forward.'

'How come?'

'Because she was such a credible witness.'

'And there was the friend, until she buggered off.'

'Exactly. The thing is, Bethany comes from a religious, Christian family. She didn't even have a boyfriend.'

'But she met Velasquez in a club. Razors isn't exactly a Methodist Sunday School.'

Tina turned one Gonk round and arranged the others behind it in a triangle.

'She went with friends from college, got changed en route. That was awkward with her mum and dad. When she turned up at A and E we phoned home, and they denied it was their daughter at first, because she wasn't wearing the clothes she left home in.'

'Do you think that's why she didn't show up at court? Too much was going to be said about her being out in a club late at night?'

'I don't know,' Tina said. 'But now he's vanished too and I've got a funny feeling about the whole thing.'

'Fancy a pint to help your brain work?'

'It has the opposite effect on me, but I'll come along for the company.' She hesitated. 'Is Ivor You-Know-What coming?'

'Yes, he suggested it. Part of his induction, learning to order a pint in the local dialect.'

'God forbid!'

'I'll see you in there,' he said. 'Rick might be along and I'll ring Lizzie, my partner. Do you know her?'

'The forensic manager? I've met her on a couple of cases. She's good with the female victims. Very kind.'

He smiled, proud for a moment, although it was none of his doing.

The Salutation pub was a stone's throw from the flat. He rang Lizzie as he and Knowles left the police station. She said she'd meet him in there, she was just getting changed. She sounded tired. He was on the point of suggesting she needn't bother, if she wanted to put her feet up, but she might take it the wrong way.

They walked past Cast, the new theatre, with its funky neon lights that gave this part of town an optimistic shine. Lizzie had been talking about taking him to see a show. There was going to be a touring production of a Shakespeare play and she said he couldn't go through life without seeing Shakespeare. He'd seen Shakespeare, he told her. Some people from Sheffield came to do *Richard III* in the hall at Chasebridge School. '*Here comes Richard between two cardinals.*' He'd never forgotten that line. There were only four actors, so the one playing Richard wore a red cloak, with a skull on each shoulder. The skulls wore little red hats and were moved by poles under the cloak, so the actor playing Richard spoke to his cardinals, moving them like puppets. It had made everyone laugh so much they hadn't heard the rest of the scene, but Sean hadn't found it funny. He'd found it sinister.

When he got to the pub, Lizzie was already there. He saw her standing at the bar, her T-shirt tucked into her jeans, sandals on her feet. Her hair was still wet from the shower. She looked lovely and relaxed. He thought he would surprise her and kiss the back of her neck, quickly, before she had time to see who it was, but as he approached someone called out to her from a table on his right. He didn't hear what was said, but the tone was enough to get his hackles up.

'Steady on, lads, I'm spoken for,' she said.

Sean saw Rick Houghton and Steve Castle, another DS in the drugs squad, at the table. Rick waved him over, but Steve concentrated on his drink.

'Now then, Steve,' Sean said. 'I didn't quite catch what you just said to my girlfriend. Was it something I should know about?'

'Steady on, mate,' Steve said. 'Just a bit of banter.'

'Was it?' Sean was at the table now, his hands gripping the back of an empty chair.

'It's all right,' Lizzie was close behind him, speaking low. 'I can handle it.'

'See. We're all right,' Steve said. 'Aren't we, Liz?'

'Oh, yeah,' she said. 'Peachy.'

But she wasn't smiling and her fingers were tight around the stem of her wine glass.

'Are you joining us?' Rick said. 'It's Steve's round. What you having, Sean?'

Sean glanced at the pumps and spotted a guest ale at 8.5%, the strongest and most expensive item on the beer list.

'A pint of Dog's Tooth,' he said. 'Since Steve's buying.'

'Same again for me, mate,' Rick said.

'How about you, boss?' Sean turned to Ivan Knowles, who was eyeing the beer list. 'Steve'll get you one in, won't you, Steve?'

'Of course.' Steve forced a smile.

'I'll have whatever Denton's having.'

'Great.'

As Steve got up to go to the bar, Rick turned to Lizzie. 'Don't mind Steve, he's all caveman on the outside, but he's got a good heart.'

'He's a twat, Rick,' Lizzie said. 'He always has been.'

Sean watched Steve chatting to the barmaid and wondered how deep his twattishness went. Steve had partnered Rick for years in Drugs, and Rick was sound, but Steve had always looked down his nose at Sean. He'd made no secret of dismissing Sean's role as a PCSO, and his banter had sailed close to bullying.

'How's it going out of uniform?' Rick asked Sean.

'All right,' he said. 'Interesting.'

Lizzie and Knowles were already deep in conversation. He wondered if they were talking shop, but he couldn't hear over the jukebox, a replica vintage machine, which was blaring out a Beach Boys song.

Steve came back with two drinks. As he turned back to the bar to get the rest, Sean turned to Rick.

'Do you know anything about date-rape drugs in the clubs in the last few months?'

'Anything specific?'

'I don't know, something that worked like Rohypnol, but a different drug. Something new. I was supposed to be in court yesterday to give a statement. Nothing too dramatic, I was just the arresting officer, but Tina Smales was working with the victim. A lass ended up at A and E, about three months ago, off her head, saying she'd been raped. The suspect was still in the club when we got there and denied everything, but later admitted he'd had sex with her.'

'What was the outcome?'

'It's been adjourned, she didn't show up. But Tina Smales said there was something odd about the drug they found in her system.'

'I'll have a look. See if any of our regular dealers were found with anything new.'

'The thing is,' Sean said, and at that moment the Beach Boys song ended and he spoke at full volume into the sudden silence, 'this is the same lad that's gone missing. The bakery boy, Velasquez.'

Steve Castle sat down and handed out the other three drinks.

'That was very discreet. Not.' Steve said. 'So what's your theory, Sherlock?'

'I don't have one,' Sean said.

'That's not like you. Twenty-four hours in Major Crimes, I thought you'd have solved it by now.'

'I'm not exactly sure what I'm meant to be solving,' he said, and concentrated on drinking his pint of expensive beer.

'It's obvious, isn't it?' Steve Castle said. 'The bakery boy's done a runner. They should have sent him back to custody.'

'Or he's topped himself,' Rick said.

'That would save the taxpayer some money,' Steve Castle laughed.

'You're thirsty.' Lizzie nudged Sean.

His pint was half-empty and he'd barely tasted it.

'We went to see Mary Dobbs earlier,' Knowles said to Rick, ignoring the discussion about Xavier Velasquez. 'You know, the woman who reported something was wrong at the school? I was wondering if you had any specific intel on dealers working from the premises. She seemed to be scared of someone and I'd like to get an idea who.'

'Someone with a massive blunt instrument who bludgeons people to death, I would imagine,' Steve said. 'Did she have a description?'

'She reckons she didn't see anything,' Knowles said, 'but I'm not convinced. She also claims there was someone shouting about a fire.'

'The scorch marks on the floor weren't recent,' Lizzie said. 'I'd say they'd been there a few weeks, probably from someone setting fires to keep warm.'

'I'm sorry,' Steve said, in a tone that suggested he was anything but sorry for what he was about to say, 'but I think that guy Homsi should have been charged, and if there wasn't enough to go on, then at least put him on the next plane back to where he came from.'

'I'm not sure there are many airports left in Syria,' Lizzie said dryly. 'Anyway, the blood spatters on his clothes don't fit him being the killer. The lab will back me up. You can't just convict people you don't like the look of.'

Sean wanted to tell Steve to fuck off, but he drained his pint instead.

'Here you all are!' Tina Smales approached the table with a bright smile, which wasn't matched by its occupants. 'This looks fun.'

CHAPTER TWENTY-EIGHT

Tuesday night

Sarah half-fills a small plastic bottle from the tap. She puts it on the table where she's laid out a chopping board and a knife. Carefully, she cups the tablets with her left hand, while bringing the knife down with her right. They need to be broken up first, then crushed with the flat of the blade. Wolf is watching her, curious to see if this careful preparation will result in food in his bowl. It's crossed her mind to try them out on the dog first, to get the dosage right, but she doesn't have time.

She can smell Joe Heron approaching before she hears him. Like the smoke from a garden bonfire, the sweet, hoppy smell of weed wafts in through the window.

'Joe?' she says quietly, knowing he's close.

'That's my name, don't wear it out.' He giggles at his own joke.

'Where have you been? Derek's going to tear a strip off you when he sees you. You were supposed to be helping Tommy with the charity race.'

'Not that it's any of your business,' he says, with a stoner's whine, 'but I took our lass back home and stopped for a few drinks in town. Had some business to do.'

She needs to keep him talking while she works, her hands hidden by the flimsy curtain.

'What are you doing round the back of my caravan?' she says.

'Was going to surprise you.'

His face appears at the window, as he tweaks the curtain aside. 'You forgot all about your washing, didn't you?'

'What's that?' She covers the chopping board with her hands.

'Sunday morning, you were in such a hurry to get it dry. And yet it's still here, hanging on a rope along the back of your van.'

'Bring it in, if you like. I haven't had time.'

She can see the top of his head and his shoulders, dipping as he bends to unclip the pegs, the burning end of his joint dancing like a firework in the dark. She presses the knife down and feels the pieces of tablet give way to powder. She shifts the knife and presses again. She has a memory of her mother, teaching her to crush garlic to make spaghetti bolognaise. Not now. She needs to hurry.

Joe heaves his shoulder against the caravan door and her repair is undone in one movement. The door flies open and clatters against the side of the sink unit.

She shields the chopping board with her right arm. 'Don't make such a racket!'

'Who's going to hear? There's nobody here but us chickens. And Tommy. But he doesn't count.' He leers at her with the joint in the corner of his mouth. He hasn't noticed what's on the table. Yet.

'Where do you want these?' He holds up the bundle of clothes in his arms, like someone who considers women's work beneath him.

'On the couch.' She nods to the curtain that divides the

211

front of the caravan from the kitchen. The fitted couch curves round under the window. Wolf has made it his bed, so it isn't an ideal place to put clean clothes, but it doesn't matter, she just needs a few seconds to deal with the powder. She looks around for some means of pouring it into the narrow neck of the bottle. Damn. She should have thought this through.

Then she spots it. A blue and white china jug on the corner shelf on the opposite side of the table. She reaches over, trying not to lean on the powder or transfer it to her clothes, but she isn't quick enough. Joe comes back through the curtain from the lounge just as she sits down, jug in hand, a small mountain of white powder on the chopping board in front of her.

'Well, you are full of surprises!'

'It's not what you think.'

'You've got no idea what I'm thinking.'

He pinches his joint out between his finger and thumb and sits opposite her.

'Tell me what you're thinking,' she says.

He looks at her for a moment, as if he's sizing her up for the first time. Then he sits back and spreads his hands on the table. She moves the board an inch towards herself, dislodging a tablet that's rolled underneath. She's too late, he's quicker and picks it up between his finger and thumb.

'Now,' he says. 'First time we met, you bought one of these off me. Did you think I'd forgotten or that I wouldn't recognise your new look? I think it's time you tell me what's going on.'

Her mouth is dry. She has to start somewhere, but she can't decide where. Joe isn't like Tommy. He's more complicated and will spot any flaw in her story. She decides it might be time to tell the truth, or some of it.

'The police came back.'

'Oh?'

'They spoke to Derek, wandered over to the new kennel block and round to the trackside. They bought Derek's DVR back, but they hung about.'

'Why?'

She shrugs.

'Did they come up here?'

'No.'

He looks relieved. 'This business in the school, it could backfire on me.'

She doesn't say anything, just pours some water from the plastic bottle into the jug and scrapes the powder in. Joe is distracted now, less interested in what she's doing with the powder.

'My DNA might be in the school, you know.'

'Why? Were you dealing to the homeless people?' She tries to sound surprised, as if all this is new to her.

'A bit of buying and selling. And a bit of rent collecting,' he says. 'First time it was just a bit of a distraction, got Tommy to put the boot in here and there, while I undid the pipes and got the sinks and that out. Then we discovered people will pay not to be hurt. It's good business.'

She widens her eyes in what she hopes looks like shock.

'Can I borrow your dog?' Joe says, as if an idea has just come to him.

'Why?'

'Need a guard dog. I've got a load of plants in that old Wallace Arnold coach by the back gate, and a pile of copper piping and old sinks in the back of the red transit. I can leave the gate unlocked, although it'll still look locked, then when the dog barks, I'll know if the filth are coming, and can drive out the back gate before they see me.'

'Do any of those vehicles actually work?'

'I'll get them working.'

'That's the weed talking, Joe Heron,' she says. 'There are three flaws in your plan. Number one, he doesn't usually bark at anything, unless he's telling me to feed him a bit quicker. Number two, you wouldn't have time, once they're in here you'd be lucky to get yourself through the gate on foot. And number three, how far are you going to get with a Wallace Arnold holiday coach full of cannabis plants? Not very.'

'You got a better idea?'

'Yes. We'll have to get the stuff moved before they poke their noses in here.'

'How are we going to do that?'

'Your pickup's got a tow bar, hasn't it?'

He nods.

'Use the horsebox. I've got something in there I need to get rid of too, so that would kill two birds with one stone.'

'I've got to go out with Derek and Lou tomorrow, got to see my dad.'

'Is Tommy going?'

What if things get out of hand? She needs Tommy here.

'Only two visitors. So that's me and Lou. Derek insists on driving us because he doesn't trust me with his poxy Jag, and I don't think the pickup will make it that far. Lou needs to get my dad to sign papers for our Melissa, so she can officially apply to adopt her.'

The weed has made him more relaxed. He's opening up to

her. She thinks this might be a good moment to tell him about Melissa's employer.

'You know that Saturday job she does, at the hairdresser's on the market?'

'What about it?'

'She's very young, isn't she? I thought you had to be sixteen to get a job.'

Joe shrugged. 'I don't suppose she has to do much.'

'But she's on her own all day, in a tiny stall, with a man old enough to be her dad. Doesn't that bother you?'

'Looked like a faggot to me.'

Sarah shudders inwardly. How could he be so stupid?

She stirs the powder and water together and pours the mixture back into the bottle. He's watching her now, the stirrings of curiosity surfacing through his stoned expression. She is so close to telling him. She can feel the blood pounding in her temples as the adrenalin rushes through her body. But she stops herself. She's better off with Tommy, he's less complicated. He's the one who promised to look after her, and everything that's followed has been part of that promise.

To her relief, Joe stands up and looks around.

'You've made it nice in here,' he grunts, before letting himself out of the door.

She watches through the gap in her living room curtains until he's back inside his own caravan. Then she pulls on a pair of steel toe-capped work boots, picks up the jug from the table, and leaves the van.

CHAPTER TWENTY-NINE

Wednesday morning

The operations room had lost its sense of urgency. Sean looked at his colleagues and noticed how few smiles there were, how tired everyone looked. The snippets of evidence, written up on the boards, seemed unconnected.

DI Khan called for silence and announced that the briefing would be very quick. He explained that no evidence of Xavier Velasquez's whereabouts had been found on the estate, or in the woods on the other side of the ring road. The door-to-doors had also drawn a blank. Enquiries should now be focused on family and friends, in case he'd simply jumped bail.

'Told you so,' Steve Castle muttered under his breath.

'Right, anything new on the Chasebridge School murder?'

Ivan Knowles raised his hand. 'I'd like to have another look at the CCTV we copied from the stadium's DVR. There's something that doesn't add up and it kept me awake last night.'

'Go ahead,' Khan said. 'No sign of Homsi? No. Thought not. And I take it your refugee centre didn't phone back?'

'Not yet, sir.'

Sean hoped DS Knowles wouldn't mind if he mentioned what had occurred to *him* in the middle of the night, when Lizzie's snoring woke him. He raised his hand tentatively.

'DC Denton?' Khan gave him an encouraging smile.

'Sir, yesterday DS Knowles and myself spoke to Derek O'Connor and he confirmed that he paid the two men, Abbas and Homsi, on Friday afternoon, but neither of them had any money on them. In other words, when Abbas was dead and Homsi was hiding, the money had gone. I'm not sure if this is relevant, but when we interviewed Mary Dobbs yesterday, she was wearing a gold bracelet, not brand new, maybe antique, but she was definitely not wearing it on Friday. PC Wentworth can back me up because he needed to grab both her wrists to get her off me.'

'You think she killed Abbas for money?' Khan said. 'But why would she alert you to a disturbance if she was the murderer?'

Sean shook his head. 'No, I don't think she's the killer. She said the bracelet was a gift from Michael Bartram, aka Longfeller.'

'Ah,' Khan nodded slowly. 'That is interesting. We have Longfeller leaving the scene around the same time as the other residents, or possibly slightly earlier. Okay, we need to locate him and have a chat. Bring him in if you have to. The good news is that we have his prints and DNA from several previous convictions, so we can alert the lab to a potential match. DC Smales, take Denton with you to speak to the parents of the victim in the Velasquez case, it'll be useful for him to watch and learn.'

'I hope someone's at home,' Tina said. 'I got fed up of nobody answering the bloody phone, so I rang BT. Turns out the phone's been disconnected and the number reassigned. I've been ringing an empty warehouse for the last few weeks. Meanwhile, the Winters family no longer have a landline.'

'Ask them about that,' Khan said. 'And Denton, when you get back I want you upstairs helping sort through the backlog of items from the school. We haven't found Homsi's shoes yet.'

'Yes, sir.'

It seemed that every silver lining had a cloud.

Bethany Winters lived across the border in North Nottinghamshire. Despite the Doncaster postcode, Sean and Tina's journey would take them into the domain of a different police force. They agreed to switch the car radio over to the local force, and keep their personal radios tuned to their own frequency. As she drove, Tina was as talkative as Knowles was taciturn. She chatted about the weather, quizzed Sean about his ambitions and finally asked him where he grew up. When he said the Chasebridge estate, followed by the marginally less doomed streets of The Groves, she accepted the answer without comment. She then told him about her own childhood, by the sea at Cleethorpes, even though he hadn't asked.

'Mum and Dad ran a cake shop,' she said. 'Me and my brother would be sent off with yesterday's leftovers and we'd play all day on the beach or under the pier. It made up for being the only non-white family in the town, having cakes to share out.'

'Sounds all right,' Sean said.

'It was some consolation,' she laughed. 'But it's no wonder I can never lose weight. I grew up on cakes and pies.'

Sean wasn't sure what he should say. He could hardly agree, it would be like falling into the trap of 'does my bum look big in this'. Tina wasn't huge, she was soft at the edges, and probably heavier than her five-foot frame should be carrying, but it suited her.

'Does your family still live there, at Cleethorpes?'

'No.' The smile dropped for a moment. 'We moved to Donny when I was sixteen. The shop got bought up by Parklands Bakeries and Dad was offered a management role at their headquarters. Bloody disaster.'

Parklands Bakeries had been a big firm across the region, but they'd gone out of business with the loss of hundreds of jobs.

'Is he working now?' Sean said.

'No. But it could be worse. At least they had money saved from selling the shop. He's not happy that I'm the main breadwinner, if you'll excuse the pun, but he's got used to it. How about you,' she said. 'What do your parents do?'

'Well . . .' Sean hesitated.

He hated telling people that his mother was dead, not because it upset him, but because it upset the person he was telling. Then he had to deal with them being sad about something that had happened years ago, something he'd spent more than half his life learning to get used to. Talking about his dad wasn't any easier.

'Is this where we get onto the M18?' Tina said.

'Yes, I think so,' Sean said, relieved by the distraction of checking the directions.

He tapped the route finder as the slip road appeared ahead. Tina focused on getting onto the motorway between a steady stream of lorries.

'Can you catch me up on our victim?' he said.

'She'd just turned eighteen when the incident happened. She was at college, doing A-levels. She's an only child of older parents, committed Christians. She was brought in to hospital by a friend and then transferred to the specialist unit in Rotherham for three nights. At first she told her parents not to come. I had to persuade her that they weren't angry, just worried. I didn't tell her that her mother kept asking me what she was wearing at the time of the assault, once it became clear it wasn't the outfit she left home in, but by the time they got to Rotherham to pick her up, we'd found her some plain navy sweat pants, a floral blouse and a chunky cardigan from Primark, so they didn't need to know. Her dress was kept as evidence, of course.'

'And it had Xavier's DNA on it?' Sean said.

'Yes.'

'I remember taking the call,' Sean said. 'She must have identified him straight away, because he was still in the club when Gav and I got there.'

'The ID came from the friend, Shelley, the one who's gone off to Devon, but Bethany confirmed it. They all knew each other. Xavier's sister, Alicia Velasquez, was at college with them. It was her birthday.'

'And the friend saw what happened?'

'She saw them together, dancing. Then she lost sight of Bethany, but when she went out for a breath of fresh air, Bethany came staggering towards her. She said she'd woken

220

up sitting against the side of a skip, her knickers were gone and she didn't know what had happened.'

'And you're sure about her story?' Sean said.

'You're joking, aren't you?'

'No,' he said. 'I mean, I'm not joking, and I don't disbelieve her, but if she's afraid of what her parents think, then she could claim to have been raped to cover a perfectly legitimate relationship.'

'She was a mess, and if she was faking amnesia she's a brilliant actress.'

After one junction they came off the motorway and Tina pulled up sharply as a traffic light ahead of them turned red. The seat belt tugged against Sean's shoulder. He felt as if he should apologise. There was no real reason to disbelieve what had happened to Bethany Winters.

They were on the outskirts of the village and the satnav showed the route twisting and turning into an estate of large detached houses by a canal. A flock of birds was picking its way over a strip of grass between the road and the towpath. A dog ran into the middle of them and they took off, haphazardly, circling over the road to land on the other side. Tina turned the car left along a wide road of houses set back behind neat lawns.

'Number eighty-three,' she said. 'Here we go, and there's even a parking space. House looks occupied, so that's a relief. Perhaps it's our lucky day.'

'Hope so,' Sean said.

The front door was opened by a woman in her early fifties, her hair was cut short and she wore no make-up. She was neatly dressed in a skirt and blouse. The smile that had been

221

ready as she opened the door, faltered when she saw Tina, who had her badge out, ready.

'You'd better come in,' she said.

Tina introduced Sean, and Alyson Winters showed them into the front room.

'Would you like a cup of tea? Biscuits?'

'Thank you,' Tina said. 'Milk, no sugar.'

'Same,' Sean said. 'Thanks.'

There was a two-seater settee and matching armchair in cream leather. The carpet was a light beige and Sean was already regretting agreeing to the tea. This was a room where you wouldn't want to spill a drop of anything that could stain.

'I'll lead on the questions,' Tina said, 'if that's okay with you.'

Sean held his hands up. 'Just here to learn.'

When Alyson came back, her polite smile was fixed in place. She sat down in the armchair and held out the plate of biscuits towards Sean. Her hand shook faintly.

'We were hoping to be able to talk to Bethany,' Tina said. 'She was due in court on Monday, but she didn't show up. We've had a few problems contacting her. Is she here?'

The smile slipped and Alyson's mouth formed a perfect, puckered circle. A frown line between her eyes made a deep crease in her face. Sean was transfixed by how strangely ugly she had suddenly become, the plate held towards him like a weapon. He took it out of her hand and placed it on the coffee table, but she seemed oblivious. She was staring at Tina.

'I don't understand,' she said. 'When you said you'd come about Bethany, I thought you were going to tell me that she'd been found. I was hoping for news . . . and dreading what you were going to tell me.'

222

Tina's usual cheerful expression was clouded by uncertainty. She struggled to speak.

'I'm sorry, Mrs Winters . . .'

Sean felt as if he should help both Tina and Alyson, who both appeared equally stricken, but he wasn't sure about the protocol.

'We reported her missing,' Alyson Winters said, in little more than a whisper.

'Perhaps you could go back to the beginning, Mrs Winters,' he said, 'and tell us what's happened since my colleague last spoke to your daughter. We're from the South Yorkshire Force, so I expect the current situation is being dealt with by your local police. We can ask them, of course, but it would be good if you could tell us, in your own words.'

She folded her hands in her lap and hesitated, then began to speak, her eyes fixed on her knuckles the whole time.

'After Bethany was in hospital, she wasn't the same. She wouldn't talk to us and she refused to come to church. She wouldn't go back to college. Then one day, she was gone. No explanation, she just packed a small bag and that was it. She didn't even take her Bible. We thought she'd gone with her friend, Shelley Martin, at first. There's a community in Devon for young people who are interested in training in mission work.'

The force with which Alyson had been holding onto her feelings suddenly broke, and tears welled up in her eyes and poured down her face. She made no effort to stop them. Tina snapped into action, pulled a packet of tissues from her pocket, and pressed one into the woman's hand. But she didn't use it. She sat, rocking back and forth, while she wept.

'I knew we should have reported her missing sooner,' she said through her tears. 'But she was so angry and I felt sure she would calm down and come home. That's what we prayed for.'

'Why did you get rid of your landline?' Tina said.

Alyson Winters blew her nose into a crumpled and disintegrating tissue.

'After the boy was arrested, we started to get phone calls. They were for Bethany, but we protected her from them. Vicious, hate-filled calls, saying she'd made it up and should be raped all over again for being a liar.'

'Did you report it?'

She sighed and shook her head.

'We really wanted the whole thing to go away. The idea of my daughter's life, her body, being discussed in such a way. It was bad enough that there was going to be a court case for the original attack, but the idea of having to go through something like that twice, I couldn't bear it.'

There was a framed photograph on the mantelpiece of a pretty young girl, with long black hair, sculpted eyebrows and thick eyelashes. She wore a clinging satin dress, which fell to her ankles. Another photo showed a much younger, fatter version of the dark-haired girl, in a red pinafore dress, holding the hand of someone taller, who'd been clipped off to fit the picture into the frame. Alyson followed Sean's eyeline.

'These two are all we have,' she said. 'The prom photo was sent by a school friend; it's not a good likeness. Why do they do that with their make-up and eyebrows? They all end up looking the same, don't they? We would never have let her leave the house looking like that, but we weren't to know.'

Sean felt it would be insensitive to agree with her, but the girl looked like every other teenager who watches reality TV shows and gets her make-up tips off YouTube.

'And how old is she in the other photo?' Sean said.

'She was five when that was taken. My cousin kept a copy. I asked her to send it.'

Sean thought it odd they had no other pictures of their daughter. Perhaps it was something to do with their religion, but he'd never come across anything like it before. As if she had read his confusion, Alyson continued in her quiet, controlled voice.

'She destroyed them before she left. Tore out every single picture from every album and every frame and tore them to pieces.'

'I see,' Tina said. 'Was that out of character?'

Alyson let out a mirthless laugh.

'Bethany was an unpredictable girl.' She picked up the picture of the younger child. 'Quite easy-going when she was a toddler, compliant and sweet-natured. But she changed.'

'Was there anything in particular that caused her to change?' Tina said.

'We couldn't have any more children.' Alyson looked at the photo in her hand. 'I nearly died when she was born. A haemorrhage. It was all such an awful mess that my whole womb had to come out.' She glanced up at Sean, as if she'd only just remembered he was there. 'I'm sorry . . .'

'Please, don't be. These things happen.'

'When she was old enough, we decided to try fostering. We took in a little boy who was in care. His name was Robert. It didn't work out.'

Sean looked at the photo she was holding, and the hand in Bethany's.

'He was older than her?'

She nodded. 'Yes, that's him, or rather he was in the original photograph. I just wanted to have Bethany in it now. Do you understand? He was a bad influence on her and like I said, it didn't work out. We had to let them take him back.'

'Mrs Winters,' Tina said, 'when we arrived, we explained that Bethany didn't turn up at court, so the case has been adjourned. But there's something you should know, Xavier Velasquez, who is accused of attacking your daughter, has gone missing.'

Alyson Winters stood up, dropping the framed picture onto the coffee table with a clatter.

'Then you must find him,' she shrieked. 'You must find him as soon as possible!'

They assured her they would do their best and promised to liaise with Nottinghamshire Police, to avoid any more surprises, then went back to the car and sat for a moment, before Sean broke the silence.

'What now?'

'I don't know,' Tina said. 'I feel like we let them both down, Alyson and Bethany.'

'It's not your fault,' Sean said.

He turned to look at her and was surprised to see that she was crying too. Without thinking, he reached out and touched a tear with his fingertip.

Then his phone rang.

As he pulled it out of his pocket, he saw her look away. She wiped her face on her sleeve and started the car, as if

226

nothing had happened. Perhaps, he thought, nothing had.

The call was from Ivan.

'Something very exciting to show you. Are you on your way back?'

'About half an hour, sir.'

'Jolly good. You'll like this.'

Knowles ended the call as Tina started the car.

'He's got a really posh telephone voice,' Sean said, hoping to get things back to normal between them. 'Even posher than he normally talks. Sounds like he should be reading the *BBC News*, not slumming it with the likes of us.'

'Speak for yourself, I didn't grow up in a slum and my mother was ferocious if we so much as dropped our aitches.'

'Well, you know what I mean.'

'I'm not sure I do,' she said. 'There's loads more Northerners on the BBC now.'

'Okay . . .'

'And Scots and Welsh.'

'Right,' he said.

'You never know, they might have a lad from Donny reading the news one of these days.'

'Well, it won't be me,' he said.

CHAPTER THIRTY

Wednesday

'Come in!'

Sean detected the excitement in Ivan Knowles' voice as soon as he knocked on the door of the viewing room.

'Ah, Denton,' he said. 'Sit down and enjoy the show. Mark, tell the constable what you just told me.'

'So here we are,' Mark Headingham sounded less excitable than the DS, but still spoke with a frisson of pride. 'We're looking out over the building site. There's an anomaly between what we're seeing and what we've been told. If the two men were working until just before five, and one goes to get the money, then we see them just after five, leaving the site, where were they in between? We might assume it's somewhere not covered by the cameras, except that Abbas appears to come from the direction of the site. So I thought I'd take another look at this footage, especially after Ivan pointed out the water bottle, do you see it?'

'Yes.'

'The time code says 15.05. Nobody there. Just that water

bottle in the ditch. Let me forward wind. 16.00 hrs, it's still there. Let's go back. 14.59. No bottle.'

'Play that bit,' Knowles said.

Sean watched the screen as the bottle appeared, Mark ran the video back and it disappeared. Ten minutes further back, and both men were on the site, working. No bottle. At normal speed, going forward, they put down their tools and left the site, wiping sweat off their brows and moving towards the car park side of the stadium building.

'They're having a break, but they don't come back,' Knowles said. 'Or at least, we don't see them come back. And the bottle, one minute it's not there, next minute it is. We don't see anyone throw it, so immediately we know there's a break in the coverage. But when? This is where Mark's sharp eye comes in handy.'

Mark moved the video forwards again until the bottle appeared.

'See the time code? It's part of the digital image, it isn't separate, so if you cut and paste that segment of the image, you get a slight mismatch in the background. At one minute to three, the light is brighter, the sun is higher in the sky. By five, it's dimmer, the shadows created by the building are beginning to impact, and it carries on getting darker. It was a bright, cloudless day, so these changes are subtle. Look, at 14.59 hours, the surrounding area of the time code, including the gaps between the numbers, is roughly in line with the light quality of the rest of the image. But after 15.00 hours, it begins to look different. Do you see? There's a shadow here that isn't picked up in the time code. Around the numbers it's brighter than the rest of the scene. If we go forward, just looking at the time code and the area immediately around it, it gradually darkens until, at around 17.15, it's a match. Then it stays in line with the rest of the image.'

'So the time code is from the original video, but it's been cut and pasted into something else?' Sean volunteered.

'Bingo!' Knowles said. 'The bottle is probably in the ditch by 17.00 hours, or soon after. But from 15.00 hours we're looking at a couple of hours of repeat footage, possibly in two chunks of an hour each. Mark's found what looks like another break, where the light on the main image changes again. It's been done by someone who knows how to edit video, but it's been done clumsily, possibly in a hurry. They knew they had to use daylight footage, but hadn't bargained for the shadows created by the main building.'

'If I remember correctly,' Sean said, slowly trying to work out the significance of what he was seeing, 'Abbas and Homsi leave just after 17.00, and presumably whoever altered the film knows this. So they don't need to worry about what happens on the building site after they've gone, only about the last two hours of their working day. How does that help us? Abbas is still alive, at 17.05, on the other camera, and that footage appears to be authentic. As for why he would alter the earlier video, Derek O'Connor could be up to anything, burying dead dogs, laying illegal cables to bypass his own electricity metre. Maybe it's just a coincidence that it happens on the same evening Abbas is killed.'

'I don't like coincidences,' Knowles said. 'And I've got another one for you that I don't like. You know the bakery van we saw being emptied out on the ring road yesterday?'

'Sunhill Bakeries, I know,' Sean said. 'It was the one Xavier Velasquez was driving.'

'This morning we got an updated delivery list from the distraught father, and Xavier was either on his way to or from the Chasebridge Greyhound Stadium. It was a last-minute order, apparently, so wasn't on the original list he emailed through yesterday, but forensics picked up a copy in the cab. The delivery to the stadium had been added in handwriting, by someone at the bakery, and given to Xavier as he was about to leave.'

'Did he ever arrive?'

'That's what you're about to find out. Give the O'Connors a call, will you? I think we're going to have to pay them another visit.'

'Mrs Winters was very keen we find him. She seemed genuinely terrified that he'd gone AWOL. She also mentioned abusive phone calls. Shall we follow that up with Notts Police? See if they logged anything?'

Knowles rubbed his eyes. 'I'll run it past the boss. This is going to get complicated if we have to involve another force.'

Sean stood up. 'Shit! Sorry, sir, I mean "damn". I've just remembered I'm supposed to be sorting through the bags of evidence from the school.'

'Make that phone call for me and let me know the answer, then you'd better get upstairs. I'll try and head Khan off at the pass so he doesn't notice I've pulled you in here. Mark and I need to get something in writing about what we've seen on the tapes. Mark, you talk and I'll write, then there's some chance we'll get the tech jargon right.'

Sean let himself out of the viewing room and went

downstairs to the ops room. Khan wasn't around, but Tina was sitting at the shared desk, typing at the computer.

'Can I use that phone?' he said. She nodded.

He was expecting Derek's slight Irish accent or Lou O'Connor's broad South Yorkshire, so the middle-class female voice who picked up took him by surprise. Then he remembered the girl who'd given him the DVR. She'd been wearing an apron and he'd assumed she was just a kitchen assistant. She'd barely spoken, so he hadn't really remembered her voice.

'Is that Chasebridge Greyhound Stadium?'

'You're through to the catering department, how may I help?'

'This is Detective Constable Denton, from Doncaster CID. Can you tell me if you had a bread delivery yesterday?'

'Yesterday? No, we didn't.'

'Were you expecting one?'

'As a matter of fact, we were. It was quite tricky, actually. But they didn't turn up and I had to defrost some bread for the evening.'

'Was that for the charity meeting?'

There was a slight hesitation. 'Yes, it's not our busiest event, thankfully, and the hot weather helped, so the breadcakes were all defrosted in time to make the burgers. But we won't be using them again.'

'Breadcakes. That's what you ordered from Sunhill?'

'Yes, or rather my boss would have ordered the breadcakes. For the burgers.'

'Thank you,' he said, 'that's most helpful.'

He texted Knowles this information and set off to the

232

fourth floor with a slow and heavy step. They seemed to be getting nowhere with either case and all he had to look forward to were the discarded possessions of rough sleepers, mixed with junkies' needles and faeces.

He took the stairs slowly and made his way to find Janet Wheeler. The smell of unwashed clothes and stale tobacco hit him as soon as he opened the door. Eight tables were each laid out with a stack of brown paper evidence bags on one side. On three of the tables, a stack of bags had been filled and labelled, while the other five tables were empty. Sean looked puzzled.

'Underneath,' said Janet Wheeler.

He ducked down and saw several large plastic bags, which looked as if they were ready to be dropped off at a charity shop.

'Right,' she said. 'Gloves on, eyes open. Everything needs a description, date, and the room number it was found in. We're looking for bloodstains, spatters, or something that's been used to wipe hands. We're looking for a weapon. And we're looking for the boots worn by Abbas. They're on CCTV, but there was nothing by the body. Oh, and if the witness evidence about men in Halloween masks is reliable, we're looking for something to match our Grim Reaper.'

Sean sighed. He was going to be here all day.

Janet Wheeler worked in silence. Sean longed for conversation, or even the radio. The pile to his right was steadily growing, bagged, marked, but totally uninteresting, as far as he could tell. He was checking the front and back of a dirty white T-shirt, when Janet cleared her throat and announced they should take a lunch break.

Sean wasn't sure he'd be able to eat anything. The smell of the dirty clothing hung in his nostrils. He could taste it. He peeled off his gloves, brushing a residue of powder into the bin after them.

'Back here in an hour?' Wheeler said brightly. 'Good work. Although you should take your time with the labelling. We need to be able to read it.'

'Yes, ma'am.'

He couldn't get to the Gents' toilets fast enough. He ran the tap and washed his hands over and over, before he went to the urinal, and then washed them again when he came back. He cupped his hands under the tap and snorted water up his nose, blowing it out again, letting the particles of dust and grime wash down the drain, but he couldn't wash away the lingering embarrassment at being pulled up for his handwriting.

He needed to get outside, into the fresh air, so he walked round the block to Nigel Gresley Square, crossing the new public space in front of the theatre, where two children, screaming with laughter, ran through the jets of water that shot up from the pavement. Now he was out of the building, his stomach rumbled with hunger. He crossed the road and slipped down the side of the library, heading for a cafe with vintage tablecloths and mismatched cups and saucers, fresh flowers in vases on every table, and staff who looked up and smiled when he came through the door. This was the new energy that was finding its way into the town, and it felt good.

He decided to take his sandwich back to the square and sit with the sun on his face outside the theatre. The children had moved on and a familiar figure, stripped to the waist, was standing over the water jets that sprang from the pavement. As the next burst of water splashed over his torso, Longfeller grinned and rubbed his chest, armpits and neck. The pattern of stars, tattooed on his cheek, continued down his arms and across his upper body. A moon on his right pectoral muscle was matched by a smiling sun across his belly. The artwork was rough and the ink was blurred, fading into Longfeller's tanned skin.

Sean approached him.

'Can I have a word?' he said.

'Just a friendly chat, is it?'

'That's right. Something you might be able to help us with.'

'Could do with a drink,' Longfeller said, 'if we're going to be talking. And maybe summat to eat.'

'Okay,' Sean said reluctantly, checking his watch. He shoved the paper bag, with his sandwich inside, into his pocket. The nearest place to eat and drink was the theatre cafe. He wasn't sure if they were ready for a half-naked Longfeller.

'You got a shirt?'

'Sort of.'

Longfeller pulled a skinny red vest with a Che Guevara logo out of the pocket of his jeans and put it on. Both the vest and the jeans looked new.

Once inside, the air conditioning was a shock. Sean led Longfeller to a table in the window.

'Stay here while I get the drinks.'

'How about a plate of chips? Or a pie. Do they do a nice pie?'

'I think it's more quiche and salad in here,' said Sean. 'What about a piece of cake?'

'All right.'

Sean was relieved that there was no queue at the counter and ordered two Cokes with plenty of ice and a slice of chocolate brownie. While he had his back turned, he texted Ivan.

'So what is it you want, copper?' Longfeller asked, when Sean got back to the table with the drinks and cake. 'I'm assuming this isn't just a social call?'

'Where were you on Friday night?' Sean said, hanging on to the glass as Longfeller's hand reached for it.

He licked his lips, eyes on the cold brown liquid.

'I couldn't be sure, one day is much like another, if you know what I mean.'

'Not sure I do,' Sean said. 'But let me help you. On Friday night the residents of the old Chasebridge School were disturbed. They mainly left the building and were seen milling around in the local area. Ring any bells?'

'Oh, yes. That was Friday, was it? A right racket going on, shouting and all that. I heard someone got hurt. Shame. It's been a nice little gaff for a few weeks, that has. If you don't mind the foreigners.'

'Sorry?'

'Couple of Arab lads.'

'Can you remember their names?'

'Nah. Summat foreign. I called 'em the Dogs of War. Dog One and Dog Two, on account of them coming from a war zone.' He stopped and rubbed his cheek, distorting the tattoo of the star, so that it crept up to his eye. 'Plumbing wasn't up to much in that place, but you can't have everything.'

Sean put the glass of Coke on the table and sat down. He

watched Longfeller drink quickly, not stopping for a breath until it was empty.

'What exactly did you see?' Sean said.

Longfeller put the glass down and paused, as if to compose himself.

'Couple of lads, young lads in these weird Halloween masks, hanging around on the field. I thought they were just having a drink or a smoke or whatever. Odd, though, because there's months to go until Halloween. Anyway, all of a sudden they came in, shouting, banging on the doors with some sort of stick or a metal bar or something like that. I didn't see what, but I heard it. Then everyone's shouting that we need to get out. So I did. Didn't take much persuasion.'

'Did you see anyone as you were leaving?'

'How d'you mean?'

'Do you remember anyone on the street, anyone you didn't know?'

'Some feller with a dog called me a bad name as I crossed over by them new houses.'

Sean nodded. It fitted with what Davies had told him. Although he hadn't mentioned specifically insulting Longfeller, it seemed entirely plausible.

'Could you identify the lads?'

Longfeller's answer was to cram chocolate brownie into his mouth.

'Nah,' he said, his mouth full. 'Hoods up. Trackies, I suppose, trainers, only caught a flash of them, but definitely had their faces covered, one was a sort of skull and the other was Frankenstein's monster. I ducked down out of sight, I did. Get a lot of grief off lads like that, what with my tattoos.'

The stars on Longfeller's cheeks may have become fuzzy over time, but still they marked him out. The skull mask could easily be the Grim Reaper that Lizzie had found in the toilet cistern. And the lads? There were two young men living right there in the grounds of the stadium, with easy access to the school.

Sean's phone vibrated and he checked Ivan Knowles' reply to his text.

'Where are you staying now?' Sean said.

'Here and there,' Longfeller replied.

'Can you be more specific?'

'The nights are warm, aren't they? I bought myself a little tent I put up in the corner of Elmfield Park.'

'Thanks,' Sean said, getting up. 'Ring 101 if you think of anything, and ask for me, DC Sean Denton.'

'Aye. I know you, even without your uniform. You've lifted me enough times.'

Nothing wrong with his memory, Sean thought.

'I wouldn't mind another Coke to wash this lot down,' Longfeller's voice was wheedling.

Sean decided to pretend he hadn't heard. He walked to the door, and with one last look around the modern interior of the theatre, with its incongruous guest sitting in the window, he stepped out into the sunlight. His hand went to his pocket and he felt the soft, damp paper bag containing the chicken sandwich he'd bought earlier. He took a bite and dropped the rest into the nearest bin, his appetite gone.

He'd wanted to ask Longfeller about the bracelet he'd given Mary, but Ivan's text had been clear. That sort of question would have to wait until he was under caution, and

Knowles had told him to slow things down, play nice, and see if he could glean any new information. There was nothing to charge Longfeller with yet. In fact, everything he'd told Sean tallied with the existing evidence. Only the second mask was new. Frankenstein's monster. Perhaps it was hiding in the bags of detritus in the exhibits room. He sighed. He'd have to hurry back, or he'd be late for Janet Wheeler.

CHAPTER THIRTY-ONE

Wednesday

She watches Joe leave his caravan and walk out of the yard. It's nine o'clock. He turns right into the car park, towards the entrance. He'll be heading up to Derek and Lou's house, opposite the country park, and from there they'll drive down south to Levi Heron's maximum security prison. They'll be gone all day and it will be a blessing to have the whole place to herself and Tommy.

He emerges at about ten, blinking and yawning in the daylight.

'I can't believe how long I've slept,' he says. 'I should get on with the jobs Derek left me.'

She smiles at him from where she's sitting on the steps of her own caravan.

'There's no rush, is there? I'm planning to take it easy.'

He rubs his face. 'I don't know.'

'Have some orange juice while you think about it. I've got some in the fridge, it's nice and cold.'

He hesitates and shoots her a shy grin, before he ambles over. Wolf raises his head and his tail thumps on the ground.

'Sarah,' he says quietly, 'I've been thinking.'

'Steady on, Tommy. You don't want to do too much of that.'

She laughs and watches his face cloud over.

'Don't say that. It's the sort of thing Joey says.'

His fists are balled by his sides. Wolf growls. At last, Sarah thinks, he's earning his keep as her guard dog.

'Hey, come on. I don't mean anything by it. Let me get you that drink.'

She gets up and goes inside. The steps creak as he follows her.

'Sit down, Tommy.'

He shakes his head. 'I need to know that you don't think I'm stupid, or a moron, or a retard, or any of the other names he calls me.'

'Of course I don't. We're friends, aren't we?'

She reaches for the carton of orange juice and takes a glass from the drainer. She turns to look at him.

'Just friends?' he says. 'I thought we were more than that. Like Bonnie and Clyde, you said.'

'Did I?' She holds eye contact with him and tries to keep her smile fixed, as she hands him the glass.

He doesn't take it. His head dips forward as he tries to kiss her. She turns and catches it on her cheek, as soft and wet as she's imagined. She fights the urge to wipe it off, curses herself for 'leading him on', and curses herself again for using that language, even in her own head. It's her mother speaking.

She hasn't promised Tommy anything. He did all the promising: to protect her, to fight for her, to keep her safe. She didn't ask him to do any of it. To her relief he finally takes the drink and wedges himself into the narrow seat at her kitchen table. He's blushing.

'You having something?' he says.

'I'm all right for now,' she says and sits opposite him.

He sips and pulls a face. 'Hurts my teeth it's so cold!'

'I turned my fridge down as low as it would go.'

The colder it is, the less he'll be able to taste any trace of bitterness. She finds herself smiling at this idea, both real and metaphorical. She misses her other life at times. The girl she was supposed to have become. The A-levels, the English degree at a shiny campus university. The poetry she was going to write. After this, she can't go back. She isn't sure how to go forward, but a plan is evolving.

Tommy rests his chin in his hands, his elbows on the table. His eyelids begin to droop.

'Do you need to lie down?'

He nods.

'Come on, then.'

She hopes she'll have the strength to manoeuvre him into the bedroom. She holds his hands tightly by the wrists and manages to turn him sideways on the seat. Then she throws his arms over her shoulders and he holds on. Gradually, she pulls him to standing.

'Come on, up you get. It's like a dance, Tommy. Look we're dancing!'

He leans into her and she struggles to take his weight, shuffling him towards her bedroom. She's afraid he might collapse on her before they reach the foot of the bed, but at the last moment, she twists him sideways and he falls like a tree in a forest. His eyelids flutter and close.

'Sleep tight, Tommy.'

She closes the door.

CHAPTER THIRTY-TWO

Thursday afternoon

It was a spur of the moment decision, getting off the bus early and walking up the road to the children's home, but since Tuesday evening, Chloe found it difficult to get the events at the dog track out of her mind. If only she'd asked for Melissa's phone number, at least she could have texted to check she was okay. She shuddered at the implicit threat in the older brother's tone, and wondered what he'd told Melissa to persuade her to get in the car so quickly.

A couple were walking towards her and she stepped aside to let them pass. The woman had bruises under both eyes and was painfully thin. The man was young and muscular, holding the woman tightly by the upper arm. Chloe walked on quickly. The woman was probably on the game. These few streets had several massage parlours and anonymous doors leading to upstairs flats, with permanently curtained windows. She felt ashamed that she'd looked away, but how could she intervene? He might not be the man who'd hit the woman, these things were always more complicated than they seemed. She wondered if this was what drove Sean. At least he could try to right the wrongs of society, whereas she could only walk past.

She thought about mentioning the evening at the dog track to Sean. There must be something about shooting dogs on your own property that was against the law, but she wasn't ready to grass up Melissa's family, the poor girl had enough problems on her plate.

She rang the bell and waited for the voice on the intercom. She was buzzed in straight away and found herself standing in the empty hall. She heard voices upstairs, followed by the slow tread of someone coming down. The sun was pouring in through the landing window, lighting up the red and blue stained glass in its arch. She couldn't see Melissa's expression against the light, but in silhouette her shoulders were hunched and her hair hung down like curtains in front of her face.

'Hey!' Chloe said. 'You okay?'

Melissa shrugged.

'Shall we sit in the garden?'

It was cooler inside, but it looked as if Melissa could do with some fresh air. As she drew close, Chloe smelt unwashed clothes, and the sickliness of someone who hasn't left their bedroom for days.

They sat on the bench amidst the chaos of toys. A little boy was digging in a flower bed with a plastic trowel, singing under his breath.

'Has something happened?' Chloe ventured.

Melissa twisted a hair around her fingers.

'I lost my job,' she said.

'Oh. I'm sorry. I thought you were still upset about the dog, Indian Whisper.'

Melissa sighed. 'Joey explained that the dog was in terrible pain. He told me it was the kindest thing to do.'

And you believed him, Chloe thought, but kept her mouth shut.

'Thing is,' Melissa said, 'someone told social services I was working with an adult who wasn't appropriate.'

'What do you mean?'

'I reckon it was that bitch, Kathy Edwards, spreading rumours about Greg.'

'The girl on the fruit and veg stall? Didn't you use to live with them?'

'They were my foster family, but they didn't care about me, just liked to get the money every week.'

'I'm sure that's not true.'

Melissa swung round and glared at her. 'What would you know?'

'I know what it's like to have no family. My mum died when I was about your age. Before that she was always working and it felt like I only saw her if I went to work with her.'

Melissa's hard stare softened a little. 'What was her job?'

'She worked in a pub. We didn't live there, but I seemed to be there all the time when I was little, sat on the bar like a doll. Sometimes I got put to bed in the rooms upstairs, or I stayed at home, with a neighbour looking in on me. By the time I was ten I was pretty much left on my own. I always wanted brothers and sisters, and a dad, so I know what that's like.'

She was about to say how happy she was to have found her half-brother and her father, but she held back. Melissa was inquisitive and Chloe wasn't quite ready to tell her that her brother was a police officer.

'Greg's all right,' Melissa said. 'He's been kind to me.'

'Is he the guy that cut my hair?'

Melissa nodded.

'Yeah, he seemed nice. Why is he inappropriate all of a sudden?'

'I don't know, they wouldn't tell me. Something about a complaint in his previous place of work.' Her eyes filled up and she suddenly took hold of Chloe's hand. 'Apart from you, he's my only friend.'

'What about school?' Chloe gave her hand a squeeze.

'I don't want to go any more. There's a tutor comes here, but he's rubbish.'

'And don't you have any friends here?'

'I don't really get on with people my own age,' she said. 'I don't mind being with the little ones, but the other girls are all bitches. I can't wait until I can go and live with Aunty Lou and Uncle Derek.'

They sat and watched the little boy pick up a green and yellow watering can. He toddled over to an outside tap and tried to turn it on.

'Do you want some help with that?' Chloe said.

He nodded.

She filled the watering can half-full and gave it back to him. He carried it slowly and carefully back to his little plot and began to water the earth he'd been digging.

'I'm going to the track on Saturday,' Melissa said, and Chloe detected a note of jealousy, as if she felt compelled to draw Chloe's attention away from the little boy.

'You're going to the dog track? On your own?'

'No, my social worker's taking me.'

'So it's an official visit?'

'Yeah,' Melissa was twisting her hair in her fingers. 'What if she finds out I've already been there?'

'You'll just have to pretend you haven't. Talk about how different it looks from what you'd imagined. Hang back, so she has to work out which door to knock on, that sort of thing.'

Melissa nodded. 'We're supposed to meet Aunty Lou and look round the track, then go up to the house for a chat.'

'Right,' Chloe said. 'So be a bit shy around her. Same with the others.'

'What if Tommy blurts something out?'

'Like he did about the dog?'

'Exactly.'

The little boy was pressing his hand into the wet patch of earth and letting the mud ooze up through his fingers. Chloe felt a sudden pang in her breastbone that took her breath away. She had never thought about having children herself and yet suddenly, as if from nowhere, the urge to pick this little boy up, and wrap him in her arms, was almost overwhelming. Her own mother hadn't been the greatest, but she'd done her best, and Chloe suddenly wanted a chance to do better, to give a child the unconditional love it needed, to play with it, and give it a proper garden to grow flowers in.

'Are you listening?' Melissa said.

'Sorry,' Chloe said. 'I was miles away.'

'I said I think he's got something wrong with him, you know, Asperger's or something. There was a boy here who had

247

it. He couldn't tell a lie and he got us all in trouble by telling our key worker we'd nipped over the garden wall one night.'

'Tommy did?'

'No, Jamie, the lad who was staying here. He's gone home now, lucky bugger. His mum's got a new partner and it's all happy families. Hey! Don't put that in your mouth!'

She jumped off the bench and rushed to the little boy, whose face twisted in disgust at the taste of mud. She scooped him up and carried him indoors.

'Let's get you some water and you can rinse all that nasty muck away.'

It was like watching herself, Chloe thought. She could hear Melissa chattering away to the boy, and followed them into the kitchen.

Melissa looked much happier than when she'd arrived, so Chloe decided it was time to go. She needed to see Jack. He'd been asleep the evening before, and she was hoping he might be a bit better today.

'Good luck on Saturday,' she said. 'And I'm sorry about your job.'

'It's okay,' Melissa said. 'It won't matter soon, not when I get back to my family.'

She didn't look up from the sink, where the little boy was sitting on the drainer, waiting for the cup of water Melissa was pouring.

Chloe felt a sense of relief when she got outside. Not for the first time, she questioned whether she should have got involved with Melissa Heron and her complicated life. She needed friends of her own age too. At least she had a bit of family to fall back on.

She set off towards the hospital and rang Sean's mobile as she walked.

'Hi, Chloe.'

'Hi. Is this a good time? I'm just on the way to the hospital.'

'Everything okay?'

'Yes, I think so. No change. He was very quiet last night.'

'Right. Look, I was hoping to get down tonight, but I don't think I'm going to make it. I've just been called into a big meeting.'

'No worries.' She tried to keep the disappointment out of her voice. It wasn't for Jack's sake, but her own. It would have been nice to share the load a bit, have a coffee and a chat with Sean, especially if Jack didn't know she was there.

'Yeah,' he said. 'I think we're about to make a breakthrough on a big case.'

'Sounds exciting.'

'It is. I can't really tell you any more than that.'

'Of course. Look, Sean, this might not be important, but do you mind me asking you something? What's a bolt gun?'

'A bolt gun?'

There was a muffled voice in the background.

'Sorry,' he said, 'got to go. The meeting's about to start. I'll ring you later.'

CHAPTER THIRTY-THREE

Thursday night

The door crashes back on its hinges and Wolf lets out a volley of barks. Sarah sits up.

'What the heck?' she says, wondering for a moment where she is. The unfamiliar itch of the dog blanket scratches her arms and she remembers falling asleep on the sofa.

There's someone in the kitchen.

'Where is he?' a slurred voice shouts.

'Is that you, Joe?'

She reaches for the light switch as Joe Heron pushes his way into the living room.

'Where's Tommy? And where's my fucking bolt gun? It's not where it should be.'

'I tried to ring you,' she says.

'You can't take mobile phones into the prison,' he says.

'I didn't want to leave a message,' she says.

'Well?'

She sits up slowly.

'There's something you need to know.'

'About Tommy?'

She nods. 'He's gone.'

'Jesus. Why would he do that?'

She can smell the brandy on his breath and decides to bide her time.

'How was your dad?'

'He was grand. We went to tell him about Melissa and he was chuffed to bits. Best news he's had all year, he said. He wants her to come and live with Lou and Derek, back in the family, where she belongs. He agreed to sign all the papers.'

He sits down heavily on the end of the sofa and his shoulders sag.

'What do you mean about Tommy?' he says. 'He wouldn't just leave, he hasn't got the brains to be out there on his own. It'd be like setting a hamster free.'

'The police phoned when I was in the kitchen. Twice. Or rather two different officers. They're coming back tomorrow to talk to Derek. I think Tommy's in trouble and he got scared.'

'Why didn't he tell me? I'm his big brother, I've always looked after him. Shit, do you think he's taken the bolt gun?'

'I don't know, maybe, yes. It makes sense. Perhaps he was getting it off the premises, in case the police started asking about that dog from Saturday night. They wouldn't tell me anything about what they were after.'

Joe frowns and rubs his eyes as if to sober himself up.

'Why would he scarper? What's he done?'

'I need to show you.'

She gets up and throws the blanket round her shoulders.

'No, Wolf, you stay here.'

The dog turns round and lies down in front of her bedroom door.

She picks up a torch from the kitchen table and leads Joe across the yard to the blue horsebox. It was built for two animals, but the partition has been removed. She opens the small door at the front of the horsebox and lets Joe peer in.

'What have you got in there, a dog?' he says, then pauses and takes a sharp breath. 'Jesus Christ! Who did that?'

He pulls his head out as if he's been stung.

'It was Tommy,' she says. 'He got angry, really carried away, and it isn't the first time.'

Joe staggers away from the horsebox and stands in the middle of the yard.

'What the fuck has he done?'

'We have to get rid of it,' she says. 'Now, before the police arrive. Maybe Tommy will come back of his own accord, or we can go and look for him, but the police mustn't find that when they get here.'

'Tommy's a liability, always has been. He's going to fuck this up for all of us, for Melissa, Lou, me. My dad wouldn't want that.'

'No, he wouldn't.' She moves closer to him and lowers her voice. 'Although I think he did this for Melissa.'

'What are you on about?'

'Get your pickup and we'll tow the trailer out of here, I'll explain on the way.'

A moment of silence settles between them.

'Is that why you wanted the pills?'

'Yes, to take the pain away. It was all I could do.'

'Fuck, I wish I wasn't so fucking pissed, but Derek was whining on at me in the car and I couldn't listen to him sober. Got me a bottle of brandy at that M&S food on the motorway. Nicked you something while I was in there.'

He opens his jacket and takes a small blue package out of the inner pocket.

'Peace offering,' he says. 'Sorry, I forgot about it.'

He holds out an M&S own brand version of a Walnut Whip, or it had been before it melted, and the walnut collapsed into the chocolate and fondant.

'Thanks.' She wants to laugh. There's something insane about the sight of the distorted chocolate, the whole mad dream of her being here, this life she's got into and is going to have to get herself out of again. She tells herself to get a grip, she must stay in control.

'Get your keys,' she says. 'I'll drive.'

CHAPTER THIRTY-FOUR

Thursday night

Sean let himself into the flat and pulled the door shut behind him.

'Hello?'

There was no reply. The door to the bedroom stood open. The bed was still neatly made from this morning. In the living room, the glass-topped coffee table shone, while in the kitchen, the surfaces were clean and clear of the breakfast things he knew he'd left out. It was as if Lizzie had erased all trace of him when he left for work. If it wasn't for his PlayStation, on the shelf under the TV set, you wouldn't know he lived here at all. He thought of the painting he'd liked, in the hospital corridor, the dark house with the bright light in the window. There was a white painted wall opposite the window in the living room that could do with something. He wondered if he could risk surprising her, or whether he should discuss it first.

He went into the kitchen and opened the fridge. It looked like she'd had a supermarket delivery. The vegetable drawers were bursting with bags of salad, and the shelves were full of yoghurts, cheese, and the thin salty ham that she liked. On the top shelf he saw something he knew was meant for him. A pepperoni, double-cheese pizza.

'Thanks, Lizzie,' he said to the empty kitchen. 'That's perfect.'

They'd both been in the briefing together, but Lizzie had stayed on to chase up some results from the lab. It really felt like things were coming together. The results from the samples taken from Homsi's boots came back as a mix of earth and building-grade crushed limestone, used as a sub-base for paths and car parks. It confirmed what the CCTV had told them, Abbas and Homsi had been working on the site. Meanwhile, the DNA from the ghoulish mask was being tested for any matches on the system, but so far had come up with nothing. Khan had sent everyone home because the next day was going to be an early start. The O'Connor family was about to get a visit from the Major Crimes Unit and its forensic team.

Meanwhile, Longfeller's tent would get a visit from the night-time response shift. If he had stolen the money from Abbas and Homsi, it would be with him in his tent. Sean's observation of his new clothes, and the bracelet he'd bought Mary had all been taken into account. Karen Friedman, from RAMA, had also been in touch. She'd apologised, but she'd been on annual leave and her boss was busy with a court case, but she was going to be in the area tomorrow, so offered to drop in. Homsi hadn't contacted her, she said, and she was surprised, because previously he'd kept in touch regularly, often phoning just to pass the time of day. Sean was looking forward to seeing her again. She belonged to the first part of his journey into the police, and he felt a little glow of pride that she would see him made up to detective constable.

'Ouch.' He'd touched the oven rack with the edge of his finger as he pulled the pizza out. 'Pride goes before a fall, you prat.'

Sucking his finger, he took his plate into the living room and sat down to eat. He turned the PlayStation on and loaded FIFA.

It was nearly nine o'clock when Lizzie came home. He paused his game and offered to make her some dinner, but she said she'd eaten and wanted an early night.

'Did you have something nice?' he said.

'Chinese. I thought I'd introduce Ivan to the delights of the New Moon.'

'Right.'

The New Moon was their restaurant, as far as Sean was concerned. What was she doing taking Ivan Knowles there?

'Did I tell you, it turns out we worked on the same case when I was in London?'

'Really?'

'I think we must have been in some of the same briefings, but we never actually met face-to-face. It was a massive job.'

'But a small world.'

She went into the bathroom and he continued playing his game, listening to the sound of the shower running. Before long he was losing against the machine and his team was three nil down.

'Bollocks,' he said, and tossed the controller onto the floor. He picked us his plate and finished what was left of the lukewarm pizza.

He heard Lizzie come out of the bathroom and go into the bedroom.

By the time he'd washed up and cleaned his teeth, she was snoring. It was amazing, her capacity to fall asleep in an instant. His body was never so biddable.

He woke in the early hours, his mind buzzing with thoughts. He lay in bed for a while, but eventually got up and went into the kitchen. He made a cup of tea and looked out over the square. The tall beech tree in the corner shimmered in the street light.

His gym bag was in the hall. He hadn't been to the gym for a while, but he kept it ready, with trainers, clean socks, shorts and a T-shirt. He had an urge to go for a run. It was stupid o'clock, but the night was warm. He picked up the bag and took it into the living room. No point in waking Lizzie.

Outside, the square was empty, but for the trees. He stretched his back and legs against the railings of the garden, and set off at an easy jog to warm his muscles. He ran towards the town centre, picking up speed, hoping it would be enough to switch off his thoughts and tire him out.

He heard a car approaching and kept his speed up, expecting the vehicle to pass. It kept pace with him, but always just behind. He refused to look round. Some wind-up merchant, probably. He wasn't going to give him the satisfaction of looking nervous.

He passed the newsagents on the corner of South Parade and glanced in the window, to see if he could catch a reflection of the car. White, marked with fluorescent green and black, and a big fat POLICE sign on its bonnet.

He laughed out loud, and turned to see PC Gav Wentworth at the wheel, waving at him.

Gav stopped the car and wound down the passenger window.

'Can I offer you a lift anywhere, you look like you're in a hurry,' he said.

'Very funny,' Sean leant in at the window. 'You on patrol on your own?'

'Haven't you heard? My partner dumped me for a cushy role in CID.'

'Bring on the violins!' Sean laughed.

'Just on the way back from a job at Elmfield Park. A little raid on the tent city that's sprung up there.'

'Ah, Longfeller.'

'Exactly. He's in the cells now, with £120 in cash to explain away.'

'He could be on a murder charge, if the forensics stack up. Just a pity he had the money to go shopping for new clothes. His old ones could have come in handy, either way.'

'Do you reckon he's the murdering type?' Gav said. 'He's got no previous for serious assault, and we've known him a long time, almost as long as I've been doing this job.'

Sean didn't have a chance to answer as the radio cut through their conversation.

Calling all cars. Anyone in the vicinity of the market? Repeat: a car to the marketplace. Blue light. Possible fatality.

Gav took the call and looked up at Sean.

'Are you coming? Or are you running?'

'Go on, then.'

Sean opened the passenger door and got in.

258

Gav put his foot down. The siren ripped through the empty streets and the shop windows were bathed in blue light. The marketplace was empty. A lone figure stepped out from the overhanging roof of Goose Hill Market Hall and waved a torch in their direction.

It was a man in his early twenties, blonde and pale, too small for the security guard's uniform he was wearing.

They parked up and got out.

'In there,' the security guard said. 'Up in the roof.'

'After you,' Sean said.

Gav got his torch out and switched it on. They peered through the latticework of the closed metal shutters.

Sean saw it straight away. A man, hanging. The face was tipped down, eyes covered with a mop of hair, but around the cheeks and mouth, the skin was yellow. He could see in the beam of his torch that the man's clothes were filthy.

'Now, then,' Gav said. 'What have we got?'

'Male, looks a mess. Do you think it's another rough sleeper?'

'Are we sure he's dead?'

'Can we get this shutter open?' Sean asked the security guard, who nodded and fumbled in his pocket for a bunch of keys.

The sound of the shutter lifting sounded unnaturally loud, while everything around them was silent.

Gav approached the hanging man as if he might suddenly jerk back to life. He reached up and felt the skin above the man's socks.

'What are you doing?' Sean said.

'Feeling for signs of life.'

'Shouldn't you be wearing gloves?'

'Can't feel a bloody thing through those.'

'Get us some gloves from the car, can you?'

Gavin wiped his fingers on the back of his trousers. 'He's stone cold.'

Sean stood back, looking up at the corpse. There was no flicker around the man's mouth or throat, no last-minute struggle for breath, but still he needed to be sure. He looked for a way to climb up and get level with the girder. The body was hanging above two adjoining stalls, one with a purple sign announcing *Hair Today* and the next, *Stan's Vinyl*, which had a fat padlock on its rear door and a bolt at head height.

Gav came back with the gloves and gave them to Sean.

Sean put his toe on top of the padlock, glad he was wearing running shoes. He gripped the bolt and swung his free hand up to reach for the lowest girder, which he used to pull himself to standing. He edged along the top of the thin partition wall.

The rope was tied a few feet away. The wooden frame of the record shop was flimsy and shifted under his weight. He looked down. He could see Stan's stock, boxes of vinyl records and CDs protected by a ceiling of chicken wire. He edged closer to the man and reached out, feeling for a pulse on the victim's neck.

'Nothing,' he said.

The beam of Gav's torch swung across the man's face and was held for a moment, like a spotlight. The face was swollen, eyes bruised and half-closed, the lips were dry and cracked. Sean couldn't be sure, but he had an uneasy feeling that he knew this young man's name.

'Should we untie the rope?' Gav said. 'Let him down?'

'Maybe we should wait for the CSI team.'

'Aye. Get your Lizzie down here.'

'She's not my Lizzie, Gav. She's her own woman.'

'Did she tell you to say that?' Gavin laughed and the sound bounced back off the concrete floor.

'It feels wrong to leave him,' Sean said.

'Too late for dignity,' Gavin said. 'He should have thought about that before he hanged himself.'

'Give us a hand down,' Sean said. 'Less I touch, the better.'

Sean glanced back at the dead man. His hair was limp and dirty, his cheeks were marked with a pattern of colour, yellowish brown, with shades of red and purple. Sean swung his legs over the parapet of *Stan's Vinyl* and jumped to the ground.

Another vehicle was pulling up outside. Doors banged and a paramedic ducked under the half-open shutter. He looked up.

'You won't be needing me, then?' he said.

'We've checked for vital signs,' Sean said. 'There aren't any.'

'Aye,' Gav nodded. 'Always follow procedure in the face of the bleeding obvious. I'm off to find the security guard, looked like he was going to throw up. If he's finished, I'll get a statement and open the log.'

'Poor bloke.' The paramedic glanced up at the body. 'There's a lot of it about. At least he didn't choose the railway line. We're getting one a week at the moment.'

'There'll be a scene of crime unit down in a minute,' Sean said. 'But I don't think this is a suicide.'

He held Gav's torch steady and flicked back over the victim's torso.

'What the hell's that?' the paramedic said.

There was something pinned to the victim's chest, a piece of paper with the word WARNING written across it.

'I'll need to stick around to certify the death,' the paramedic said. 'I'm over the end of my shift, but I'm in no rush.'

They didn't speak for a few moments. Sean stepped back from the market stalls, into the centre of the aisle. From here he could watch and listen, keep the area clear. The sky was beginning to lighten and the market traders would be arriving soon.

'Been on the job long?' the paramedic said, cutting through Sean's thoughts. Probably thought he was a rookie.

'Two years as a constable on the response team,' he said. 'Community Support before that. Just moved over to CID.'

'Seen a few of these, have you?'

'One or two.'

The sounds from the street beyond the market hall seemed far away: a door slammed, a motorbike started up. There were no sirens. This wasn't an emergency. Whatever struggles this man had experienced in life, they were over now.

He heard a car pull up. The paramedic went to see who'd arrived.

Sean wondered if Lizzie would be on this job. When he got out of bed, he'd been careful not to let the cold air creep under the duvet and wake her. He let out an involuntary sigh. He wanted to keep his thoughts there, in the clean flat, away from the steadily growing scent of death, hanging from the girders.

'This lot you've got playing now, they don't even get their knees dirty.' It was Donald Chaplin, a CSI who was an ardent cricket fan. He was talking to the paramedic. 'No, cricket's a game for those with real stamina,' he continued. 'You can keep football. Hello, Sean, what have we got here?'

'Male, late teens, early twenties. Bruising to the face, some yellow, some darker patches, could be more recent bruising or something else, sepsis maybe? Really dry round the lips, flaky skin. Possible wound to the abdomen. He was in bad shape before he died.'

'Who found him?'

'Security guard. Gav's getting his statement now.'

'We'll need to get him down. But pictures first.' Donald took out a camera and looked at the flimsy walls of the shop units.

'Shall I?' Sean said. 'I've been up there already, so it's one less set of prints.'

'Aye, go on, you've got the right shoes on for climbing. I'll pass this up to you.'

It wasn't easy balancing and taking pictures, with Donald directing him, and he nearly lost his balance when he heard voices from the pavement. He looked over and saw Lizzie with DS Ivan Knowles. They were ducking under the half-open security grille to come inside. He tried to raise his hand to wave, but letting go of the girder was a mistake. He stumbled and grabbed the air in front of him, missed the girder but caught the rope. The dead man jerked as if he was alive and Ivan Knowles looked up.

'Morning,' Knowles said.

'All right?' Sean said, letting go of the rope.

'Leave him as he is, Sean,' Lizzie said. 'We'll have him

down in a minute, but I want to get a proper look first. Can I have everyone back, please.'

He couldn't tell if she'd seen his fumble and was covering for him, or whether she really thought he'd been trying to untie the rope. He passed the camera to Donald and climbed down.

Knowles looked at Sean's T-shirt and shorts. 'Do you often go for a run in the middle of the night?'

'Now and again,' he said. 'Bumped into Gav, my old partner on response, just as he got the call. It made sense to be first on scene, we were just round the corner.'

'Right, well make yourself useful and get the security guard to give you a tour of the exits, we need to know how this body got here, dead or alive.'

'My money's on dead,' Donald Chaplin muttered under his breath.

'Sir,' Sean said quietly to Knowles. 'It's hard to tell with the damage to his face, but I think I know him. I think it's the lad from the bakery van, the one who's on bail for Bethany Winters' rape.'

'Xavier Velasquez?'

'Yes. I arrested him back in March and I saw him again in court the other day. I could be wrong, but he looks the right height and colouring.'

'Shit. What the hell is going on in this town?' Knowles turned away and got on his radio. Sean sensed he had been dismissed.

Outside, Gav was finishing off the paperwork.

It had grown lighter, and the sky was tinged with a pinkish grey like the belly of a fish. The security guard was sitting on the kerb on the edge of the pavement, his head between his legs.

'How's he doing?' Sean said.

'I think he's had better days,' Gav said. 'Keeps talking about a mouse.'

'Do you want to tell me what you saw, Mr . . . ?'

'Bakowski. My name is Lukasz Bakowski.'

His Polish accent was very faint, overlaid with South Yorkshire.

'I was at the other end of the buildings,' Bakowski said, 'by the Exchange and I thought I heard a car engine start up. I walked around this side and when I got to the Goose Hill Market Hall, I flicked my torch through the shutter. There was a mouse, and I followed him with my torch. Your colleague thinks I'm mad, but let me tell you, this job is very boring. The mice are the best company I get on a night shift. Sometimes I give them names and make up stories about them.'

Sean caught sight of Gav pulling a face.

'Anyhow, I follow its path, behind a stall and out again. Then he stops at a pool of liquid on the floor. His whiskers twitch and he sniffs it. He looks up, this little mouse, and I look up too. And there is a man hanging from the roof.'

'Mr Bakowksi, can we keep it simple?' Gav said, his pen poised on the statement pad. 'Can we agree that you approached the side of the Goose Hill Market Hall, shone your torch inside and saw the body?'

Lukasz nodded his head.

'Right,' Gav said. 'Sign here.'

The security guard took the pen and signed in a trembling scrawl.

'Do you think you'd be able to walk me round the outside and show me all the entrances?' Sean said. 'We need to check how someone came to be in there in the middle of the night.'

The other man nodded and accepted Sean's hand to get to his feet. He wiped his mouth.

'Sorry. I am sorry. It's shock.'

'I'm sure it is.'

Sean led the way. He remembered he had a packet of mints in the pocket of his shorts. He offered one to Lukasz.

'Sugar might do you good.'

'Thank you,' Lukasz took one and sucked hard on it. 'Here, this is the fire door. The internal doors are all locked, outside grilles are down, all padlocked, except what I opened for you to get in.'

They were at a double door with no handles on the outside, closed tight with no sign of having been forced. Sean put his fingers in the gap between the door and the frame at the top, and pulled as much as was possible, but the door wasn't moving.

'Any more?' he said.

'Another one at the bottom, round the corner.'

'Let's give it a look.'

As they made their way back past the scene, Sean noticed they'd attracted a couple of bystanders. They looked like butchers or fishmongers, white coats sticking out beneath their warm jackets.

'I'll have to ask you to step back to the other side of the road, gentlemen,' Sean said.

'What is it, then? Break-in?'

'I'm sorry, can you move back?'

266

They went on their way, looking over their shoulders to get a glimpse inside.

When Sean and Lukasz reached the corner opposite the Red Lion, a car pulled up and a man got out. He watched Sean and Lukasz approach.

'You the lad from Securico?' he said.

Lukasz nodded.

'Bob Aston, Market Manager,' he said. 'Your control called me. Told me the police were down here. Do you mind telling me what this is about?'

'A fatality, sir,' Sean said.

'In the market hall? How the fuck did anyone get inside?' he said to Lukasz, who looked ashen and did not reply.

'You'll need to talk to the officer in charge,' Sean said.

'Who are you?'

'Detective Constable Denton.'

Bob Aston looked him up and down. Sean was acutely conscious of his running shorts and T-shirt.

'Right,' Aston said. 'Where is he?'

'Over there. There's a constable outside. He'll let the DI know you're here.'

Bob Aston got back in the car and turned it round, in order to drive a hundred metres to the corner of Baxtergate. *Lazy sod*, Sean thought.

As he pulled level with them, Aston opened the driver's side window and pointed a leather-gloved finger at Lukasz. 'And if I find you've left something unlocked I'll have Securico fire you,' he said.

He accelerated to the corner, slamming on the brakes as the car turned and squealed to a halt.

'You want to look at the doors?' Lukasz said quietly.

'Aye, go on, then.'

'All shut, and locked, I can tell you for sure.'

Sean walked away from the smell of sick and peppermint on the other man's breath. He took in every detail: a crisp packet in the gutter, three fag butts, a discarded orange, its squashed pulp grey with dirt.

'So talk me through this, Lukasz, your job is to go round the outside of the buildings, is it? Which areas do you have keys for?'

'Just the public areas, not the inside shops or the manager's office. I'm only supposed to go inside if there's an emergency. The ones who are there at the end of the day, they do the locking up and clear people out.'

'Could they have missed someone?'

Lukasz shrugged. 'There are two guys for the whole place, but they do the halls in order, sweep up and down. Check the toilets. Lock inside each hall, and go on to the next one.'

'When you walked round the time before there was nothing unusual?'

'Nothing.'

He kept pace with Sean as they walked. Sean was still looking at everything, the ground, the walls, the windows, testing the outside of each fire door, the padlocks on each metal grille.

When they got back to where Bob Aston's car was parked askew, they saw that it had been joined by a police van and a black Land Rover Discovery.

'When can I go home?' Lukasz said.

'Don't get your hopes up, this is a serious crime.'

268

PC Gavin Wentworth stepped out from behind the van.

'There you are!' he said. 'You're missing all the fun.'

'What's happening?' Sean said.

'Your Lizzie confirmed definite signs of foul play. Not a suicide. DI Khan was here in seconds. I told you he never sleeps, and Ivor Biggun is bouncing around like Tigger trying to impress him.'

'Knowles? He didn't look very bouncy.'

'He seems to have perked up now it looks like a homicide.'

'Right,' Sean said.

He was annoyed with himself for taking so long in finding absolutely nothing of importance on his walk, except that there was no sign of a break-in.

'Where's Khan?' Sean said.

'Inside,' Gav said.

The empty market halls were like a miniature town, a grid system of abandoned streets. Three blocks down, the hard white of an arc light shone on the sign of *Hair Today*. As he came round the screen, he could see Lizzie's narrow shoulders cocooned in a white forensic suit and beside her, the broader frame of Donald Chaplin. They had the body on a plastic sheet on the ground and were kneeling over it.

'Morning, Denton,' DI Khan was standing on the other side of the light. Sean hadn't seen him in the shadows.

'Sir,' he said. 'Just been round the outside of all the market buildings with the security guard. No sign of forced entry and all the doors are locked. They're either push-bar fire doors, sir, which can only be opened from the inside, or they're padlocked.'

'So?' DI Khan said.

'So either he was in here already, with his attackers, or someone else stayed in the building and let them in.'

'Knowles tells me you think you can ID him. You reckon it's Velasquez?'

'It could be, sir. Like I said to DS Knowles, the face is so swollen, it's hard to be sure.'

Light seeped under the shutters of *Hair Today*. Someone was moving around inside. A door opened and Knowles stepped out, masked and wearing plastic shoe covers.

'The note on his chest may have come from here, there's a message pad on the counter, which is a match, but apart from that it's very tidy, no sign of a struggle in the stall itself. If he's been in a fight, it wasn't in there.'

'If he's been in a fight,' Lizzie said, 'it was very one-sided, and it's been going on for several days.'

Khan and Knowles immediately stepped forward to take a closer look at the body. Sean checked his own instinct to go nearer. He thought about what he'd seen when he'd been up close, teetering on the roof of *Stan's Vinyl*, the rainbow of bruises, some healing, some still fresh, and a dark patch on the front of the man's trousers. Markers outlined the area where the liquid had dropped onto the concrete. He wondered whether there would be mouse paw-prints in the blood.

DI Khan sent Knowles to speak to the market manager, and Sean was told to let Lukasz go home, but make sure they knew where to find him.

'And Sean?'

'Yes, sir?'

'Thanks for coming in when you were off duty.'

'Right.' He wasn't sure whether he should explain about being out running, and Gav passing by.

'But you might want to get changed before the briefing. See you back at the station at eight-thirty.'

'Yes, sir.'

He tried to read Khan's expression, but the shadows from the arc light gave nothing away.

CHAPTER THIRTY-FIVE

Friday

He woke up on the sofa. Lizzie was nudging his arm.

'You back already?'

'You've been asleep,' she said.

He tried to focus. 'What's the news?'

'Unexplained death,' she said. 'We need to find the explanation, but it looks like murder.'

She went through to the kitchen and he could hear her taking plates out of the cupboard.

'I got some nice fresh bread on the way back,' she said. 'Do you want some toast?'

He sat up and rubbed his face to wake himself up.

'You want to know what I think?' Sean called to her. 'I think someone else was in the market hall. They must have been. Lukasz swore the place had been checked in the evening and nobody could have got in after that, unless they were let in. The fire doors are push bar from the inside.'

She was standing in the doorway with a slice of bread in her hand.

'Look, do you want this toast or not? I've got a briefing to prepare for.'

'Aye, go on, stick some Marmite on it, will you?'

'If you say please.'

'Please, love of my life.' He tried to sound cheery, but he didn't have the energy. 'What does the doc say about cause of death?'

'Sean, wait till we get back in to work.'

He sat up and looked at her.

'When did you get to be such a stickler for the rules?'

She didn't catch his eye. 'You know I think we shouldn't bring work home.'

'Who says?' Sean took a mouthful of toast, but she'd put too much butter on it. It tasted greasy.

She didn't reply.

'I need a shower,' she said finally.

'Me too.'

'Well you'll have to wait. I'm going first.'

Not together, then. When did they stop having showers together? Two months ago? Maybe three. He put the plate of toast on the floor and turned on his side with a cushion over his head, but he knew he mustn't go back to sleep.

'That's more like it,' DI Khan said, looking him up and down. 'Come in and take a seat before we get going in the ops room.'

'Thank you, sir.'

He'd run the shower cold to wake himself up, put on a clean pair of jeans and an ironed shirt and now he was here early.

'You might be interested to know that the cause of death

273

is confirmed as asphyxiation by hanging, but if he hadn't run out of breath, he would have died from the wound in his abdomen.'

Sean nodded. He wanted to say that he'd noticed that, but he stayed quiet, staring at the spider plant on Khan's desk and the photograph of his wife, holding their baby son.

'The reason I wanted to talk to you, is that technically you're supposed to be going on induction in Sheffield in a couple of days, but it's all desk-based and frankly, it can wait. I want you here. Things are getting complicated.'

'Yes, sir. Happy to be here,' Sean said. 'What about the identification? Is it Velasquez?'

'We need a DNA match to ID him officially, but everything points to it. We've got some of his effects to show the parents. There's no way they can see him like he is, and anyway, it's going to be a very slow and detailed autopsy.'

Sean thought of the mother, opening her arms to her son on Monday, as he was released on bail, holding him tight as if she couldn't bear to lose him.

'As he's your body, you may be interested to know that the wound, according to Doctor Huggins at least, looks like it's come from a bolt gun.'

Sean sat up.

'Did you say bolt gun?'

'Yes, a captive bolt gun. Not to be confused with the kind used in abattoirs, where the projectile retracts. No, this gun leaves the bolt in the brain of the animal and kills it slowly, unless a vet's kind enough to add a lethal injection to take the pain away.'

Sean felt slightly sick. Khan looked at his watch.

'Briefing in the ops room in five minutes,' he said. 'Can you pick me up a coffee on the way? Americano. No milk.'

'Yes, sir.'

He would be able to get the coffee and phone Chloe at the same time. He needed to find out what she meant yesterday. He'd only partly heard what she'd said, Knowles had been demanding his attention, but he was sure she'd been asking him about a bolt gun.

The briefing was quick and to the point. Sean sat in the third row. He tried to make eye contact with Lizzie as she delivered the forensic report, but she didn't look his way. Chloe hadn't answered her phone, so he'd left her a message, asking her to ring back in half an hour.

'Donald Chaplin and Janet Wheeler are still at the market hall, focusing in on the area around the hairdresser's stall and the girder itself,' she was saying. 'The rest of the market is now open, but we've isolated a twenty-metre crime scene. We've got a multitude of fingerprints, dust particles and hair-clippings that we'll be cataloguing and sending for testing. One thing that's worth mentioning, I think, is the smell on the body. Human faeces, urine, a build-up of body odour that may be a couple of days old. If it's Velasquez, and he's been missing for over forty-eight hours, we need to test for any matter on his clothes and skin that tells us where he's been.'

Rick Houghton had his hand up.

'Could he have been sleeping rough? Can we connect it to the homicide in the school?'

'Too early to say,' Khan replied.

275

Knowles put his hand up and cleared his throat.

'I'm interested in the note on his chest. WARNING in capitals. The paper may have come from inside the stall, although the door was still locked until the market manager let us in. There was a pad in there with flowers in the corner and the logo says Edwards and Sons. It's the same as the paper the note was written on, but we need to check it came from that pad.'

'Edwards is a fruit and veg stall in the food hall,' Sean said.

The board was filling up with images. Sean recognised the photographs he'd taken with Donald's camera. There were more now. Xavier Velasquez from a local newspaper article about his arrest, the van parked askew on the edge of the dual carriageway, a newspaper headline. In his sleep-deprived state, it was as if the images were spinning in a kaleidoscope.

'Denton and Knowles,' Khan said, 'I want you on the market, talk to Edwards and Sons, talk to the other stallholders. We've got a mobile number for the hairdresser. In case he hasn't heard, ask one of the uniforms to ring and tell him his shop's in the middle of a crime scene.'

They walked to the market, after Sean reminded Knowles that it would take longer to negotiate the one-way system in a vehicle.

'How many stalls on Doncaster market, Denton?' Knowles said, as they cut through from Silver Street.

'Hundreds.'

'More than four hundred, according to Visit Doncaster's website.'

'Less in the Goose Hill Market Hall. Maybe twenty-five, thirty tops.'

'Fewer, Denton, not less.'

'Sir?'

'Call me Ivan, for God's sake.'

'Less than four hundred, Ivan.'

Knowles laughed, and hitched his laptop bag over his shoulder.

'Let's go, shall we? We'll talk to as many stallholders as we can find.'

They started with the second-hand bookstall. Sean glanced across the garish images on the book covers and wondered if any of them could match the sad drama of the young man hanging from the roof.

The owner of the bookstall was a stout man with a beard.

'Excuse me,' Sean said. 'Can you tell me what time you arrived this morning?'

'Got here at six and I've only been open an hour, your lot kept us waiting,' he said. 'Bloody typical. I knew I should have gone fishing.'

'So you know what's happened?'

'Aye, some fellow hung himself.'

'Can you tell me, when you left last night, did you notice anything – or anyone – unusual?' Sean said.

'Can't say that I did. Try Pat, she's the nosy one.' He nodded over at the pet shop opposite.

Sean crossed the aisle and introduced himself.

'Was he a friend of the hairdresser's?' Pat said, slurping a large mug of coffee. 'I don't really know him, but they did say it was a young man. I have my hair done at home, you see. My friend does it. That Greg's only got the one chair, hasn't he? This coffee's nice. I get it over in the Red Lion, that's a good deal they do there, you know. Only seventy-five pence and endless refills.'

Sean's pen hovered above his pad. He knew the price of coffee in the Red Lion well enough, and the price of a pint. He missed the next thing Pat said.

'Sorry?'

'The girl he had helping him, you should ask her.'

'Which girl? Bob Aston said he worked alone.'

'He's had her helping out,' Pat said. 'Last few weeks, Saturdays mostly. He had an apprentice before her, but he didn't keep her long. Supposed to help them get a qualification, but he's not geared up for all that. I don't think he was doing too well, to be honest.'

'It's tough going,' the bookseller called across. 'Bad time to start a new business.'

'Aye,' Pat drained her coffee mug.

'Has he been here this morning?' Sean said.

She shook her head. 'I haven't seen him but you could ask Bob.'

Sean tried with the next three stalls, but nobody had seen anything unusual as they left the night before. He arrived at the police incident tape that was wrapped round *Hair Today* and *Stan's Vinyl*. A solitary PCSO was standing guard.

'Hey, Sean!' she called as he got nearer. It was Carly. 'There's a fellow over on the food market wants a word with a detective. Dave Edwards, fruit and veg. He wouldn't tell me what it was about.'

Sean looked down the aisle to see if he could see Knowles, but there was no sign of him.

'Well,' Carly said. 'You're a detective, aren't you? What are you waiting for?'

He walked through the connecting door into the Food Hall, where he soon found *Edwards and Sons, Quality Fruit and Vegetables*. It was a neat stall, with an older man and a young woman serving. Sean guessed they were father and daughter, the daughter looking very much like the father, with sandy hair instead of grey. The young woman looked up when she saw Sean coming and nudged her father. Sean wondered how she knew; he thought plain clothes were meant to give him some sort of anonymity.

'Mr Edwards? I'm Detective Constable Denton.'

'Dave Edwards,' he shook Sean's hand. 'Can we talk around the back?'

'Sure,' Sean said.

The girl was watching him. She touched a small silver cross hanging round her neck.

'Sad, isn't it?' she said. 'We'll pray for him.'

As he slipped between the fruit and veg stall and a Polish meat counter, Sean spotted Knowles heading in his direction.

'Excuse me a moment, Mr Edwards,' he said. 'Over here, sir!'

'Thought I'd lost you,' Knowles said. 'The PCSO said you'd be here. Ah, Edwards and Sons, they're top of our list.'

At the back of the stall the three men stood close, to avoid being overheard by the neighbouring businesses.

'I had a phone message,' Edwards said, 'about our merchandising being found at the crime scene. What's that about, exactly?'

'A piece of paper with your logo on it, from a message

pad. Did you give them out to all the other market traders, or just a few?'

Mr Edwards frowned as if trying to remember. It was a simple enough question, but he hesitated before responding.

'We gave them to customers at Christmas,' he said.

'There was a pad in the hair salon,' Knowles said. 'Was the owner one of your customers?'

'No, not exactly,' Dave Edwards said slowly. 'I think it may have been the girl who worked there, she may have been given the notepad.'

'Pat, the pet food lady, mentioned a girl,' Sean said.

'So she was a customer?' Knowles said, with a note of impatience at Dave Edwards' ponderous manner.

'No,' he pressed his fingertips together and took a long, slow breath. 'But we know her quite well.'

The silence that followed was broken by Ivan's phone ringing.

'Do you have any of these notepads left?' Sean asked.

'A few, we've been using them up, but I've usually got one on the go.'

They walked back round to the side of the stall.

'Can I have a look? Just to check we're talking about the same thing.'

'Sure.'

He went inside and manoeuvred past his daughter, who was serving a customer.

'Where's the notepad, love?'

'I haven't seen it,' she said. 'I've been writing on paper bags all morning. That'll be four pounds and fifty-two pence please.'

She handed three brown papers bags of vegetables to a customer.

Dave crouched down behind the counter and pulled out a new notepad, still in its cellophane wrapper.

'Here you are,' he said and handed it to Sean.

'Can I take this?' Sean said.

'Of course.'

'Denton?' Knowles had finished his call and stood behind him. 'We need to go and talk to a Mr Greg Smart. He's in the market manager's office. He's our hairdresser.'

'Okay,' Sean said. 'There's just one thing, can you give me any details of the girl who worked at *Hair Today*?'

'Melissa Heron. She lives on Highfield Road. It's a council place. A children's home, you'd call it, although it's not much of a home.' He took another of his long, slow breaths and Sean could sense Ivan Knowles itching to leave. 'When I say we know her, in fact she was my foster daughter.'

'Right,' Sean said.

'I wasn't delighted about her working there, but there was nothing I could do. She was out of my hands by then. She's packed it in, though, the job. Her social worker wasn't happy with Greg Smart as an employer. I can't say I'm surprised.'

'Come on, Denton, we need to get on.'

'Thank you, Mr Edwards, you've been very helpful.'

Sean turned to go, but as they passed the front of the stall, he stopped and leant in to speak to the daughter.

'Sorry, I didn't catch your name.'

'It's Kathy Edwards.'

'Kathy, did you happen to see anyone here last night, hanging round as the market was closing up?'

She shook her head. 'Not particularly. Unless you count Melissa.'

'She was here? But your father just said she doesn't work on the market any more.'

'It's a public place, you can't stop people coming in. She's the sort that likes to hang about like a wet rag because she's got nowt better to do.'

'Denton!'

'I'm coming,' he said. 'And thank you, Kathy, that's very helpful.'

CHAPTER THIRTY-SIX

Friday

In the stadium kitchen, Sarah draws the cloth across the kitchen worktop, runs it under the tap and wrings clean water through it. She turns back to the worktop and wipes it again. She's been waiting for them since she got up, but they still haven't appeared. Every vehicle that drives across the car park brings her to the back door, but it's never the police. She told them Derek would be here all morning, so why don't they come? Her plan is to speak to them before they get to Derek, and show them what they're looking for, so they don't have to waste time asking questions, but it's becoming impossible to stay near the door. She's run out of jobs to do in the kitchen and any minute now Lou will come in, and send her upstairs to the bar. She can't understand why they aren't here yet.

She sighs and folds the cloth carefully over the tap. Then she goes to the drawer and takes out a receipt pad and a pen. She scrawls a note on the top page and puts it on the surface by the hatch.

GONE TO CHECK ON WOLF. HE WAS OFF HIS FOOD THIS
MORNING. BACK IN FIVE.

Wolf is on the settee. He climbs off and lollops across to
her, ears pricked to see what's happening. She ignores him
and checks the fridge. There's still some orange juice left in
the carton.

'Sarah?'

Lou is outside. She shuts the fridge and goes out.

'Is he okay, the dog?'

'Yes, he seems fine now. He's eaten everything.'

'Aye, they get like that. Turn their nose up at their regular
food but if they're hungry enough they'll eat it.'

Sarah pulls the door shut behind her. She's tried to fix it
again, after Joe burst through it, but it's more temperamental
than ever.

'I've finished in the kitchen,' she says.

'Yes, looks lovely, the cafe too.' Lou is standing a few
feet away from Sarah's caravan, looking around at the yard.
'Something's changed. What is it?'

'I don't know,' Sarah shrugs. 'It always looks the same old
jumble of things to me.'

'Aye, well, it'll come to me. I was looking for the boys, as
it goes. Are they about?'

'Haven't seen them today,' she says. 'Do you want me to
clean upstairs?'

'Please. Give Derek a knock and if he doesn't mind being
disturbed, that office could do with a dust.'

'Of course.' She smiles and her smile is genuine. The
windows of Derek's office overlook the car park and she'll be
able to see the police arrive before he even knows it.

She hesitates on the edge of the scrapyard. When she looks back, she sees Lou banging on the door of the boys' caravan. Joe opens it, his hair tousled, his face crumpled from sleep. She crosses her fingers hard and hopes she can trust him, at least until she doesn't need him any more.

CHAPTER THIRTY-SEVEN

Friday

Bob Aston, the market manager, was sitting behind his desk. Opposite him the cowed figure of a man, in neat T-shirt and pinstriped trousers, sat with his head in his hands. He looked up as Sean and Knowles came in. He'd been crying.

'This is Greg Smart,' Aston said. 'I heard you wanted to talk to him so I asked him to wait.'

'Thank you,' Knowles said, and when Aston showed no sign of getting up, he added, 'Is there somewhere we can speak privately?'

'I'll leave you to it.' With that, he picked up his copy of the *Daily Mail* and left the office.

Once Aston had gone, Ivan's demeanour softened. He perched on the side of the desk. Sean had noticed this knack he had of mirroring the energy of the person he was dealing with.

'This must have come as a bit of a shock,' he said gently.

Greg Smart nodded. 'I had no idea. I stayed with a friend last night and hadn't turned my phone back on. Bob Aston had been trying to ring me, but the first thing I knew was when I saw the police cordon. Then one of the other stallholders said a young man had hung himself from a girder above my shop.'

'Is that all they said?'

'They said there was a note on his chest saying it was a warning to me.'

Knowles and Sean exchanged glances. How had that leaked out? Had Lukasz, the security guard, told someone? Or had Bob Aston seen it? He was trying to remember the order of events and who else could possibly have seen the body. Then it came to him, the two market traders who'd turned up before the screen was in place.

'Is there any reason that it would have been a warning to you?' Ivan said.

'This might be the twenty-first century, but there are still some very nasty people around. My first thought was that the victim might be someone I know. A lover, or a friend.'

'You need to keep this entirely confidential,' Knowles said, 'because we haven't yet made a definite identification, and if this gets back to the family, I will know it came from you.'

Greg held his hands up. 'You can trust me! Please, I just need to know his name.'

'Does the name Xavier Velasquez mean anything to you?'

Greg shook his head. 'I don't think so.'

Sean took his phone out and found a photo of Xavier on the Doncaster Free Press website. It was taken at the time of the initial court hearing. He showed it to Greg.

'No, I've never seen him. Hang on, is this from the local press? What does it say?'

Sean scrolled up to the headline and back down to the text of the article.

'Oh my God!' Greg sat back in the chair and stared into space. 'It's not what I thought, oh God. It's much worse.'

'Slowly, Mr Smart,' Knowles said.

'I thought, although it doesn't really matter now, but I thought it was going to be a boy I'd fucked, or been seen with at least, the victim of some nasty little vigilante brigade. It still goes on, you know, queer-bashing.'

'I know,' Knowles said.

'But I think it's more complicated than that. I think I understand the warning.'

The old clock above Bob Aston's desk ticked slowly on while Greg Smart summoned the words to explain what he thought had happened.

'The girl in the article, Bethany Winters, used to have a Saturday job in the hairdresser's I worked at in Sprotbrough. She reported me to the salon owner, a lady called Charlotte Johnson, for inappropriate behaviour. I lost my job. I've had to borrow heavily from the bank to set up here, because I can't get a chair in any salon in Doncaster with that hanging over me. She said I stood too close and touched her up when the clients weren't looking.'

'And did you?'

'I'm gay,' Smart snapped.

'I know that,' Knowles said, 'but answer my question.'

'No, of course I hadn't. There are girls like that, you must have come across them. They mistake affection, or someone being tactile, and they get an idea in their head, an obsession. When they can't get what they want, the accusations come flying. This poor boy,' he gestured to Sean's phone, 'he must have fallen foul of her too.'

'There was sufficient forensic evidence to show she'd been date-raped by him,' Sean said.

'Well, why wasn't he tucked up safe in prison, then? Instead of hanging over my stall?'

Knowles shot Sean a look, and he wondered if he'd already said too much.

'Mr Smart,' he said. 'Greg, look, we may need to take an official statement from you in due course.'

'Yes, of course, that's fine,' he said, and gave Knowles his address and landline number, to add to the mobile number that was already on the incident board at the station. 'And maybe you could have a word with Bob Aston too, he's just given me notice to quit the market with immediate effect because I've tarnished its reputation.'

'I'll do my best,' Knowles said. 'But I can't promise.'

He gave Smart's shoulder a light squeeze as he passed his chair, and they left the office. Bob Aston was outside, close enough to the door to have been listening through the keyhole. Knowles spoke to him quietly and Sean moved away. Aston was more likely to agree to something if he thought he was doing a more senior officer a personal favour. He was that kind of oily sycophant.

Sean went out into the square in front of the Exchange Building. The heat of the last week had subsided a little and there was a cooler breeze picking up crisp packets and chip papers and tossing them aside again.

When Knowles came out, he was talking into his phone.

'Yes, sir, a priority to find Bethany Winters. Can we bring the parents back in, particularly the dad, and see if this is some kind of revenge attack? Get local police to track down the witness who went to Devon, find out who her friends were. She's the key to this, or someone close to her.'

There was a pause.

'Yes, sir, sorry sir. Just got a bit carried away . . . yes, he's fine, great actually,' he shot Denton an unexpected wink. 'We'll go there next. She's connected to Smart and may have been in the market hall last night.'

He ended the call and rolled his eyes.

'DI Khan didn't like me telling him how to do his job.'

'Ha! No, I imagine he didn't.'

'I forget my rank sometimes.'

Sean looked at him, staring over the craft stalls in the square, as if he was miles away.

'You don't have to answer this, Ivan, but did you once hold a higher rank?'

'Well spotted,' he sighed. 'I was a DI in a homicide squad in London, but I made a tactical error. I got too close to a witness who turned out to be manipulating me. It could have been worse. I owned up before anything went too badly wrong, so at least I kept my job, but I went back to constable for a while.'

'Is that why you came up here?' Sean said.

'Fresh start. Yes.' If he was going to say more, he stopped himself. 'Come on, we need to pay a visit to Melissa Heron.'

At the Highfield Road children's home, Sean and Knowles were shown into an overheated lounge. A support worker, who introduced himself as Pete, hung around by the door, reading something on his phone, while the girl sat back in a deep armchair, her long hair hanging in curtains either side of her face. Knowles perched on the edge of a battered sofa.

'Hello, Melissa, my name's Sean and this is my colleague,' Sean said, unsure whether he should introduce him as Ivan.

It was Knowles' idea that Sean should lead the conversation.

'My accent will put her off,' he'd said, as they walked across town. 'You sound more . . .'

'Common?' Sean said. Knowles let it pass without comment.

'We're detectives,' Sean said to Melissa. 'We know you've been working on a Saturday for Greg Smart on the market.'

She turned to look at Knowles.

'Don't worry,' Sean said. 'You're not in any trouble.'

'Greg Smart?' DS Knowles said. 'You were helping him out.'

She nodded.

'There was an incident there last night,' Sean said.

'I know,' she said.

'I suppose news travels.'

She held up her mobile phone by way of an answer.

'Can you tell me when you were last there?' Sean said.

'Saturday.'

'Are you sure?' Knowles said.

'Yes.'

'And you haven't been there since?' Sean said.

'Of course not. I just do Saturdays and anyway, I've lost my job, thanks to some interfering little bitch.'

Pete the support worker looked up from his phone. 'Mel, there's no need . . .'

Knowles turned to Pete. 'Can you confirm that?'

'She has stopped working there,' Pete said. 'She has to

291

have special permission and the social worker asked us to withdraw that permission.'

'May I ask why?' Knowles said.

'Someone said he'd been sacked from his last job for touching up the girls,' Melissa said, eyeing Pete as if daring him to stop her. 'It's a lie, though.'

'But you don't know who reported him?'

'It was an anonymous tip-off,' Pete said, 'but I believe the council's child protection officer confirmed it with the salon owner at his previous place of employment.'

There was not much else to ask and Knowles indicated it was time to leave. As Pete showed them out at the front door, Knowles gave him a card.

'Give me a call if she says anything else that might be of interest.'

Pete grunted and shut the door.

'What a despicable little man,' Knowles said, as they walked along Highfield Road.

'Who?'

'Pete,' He spat the name. 'He stank of cannabis. We should have pulled him in and got a blood test. Looking after vulnerable kids while he's off his head. He should be struck off, or whatever they do to care workers.'

'If they pose a safeguarding risk, they put them on the barred list,' Sean said.

Knowles stopped and turned to look at him.

'You seem to know a lot about it.'

'Been on a course.'

'Good,' Knowles said. 'Looking to specialise, are you?'

'Just been trying to improve my CV,' Sean said and

thought about Pete, wondering if he'd misjudged him. That laid-back quality seemed to be a good fit in a children's home. 'At least he's kind.'

'Because he's stoned?' Knowles said.

'No, I didn't mean . . .'

'Don't worry,' Knowles said. 'I'm not about to tell the CID recruitment panel that my trainee detective is soft on drugs.'

There was a moment of silence while Sean wondered if he'd said the wrong thing, but to his relief, Knowles laughed. He was beginning to get used to his sense of humour.

When they got back to the station, there was a message to say that someone was waiting for Sean at the front desk, a Mrs Karen Friedman.

'It's about Homsi,' he said to Knowles. 'She was supporting his asylum claim. Do you want to meet her?'

'No, you go ahead. Take her into one of the interview rooms. I need to report to DI Khan.'

'Make your peace with him?'

'Something like that,' Knowles said. 'And Sean, we don't have much resource for the Abbas case now, remember that. The focus has to be on Velasquez.'

'Yes, sir. I mean, yes, Ivan. I'll keep it brief.'

She was standing with her back to him when he arrived in the foyer. He'd remembered her as a careworn, middle-aged woman in a beige mac, but as she turned round, she seemed younger, more relaxed in a summer dress of dark-red flowers, bare legs and wedge-heeled sandals.

'Hello, Sean,' she stepped forward with an outstretched hand.

'Nice to see you again, Mrs Friedman. Let's go and sit down somewhere quiet. Can I get you something to drink?'

She decided to risk a coffee from the vending machine and he got one for himself. They went into one of the interview rooms.

'This brings back memories,' she said.

'I'm sure.'

She opened her bag and brought out a folder.

'When I got your call, I reminded myself of Homsi's case notes. We had a mobile number for him, so I tried it. Someone answered, but the voice was different. When I said, "Is that you, Elyas?" He said "Yes." But the voice, the accent even, was all wrong. I've worked with many people from the Middle East and this wasn't a Syrian accent. It was closer to Afghan or Pakistani. I said who I was, and asked again to speak to Elyas Homsi, but the line went dead. I tried to ring back, but it was turned off.'

'Go on.'

'I thought I should show you the documents we have, including a copy of Elyas Homsi's ID card.' She reached into the folder and pulled out a sheet of A4 paper, which showed a scanned copy of a card with a photo in the centre and Italian writing. 'It's the card he was issued with when he arrived in a leaking rubber boat on the island of Lampedusa.'

Sean peered at the photograph. The vending machine coffee turned sour in his mouth as he realised that, for the second time that day, he was looking at the features of a man whose face he'd seen destroyed in death, only this time he was sure of the identification, thanks to the few seconds of CCTV footage that showed this man alive.

'This is Abbas,' he said. 'Or rather, it's the man we've been calling Abbas.'

'Who told you that was his name?'

Sean sat back. 'Homsi. No, not Homsi. The guy who was calling himself Elyas Homsi. He had the letter from you at RAMA, saying that the first stage of his appeal had been successful. He was worried about getting it back, but it's currently being held as evidence.'

'Did you give him a copy?'

'No, thankfully, so he can't pass himself off as Homsi any more. I just gave him your number.'

'And it's obvious now why he didn't call us,' she said. 'So where's the real Homsi?'

'I'm sorry, Mrs Friedman, but he's dead.'

CHAPTER THIRTY-EIGHT

Friday

She polishes the window and finds a smear, so polishes it again. Derek clears his throat.

'Are you nearly done, pet?'

'Yeah, sorry,' she says.

Outside the car park remains empty apart from Derek's green Jaguar and Joe's pickup. If the police aren't coming, then her plan isn't going to work. Maybe it was a stupid idea. It might be better for her to get away cleanly. The keys to the Jaguar are on Derek's desk.

'If that's all?' Derek says.

He's turned in his chair, smiling at her in a way that pulls his moustache tight across his upper lip. He stands up and comes closer.

'Is everything all right? You can tell me, you know.'

If he wasn't five foot four and no higher than her chest, she might feel repulsed by him being so close, but she's not afraid of any man now. She is invincible. She picks up the window spray and amuses herself by aiming at him like a gun. He flinches.

'I wouldn't, honest,' she says, laughing. 'Just having a joke!' The smile drops.

'I think Lou has some jobs for you in the bar,' he growls.

She leaves the room without further comment, trying to suppress the grin on her own face. She feels giddy. Christ, she needs to get out of here before she says or does something crazy. She laughs at herself. Not that she hasn't done things that would be considered insane, but nothing that isn't justified.

In the bar, there's the whole wide viewing window to polish. She watches Joe drive the tractor round the track, raking neat furrows in the sand. There's no sign of Lou, so after a few minutes, she puts down her cloth and makes her way over to the emergency exit. She leans into the handle and opens it onto the fire escape. She hesitates. If she's fast, she'll be able to run across the car park and get to the yard before anyone notices. She needs to get the keys to the pickup. If the lock to the boys' caravan is as weak as the one on her own van, she should be able to give it a sharp kick to get it open. Then what? Logically, she knows that if the police don't come, she will have to shelve Plan A and then there will be one more act she must complete. She considers how she would do it, but there's something not right. She can only do it if she feels anger, and it's just not there for Tommy.

'Sarah?'

Lou is calling her from the door to the bar.

'Just getting a breath of air.'

'Derek said he thought you'd been drinking,' Lou said.

'I don't drink,' she says.

Lou raises one eyebrow, as if she doesn't believe that

anyone doesn't drink. It annoys Sarah that after three months of living here, Lou hasn't even noticed that she's never touched a drop.

'I'm worried about our Tommy,' Lou says suddenly, and sinks down into one of the chairs. 'Joe says he's staying with a school friend in Bentley, but I don't remember him having any friends there and he barely ever showed his face at school. Joe says this lad offered him some work doing up a house and they're staying on-site.'

Sarah is impressed that Joe's given Tommy such a plausible story. She wishes she'd thought of it.

'I'm sure Joe will know,' she says. 'Tommy tells him everything.'

'He didn't tell you?'

She shakes her head.

'I can't understand why he didn't tell me.'

'He must have gone while you were visiting his dad in the prison.'

Lou looks at her sharply and she wonders if she's said too much. But it doesn't matter any more, she can stop treading on eggshells, because tonight she'll be out of here for good. It will be easier when everyone's in bed. There's no racing until tomorrow, so no punters getting in the way. She feels the draught from the door behind her and thinks about the week that's just passed. When it's over, she will never need to think about any of it again.

CHAPTER THIRTY-NINE

Friday

Sean walked into the busy ops room. The boards had been changed and now Xavier Velasquez occupied a whole wall; lying on the ground in the market hall, arms out, he looked like a battered Christ. Sean looked around for the school case and found a single flipchart stand, the images and notes compressed, a red circle around the name Elyas Homsi, already a suspect, and now, with the information Sean had just received, about to switch to being the victim.

He made some space and stuck the copy of the ID card, which he'd made from Karen Friedman's scan, at the top. He took a board eraser and a pen and changed every incidence of Homsi's name to Abbas, and every incidence of Abbas to Homsi. He was suddenly aware that the room had gone quiet.

He turned round as DI Khan and Lizzie enter the room. He waited for Khan to speak.

'Don't let me stop you,' Khan said.

'I've just had a visit from Karen Friedman,' Sean said. 'She's a refugee case worker who's been working on behalf of Elyas Homsi. The letter he had in his possession came from her organisation. She showed me a copy of his ID card. There's no doubt. Homsi is the name of our victim, not the suspect. It's my guess, and Mrs Friedman's, that the man who is alive, who tried to hit me with a bottle in the old history classroom of Chasebridge School, is Mohammad Abbas, Homsi's friend, and he took the letter to pass himself off as a man who was on the way to being granted leave to remain.'

'That's awful!' DC Tina Smales was looking up at him wide-eyed. Despite the things she'd seen, he was impressed she could still be shocked.

'Mrs Friedman explained that the Syrians are more likely to get refugee status than Afghan or Pakistani asylum seekers,' Sean said.

'Well, we also have evidence that he didn't do it for the money,' Rick Houghton said. 'I've just had a very enlightening chat with Longfeller. Threatened with a murder charge, he confessed to robbing Abbas, sorry, I mean Homsi . . .'

'Why don't we stick with victim and suspect?' Steve Castle grumbled from the back of the room.

Sean thought about how quickly people wanted to deny these two men their names. Derek O'Connor called them Fred and Bert, Longfeller called them the Dogs of War.

'Did he take the money before or after Homsi was assaulted?' Khan said.

'Before,' Rick said. 'He was adamant. He'd seen the two men counting the money earlier in the evening, when they thought nobody was watching. Homsi slipped it into the hood of his sleeping bag. He's a bit of a night owl, our Longfeller. It's a result of all that raving in his youth, his mechanism's fucked. So he paid the sleeping Homsi a visit and managed to slip the money out of the pouch in the hood. He was at the back of the hall when he heard the shouting in the corridor and he slipped out of an exit next to the stage.'

'That might explain why Abbas was hiding in the building when we arrived. He was still looking for the money,' Sean said.

'Or,' Lizzie said, 'he was looking for clothes that weren't covered in blood. The expiration was on his top, but maybe the trousers weren't his.'

'We've got a description of the man we now know as Abbas and we've shared that with all forces,' Khan said. 'He could be calling himself anything now, so the name is not that relevant. Sean, I'll leave it with you to liaise with Mrs Friedman about informing Elyas Homsi's family members, if there are any. It's a sad business that someone would be made so desperate that they would kill for an identity.'

'Yes, sir.'

'But for now, we need all the brain power we can muster to work out what's happened with Xavier Velasquez. We've got Mr and Mrs Winters coming in any minute, the rape victim's parents, and I want everything they can tell us about their daughter, her associates, other boyfriends. Watch the father closely, if it's a vigilante thing, he's got to be in the running. Denton and Knowles, you take them into Interview Room Three. I'll listen in.'

Sean felt his phone vibrate with an incoming call, he slipped it out of his pocket and glanced at the screen. It was Chloe.

'Sir? Can I take this? It might be relevant?'

'Go ahead.'

He walked towards the door.

'Hi, there. Thanks for calling back. You said something about a bolt gun, what was that about?'

He stood in the corridor with his back against the wall.

'A bolt gun?' she said. 'It doesn't matter now. I'm ringing about Jack, he's not so good. Any chance you could make it over to the hospital?'

He looked at his watch. 'I'll be there in an hour.'

He hoped that was enough for the interview with Bethany Winters' parents.

Sean showed them into the interview room, Mrs Winters, who insisted he call her Alyson, and her husband, Graham. He wore a tie with his short-sleeved white shirt and she wore a fuchsia pink blouse and neat cotton skirt. They looked as if they were dressed for church, too clean for the decrepit decor of Interview Room Three.

Knowles sat centrally on one side of the table and Sean sat a little to his left, his chair turned at an angle. It was the plan that Knowles would ask the questions, and Sean would watch for their reactions.

'Tell us about your daughter,' Knowles said.

'We've brought the photographs, as you asked.' Graham Winters reached inside a slim black briefcase and took out the same pictures Sean had seen at the house. There was the reality TV lookalike, with perfectly sculpted eyebrows, false eyelashes and matt make-up. Her long black hair was smooth and shiny. Then there was the more awkward five-year-old, holding the hand of the invisible foster brother. It was hard to see the little child in the young woman.

'They're all we've got, as my wife told the officers who came to the house. Before Bethany left, she destroyed all the pictures in frames, and pulled all the photos out of albums. She destroyed them all.'

'What about online?'

'Oh, she's clever with computers, my daughter,' he sighed. 'She takes after me. I work in IT. I've taught her a lot.'

'What exactly do you do?'

'I work for a company that installs and manages security systems, but my real interest is programming. I've made a few apps for our church organisation.'

He smiled, used to expecting praise perhaps, but Sean was watching Mrs Winters, who was looking at her hands.

'She hacked into my iPad and Graham's laptop. She erased every single picture of herself.'

'Social media?' DS Knowles opened his hands as if to say, there must be something, somewhere.

'We don't use it,' Mrs Winters said quickly.

'Did Bethany?'

'No.'

'As far as we know,' Graham Winters said, patting his wife's arm.

'I think we can be certain that she meant to disappear,' Knowles said.

The couple nodded.

'And yet up to a week before the trial, she was answering her mobile phone to one of our officers. If we'd known she was missing, we could have done a cell site analysis on those calls and worked out where she was, but by the time you reported it to Nottinghamshire Police, she'd turned her phone off.'

'We should have reported it straight away,' Alyson Winters said. 'I realise that now, but she wasn't exactly missing, was she? She'd walked out. It was intentional and it was meant to punish us.'

Knowles looked at her sharply. 'Explain what you mean by that?'

Alyson Winters said nothing but looked at her husband. He cleared his throat. There was the sense of something rehearsed, as if this was what they'd come for.

'The boy in the photo, you can only see his hand and arm here,' Graham Winters said. 'His name was Robert. We took him in because we felt, as Christians, that we should share our good fortune. We were not well advised. He was a very damaged boy. By which I mean he'd been sexually abused.'

Outside the room a door banged and the distant sound of voices reached them from the corridor.

'Go on,' Knowles said gently.

'Bethany's behaviour changed. She wet the bed, had night terrors, began to have tantrums, which at five, is very late.' Graham Winters spoke quickly and quietly. 'Then the school asked us to come in. She'd been playing games with the other children that showed a level of sexual knowledge much greater than her age.'

He paused to catch his breath.

'We informed social services. Robert was moved elsewhere and Bethany received medical treatment. She had some counselling, but in the end we felt it wasn't helpful. We believed that with Christ's love and our care, she would forget all about it and grow into a beautiful young woman.'

'Which it appears she did,' Knowles said, touching the prom photo.

'She found it hard to make friends,' Alyson said. 'There was Shelley Martin, and Kathy, another girl from church – she's known them since she was a baby – but apart from them, no friendships lasted. Each new school ended up with her in a fight, or with accusations flying about.'

'About her behaviour?'

'Sometimes, or she would accuse other children, especially boys. At secondary school she accused a male teacher of molesting her.'

'What happened?'

'He was suspended and then he left. The school would have supported her to take him to court, but she changed her mind.'

'False accusations are relatively uncommon,' Sean said.

'Indeed,' DS Knowles said, 'but when they do occur, it's usually as a long-term effect of childhood abuse. It's called "acting out". The sense of injustice and hurt is deeply ingrained. The person who committed the original abuse can't be blamed, so other targets are sought. Sometimes a child believes they are in love, and when that isn't returned, the anger and confusion of the original trauma is relived.'

Mr and Mrs Winters were nodding.

'That's what we were told,' Graham said. 'We tried to protect her, sent her to a girls' school. Her hobbies were all in church groups, which were run on a single-sex basis, but then she wanted a Saturday job. Alyson's friend Charlotte is a hairdresser and offered some hours in her salon.'

'Ah,' Knowles nodded, 'and this is where she met Greg Smart.'

'Exactly.'

'Also, she had access to the Internet, she knew about boys,' Alyson said. 'It seems she'd learnt a lot about how to find her way round a computer from my husband.'

'That's a little unfair,' Graham said, colouring slightly. 'I taught her about safe Internet use. If she guessed passwords, that's not my fault.'

'Did you believe her when she accused Greg Smart of touching her inappropriately?'

Sean watched them both hesitate.

'I felt,' Alyson said, 'that we should give her the benefit of the doubt. That's what you do, isn't it? Charlotte agreed, it was the reputation of her salon at stake.'

'We argued about it,' Graham Winters said, and his wife looked crushed. 'I felt my wife should have prioritised my point of view over Charlotte Johnson's.'

'We need to move on,' Knowles said. 'We need to talk about Xavier Velasquez and find out who killed him.'

His energy had changed, as if he'd lost sympathy with Mr and Mrs Winters. He put a photograph on the table and turned it round to face them. It was the image of the dead young man in his crucifixion pose, laid on the plastic sheeting on the floor of the market hall.

'God have mercy on him.' Graham Winters spoke in a whisper. His hand went to his throat and he loosened his tie.

'Did you have any contact with the victim?'

'No, none at all!'

'You're sure?'

'Yes.'

'So you didn't visit him when he was on remand at HMP Doncaster?'

Sean glanced at Knowles but his face was a mask.

'I . . .' Graham Winters loosened his tie again. 'I visit the local prisons as part of my church outreach work. We have discussion groups and prayer groups. A lot of men come to Jesus during the time they're in prison.'

'We've been in touch with the deputy governor and he said you spoke directly to Velasquez at a chapel service. It was brought to his attention after you left the premises, otherwise he'd have hauled you over the coals. But the boy put in a complaint, said he felt harassed.'

'I wanted to pray with him, for forgiveness.'

'Whose?' Knowles raised his voice. 'His or your daughter's? Or yours? Where were you on Thursday night, Mr Winters? And where were you on Tuesday afternoon, when Xavier went missing?'

'You don't think this is anything to do with me?' he stammered.

'I don't know what to think, but I will need a full list of where you've been since Monday of this week and a list of people who will corroborate this.'

He passed a piece of paper and a pen towards him. 'Before you leave.'

'DS Knowles, sir, can I have a word?'

Sean and Knowles stood in the doorway as an ashen-faced Graham Winters wrote in a slow scrawl, occasionally checking the diary on his phone.

'It's my sister, she rang from the hospital. My phone's been buzzing with texts since we've started in here. My dad's very sick, can I be excused?'

'Yes, of course. Why didn't you say? Give Tina a shout on your way out and she can sit with these two while Mrs Winters does the same exercise.'

He texted Chloe.

I'M ON MY WAY.

CHAPTER FORTY

Friday

It would take half an hour to walk to the hospital, but Sean could make it in fifteen minutes if he ran. The urgency in Chloe's tone had increased with each text. First she'd reminded him of the ward number, then which floor it was on. The last text read: ARE YOU NEARLY HERE? He took the front steps of the police station two at a time and headed past the law courts. There was a taxi rank around the corner and he prayed there would be a cab waiting.

There wasn't. Just an empty bay and an old woman with a shopping trolley, standing patiently, as if she'd been there for hours. If he went the other way, he could be at Princes Street in five minutes, where he could pick up a bus. He doubled back, past the front of the police station. A car was coming out of the yard. It stopped and the driver's window opened.

'Something wrong?' DI Khan peered out at him.

Everything, Sean thought. 'It's my dad. It's serious.'

'Get in.'

It wasn't an offer, it was an instruction. Sean did what he was told, relieved that someone else was taking control.

Five minutes later, DI Sam Nasir Khan strode ahead of Sean, through the electronic doors of the hospital and across the entrance foyer towards the lifts. Sean didn't have time to question why his boss was coming with him to his father's bedside, but he was grateful. He'd tried to phone Chloe while Khan was driving, but her phone went to voicemail. That worried him even more. He imagined her, hunched over the bed, holding Jack's hand. It should have been him. All the recriminations, the wishing things could have been different, couldn't change the fact that they were father and son.

The lift arrived. Inside they watched the floor numbers light up in sequence.

'My father died when I was your age,' Khan broke the silence, his voice thick with emotion. 'Exactly your age. He ran out of air. It was byssinosis, also known as brown lung. He worked in a cotton mill in Oldham for twenty years on the night shift. They didn't give them masks until it was too late.'

Sean didn't know if he was expected to say anything.

'He went back to Pakistan to die,' Khan continued. 'At the end, I realised I should have gone with him, but I was too busy, too ambitious to ask for the time off. He was surrounded by his family, but not his son. I have never forgiven myself.'

The lift doors opened and Khan stepped out first, his face set in its familiar mask, as if the revelation about his private life had never happened. Sean followed him. Even if his father was too far gone to understand him, Sean wanted to say something important to Jack. He wanted to say sorry. He wanted to say, that despite everything, he loved him.

At the entrance to the ward Khan stepped aside and let Sean

go first. A nurse stepped out from behind the nurses' station.

Sean said his father's name. She hesitated.

'I'm sorry,' she said.

She had brown eyes with tired shadows beneath them. She had a mole on her left cheek. He felt as if her face would be imprinted on his mind for ever.

'We lost him,' she said.

'Where . . . ?'

She took his arm, as if he were an old man, or a very young child, and he sensed Khan holding back. They walked to the end of the corridor and into a side room with just one bed. At least Jack had been given some privacy at the end.

'It was just a few minutes ago,' the nurse said softly.

Chloe was there, just as he'd imagined she would be, sitting on the opposite side of the bed, holding Jack's hand, her fingers woven into his, as if in death he'd finally released the clenched fist of his old injury. His other arm lay flat on the bed, a cannula and tube leading to a drip-stand with a bag of saline. The liquid was still, no bubbles breaking the surface.

Sean forced himself to look at his father's face. His head was turned slightly to one side, an oxygen mask hung below his chin. This was Jack. His dad. Yellow skin slack around the bones of his face, the fight finally gone out of him.

Tears rushed to Sean's eyes and he wanted to howl. *What a waste. What a fucking, terrible waste.*

'I'm sorry.' It was Chloe, her voice so quiet he almost missed it.

Sorry, that word again. He wanted to tell her not to be. It wasn't her fault. But he didn't trust his mouth to form the right words. He shook his head and wiped his eyes on the back of his hand.

'What happens now?' he managed to say.

He hadn't noticed the nurse still waiting in the doorway. She came further into the room.

'Would you like to step out while I tidy him up? Then you can sit with him a bit longer.'

The little words jangled in his mind. Step. Bit. Sit. Like rhymes in a storybook for a small child. Did she think he didn't know what happened to a body after death? The smell, that would soon become overpowering, had already begun to seep through the cotton blanket covering Jack's body. He wanted to tell her, this heap of skin and bones and shit was not his father any more. Jack Denton was long gone.

'Chloe?' he said, and offered her his hand. She stood, shakily, and he guided her around the end of the bed. 'We'll wait outside.'

'There's a family room at the end of the ward,' the nurse said.

Khan was already there. He'd made three cups of tea and was putting them on a low coffee table in front of a blue settee.

'I've put sugar in,' he said.

'Thank you,' Chloe said. She looked at Sean, as if waiting for an explanation.

'The DI gave me a lift,' he said.

Chloe held the mug of tea in both hands and sat down. The room was cold. The sun didn't reach this side of the building. She closed her eyes as the steam wafted over her face.

'You wanted to know about the bolt gun,' she said. It was almost a whisper.

'It can wait,' Sean said, sitting next to her.

'They killed a dog.'

'Who did?'

'The lads at the race track, Melissa's brothers. No, not both of them, the older one. I think he's called Joe.'

Sean looked at Khan, who put his tea down and watched Chloe closely.

'Does your friend Melissa have another name?' Khan said.

'Yes,' she said. 'Heron. I remember because it's the name over the scrapyard, by the dog track. Her dad's called Levi Heron.'

'Did you go back to the track?' Sean said.

'Yes, on Tuesday evening. We were going to watch a race with all the retired and rescue dogs. It's a charity thing, but Melissa got upset because she found out about Indian Whisper. It was the dog we saw on Saturday, do you remember? He broke his leg by running into the lure, and they took him to the vet's room.'

Sean nodded. 'Yes, I remember.'

'Well, they shot him, with a bolt gun. Melissa's brother convinced her that it was the kindest thing to do, but it's not right, is it? Surely it's not legal.'

She began to cry and Sean wasn't sure if it was for the dog or for Jack.

Khan knelt down in front of her and she looked at him.

'Now, Chloe,' he said. 'I'm sorry to come over the policeman, but in a minute the nurse is going to come back, and you and Sean are going to spend some time saying goodbye to your father, and that's how it should be. But meanwhile, I have a very unpleasant murder to solve, in addition to the illegal destruction of a dog, and it's beginning to look like the Herons could be involved, so I'm going to ask you some very quick questions, then I promise I'll leave you alone.'

She nodded and wiped her nose on a tissue.

'Where and when did you meet Melissa?'

'At the market stall, where she was working. I had my hair cut there on Saturday and she was at the dogs on Saturday night. She lent me her jacket. I went off with it by mistake, so I went to find her at her work, that was Monday. She wasn't there, but a girl from another stall was passing and told me where Melissa lived.'

'Do you know that girl's name?'

'No, but she knew Melissa well. She had a mark on her neck that she said Melissa had done.'

'What was she wearing?'

'Like a coat thing, a sort of overall. I think there was a logo, maybe a flower on the pocket. She worked on a fruit and veg stall in the food hall. Edwards, I think it's called.'

'Have you ever heard of a young woman called Bethany Winters?'

'No.'

'How come you went back to the track with Melissa?'

Chloe drank from her tea. A thin frown appeared and Sean wondered if she felt under pressure from Khan's rapid-fire questions.

'It's okay, Chloe, you're not in trouble,' he said.

'I know.' She took another drink and looked back at DI Khan. 'I went to the care home where she lives. We got on well. We have a few things in common, I suppose. She asked

314

me if I wanted to come to the charity race and we could see how the injured dog was getting on.'

'And when you got to the track on Tuesday evening?'

'We were early. And it was weird, a really odd atmosphere. There was this lass there with a big dog, more heavy-set than a greyhound, and she gave us a mouthful, then the younger brother came straight out and told us Indian Whisper was dead and Joe had killed him. Melissa was upset and I was going to see her home, but the older brother turned up in a pickup truck and talked her into getting in and having a lift, while I was left standing there like a lemon. He mouthed off at me, and I just thought they were a nasty bunch, to be honest, covering up for killing a dog that could have got better.'

She sat back, as if the energy had left her, and drank the rest of her tea. Khan got up. Sean walked with him to the door.

'It gives us a reason to turn the whole place upside down, with or without Derek O'Connor's co-operation,' Khan said. 'I have a feeling that we're going to find more than a dead dog in there.'

'There's something else, boss,' Sean said. 'When I spoke to the girl that worked there, she said the bread van didn't deliver and she had to do a load of defrosting. Now, Ivan and I saw the van being looted on our way to the dog track. If we'd realised its significance, we'd have stopped. But the thing is, when we arrived, there were trays of breadcakes on the kitchen surfaces. Fresh, not frozen.'

'So she lied. The bread van had delivered.'

'And not long before we arrived. There was another woman there, a Polish girl they called Agnes. She'll be able to confirm it. 142 Selby Avenue, Hexthorpe.'

Khan put his hand on his shoulder. 'You're sure of the address?'

'Yes, I knew I'd remember it. I had a friend lived on the same street.'

'Thanks,' Khan said. 'This means Xavier Velasquez was at the track and the van was dumped shortly afterwards. I'm going to need a bigger team.'

'I want to be in on it.'

'You need to be with your sister.'

'And if I happened to be passing?'

'Like you were the other night at the market?'

'That really was a coincidence,' Sean said. 'I didn't hand my radio in when I left just now, and as soon as I leave here, I'll either be at my dad's flat or down at my nan's. Either way, I'll be close. I want to be there when this goes down.'

'Nothing I say is going to stop you, is it?' Khan said and smiled.

Sean didn't have to reply.

'Keep it turned off now. You're officially off duty,' Khan said. 'And don't turn it on until you're ready.'

At that moment the nurse came back.

'Would you like to come in now?' she said.

CHAPTER FORTY-ONE

Friday

Sarah is sitting on the side of the bed, holding his hand. The air is stifling and smells of his stale breath and sweat. Every time she comes back to the caravan, she manoeuvres him to the bathroom in time to pee. Thankfully he hasn't needed to take a shit. It won't have done him any harm not to eat for a couple of days, and she's kept him hydrated. The other one didn't deserve this kind of care, there was no point with him, knowing there was only one way it was going to end.

The evidence is all around him, she's used the gloves she keeps under the sink, the latex hairdresser's gloves she lifted when she finished working for that silly cow in Sprotbrough. The box is nearly empty because she's been careful, she's made sure none of this will come back to her. She's even wearing them now as she strokes his forehead. When the police come, they will find him and they will be able to come to their own conclusions. She won't be here. They will never find her, because Sarah Sutton doesn't exist.

'There now, Tommy,' she strokes his cheek. 'It's nice and quiet in here, nothing to disturb you.' He doesn't reply but she keeps talking in a low tone, so that no one outside will hear her. 'You should have heard the row just now. I thought Lou was going to haul Joe off the tractor while it was still moving. She worked out what was missing, you see. Went mental because he said he'd sold it, the blue horsebox, and she threatened to tell your dad that you two were selling his stuff while he was in jail. Joe's a good liar. I admire that. He had a whole story about a gambling debt. You should have seen him go for it!'

His head rolls back and his breathing catches in his throat. He begins to snore. She takes his arm and pulls him onto his side. His snores could easily be heard outside the van if she's not careful.

She thinks of him in court and knows he won't stand a chance. He won't be able to follow the instructions of his defence counsel and he'll want to tell the truth. But he'll protect her, and keep her name out of it, he's promised her that. It's only when she imagines him in prison that she falters. He is like a big child and prisons are cruel places. She has become fond of him, and that's a mistake, because it's chipping away at her resolve.

The bolt gun is on the floor by the bed. She looks at it, bends down and picks it up, weighing it in her hand. It's not the right thing, and anyway, she doesn't know how to reload it. It serves a different purpose here, it can't be used for this.

'Sleep now, Tommy,' she whispers, and his eyelids flutter. 'I'll be back in a little while.'

CHAPTER FORTY-TWO

Friday afternoon

Chloe was standing at the window in Jack's living room. She'd been holding the net curtain to one side but now she'd let it drop behind her. Sean thought it looked like an old-fashioned wedding veil. He sat on the settee, taking in the room. A fresh coat of paint and some framed posters on the walls indicated the small improvements Chloe had been able to manage in Jack's life.

'Will you stay here?' he said. 'I could talk to the housing office about getting your name on the tenancy.'

She shook her head. 'There's a cottage going at Halsworth Grange. I'll get a good discount on the rent. I don't want to stay here. What about you?'

'Me?'

'Is everything all right with Lizzie?'

'Yes, fine. Why do you ask?'

She emerged from behind the net curtain and smoothed it back into place.

'It's just that you haven't rung her, have you? I mean, your dad died two hours ago, and you haven't told your girlfriend.

I would have told mine straight away, if I had one.'

'She's at work, she's really busy, we've got two complicated cases . . .' He stopped himself saying any more.

'Sorry. It's none of my business,' she shrugged.

He sank back into the settee and took out his phone. He selected Lizzie's number.

'Hi!' She sounded excited. 'Have you heard? Khan's got a warrant to raid the dog track. Where are you, by the way? I thought you'd be at the emergency briefing.'

'What happened to keeping home and work separate?'

'I was wrong, and anyway, this is your case,' she said.

'Lizzie, love,' he said. 'I've been meaning to ring you.'

'Mmm,' she said.

'It's Jack, my dad. He's dead.'

He heard an intake of breath, counted three seconds of silence.

'I am so sorry,' she said. 'I mean, in some ways, you know, it's got to be a blessing, but all the same. Are you all right? And Chloe, is she okay?'

The rush of energy in her voice startled him. There was something about it that seemed too perfect, as if she had been rehearsing the right thing to say for this moment. Or maybe he imagined it. He was still unsettled by Chloe's observation that he hadn't thought to ring Lizzie immediately. He had no problem justifying that to himself: he wanted to be there for his sister in the immediate aftermath of losing Jack. She had nobody. That's why he'd delayed phoning anyone else. He hadn't even phoned his nan yet, and phoning Nan usually came ahead of phoning Lizzie.

'Sean?' Lizzie's voice jolted him.

'Yeah, I'm okay. I'm with Chloe at Jack's flat.'

'What about work? Does the boss know?'

'I'm still on the job,' he said. 'Khan knows I want to be in on the raid. I'm just waiting for the call.'

'Look after yourself,' she said. 'And give Chloe a big hug from me.'

'I will. Bye.'

'Bye.'

Sean put his phone back in his pocket.

'She said to give you a hug.'

'Thanks, tell her you already did,' Chloe said. 'I think I'll pack a bag and go down to Maureen's for now, if she'll have me.'

'Do you want me to let Nan know what's happened? Tell her you're coming?'

Chloe nodded and made her way to her bedroom. Sean's old room. He took up her position at the window and looked out over the playground, down towards the community centre. He pressed his hand against the glass. Chasebridge Estate held nothing but sadness for them both. He hated it. After burying his father they could clear the flat and walk away. And when he'd passed his probation in CID, he could make sure he never had to come back here again. There were other districts, other regional forces. He fancied somewhere near the sea.

He snapped back to the present. There were things to do. After ringing Nan, he was going to turn his radio on and let Khan know he was ready.

CHAPTER FORTY-THREE

Friday afternoon

A sparrow is having a dust bath by the edge of the fence, whipping up a flurry of dry soil with its tiny wings. A Sunday school hymn trips across the back of Sarah's mind. 'All Things Bright and Beautiful'. She kicks a stone at the bird and it flies up, protesting, and perches in a buddleia bush, warning the other sparrows of her presence. She needs to tread more carefully if she's going to get what she needs from the stadium building. There'll be more than just sparrows listening and watching over there. Perhaps she should have brought Wolf with her as a decoy, but he is lying outside the bedroom door in the static caravan. He seems to take more care of Tommy than he has done of her. She likes to think he's keeping watch, and will at least bark if someone tries to open the front door. It's fixed as well as she could manage it, but there are no guarantees.

She sets out across the car park, her nylon work overall sticking to her arms. She needs to look as if she's come back to finish the cleaning. There are two cars in the car park, a small blue hatchback and a large black saloon car. Perhaps Derek has visitors, corporate types, looking to book the bar area for a function. They're supposed to be diversifying and finding more ways to get people in, but Derek's a dinosaur without the first idea of how to use social media. She could have done so much more here, if they'd asked her. Too late now.

She steps into the kitchen, her eyes adjusting from the glare of the afternoon sun. A fly snaps and dies in the electric fly killer. Against the neon blue she can just make out its tiny limbs flailing. There is no sign of Lou, nor is she in the cafe. Sarah listens, but there is just the uneven click of the electric clock on the wall. She steps into the storeroom and waits. There is no need to turn the light on, she knows where she's going. She creeps forward until her hand rests on the lid of the old deep freeze. When she first arrived, she wondered why Lou kept such a large chest freezer that didn't work, but then she understood. It was always useful to have storage, especially for something you weren't meant to have. She lifts the lid, marvelling that Lou has never thought to keep it locked. She's just too trusting. There are empty ice cream boxes neatly stacked, three deep. She moves them carefully aside, trying not to make any noise, pausing every few seconds to listen. And then her fingers touch a different texture, wood, and her hand closes round the stock of the shotgun.

A dog barks. It's Wolf. She pulls the gun out of the deep freeze, opens it and sees that both barrels are loaded. She rips open the press-studs of her overall and holds the gun against her chest, the barrel between her breasts. Closing the front of the overall over the gun, she walks as fast as she can across the car park to the scrapyard, where the dog's barks are now rising in a continuous volley.

As soon as she turns into the yard, she sees the caravan door is open. She runs across the yard and up the steps. Wolf's bark has settled into a menacing growl.

Once inside she can see straight away that he's failed as a guard dog. She brandishes the stock of the gun.

'You stupid fucking animal!'

She catches him on the jaw and he whimpers away under the table. The bedroom door is partly open. She turns the gun round and pulls back the catch. This is not what she'd planned.

'Joe!' she calls, pushing the door wide.

A familiar-looking man is leaning over the bed, taking a pulse from Tommy's neck. He looks up, his eyes on the gun.

'Hello again,' he says. 'It's Sarah, isn't it?'

Her finger is slippery with sweat as she pulls against the trigger. Its resistance is greater than she imagined and for a moment she could still stop this from happening. The man is saying something, but she doesn't hear it. A huge bang rips through the air and the recoil hurls her into the door frame.

CHAPTER FORTY-FOUR

Friday afternoon

'Victor Charlie Four Three, come in please.'

'Four Three receiving.'

'What's your location?'

'Eagle Mount flats. Block one, first floor.'

'Stand by Four Three.'

Sean walked into the kitchen and looked out of the window. From here he could see the dual carriageway. The two lanes leading away from the town centre were almost at a standstill. It was five-thirty, the rush hour. Stupid name for it. No bugger was rushing anywhere.

'Victor Charlie Four Three? Can you be outside the flats in five minutes?'

'Received.'

'Three One will pick you up.'

A blue light, nudged slowly between the cars, followed by another. No sirens.

'Chloe,' he stood in the door of Jack's room, where she was sitting on the bed. 'I've got to go now. Nan's expecting you any time.'

'I'll just tidy up a bit,' she said. 'Take care, Sean.'

'Thanks,' he said. 'You too.'

The patrol car pulled up onto the kerb. Sean jumped back to protect his toes. He opened the rear passenger door.

'I see your driving hasn't improved,' he said to Gav. 'Hi, Tina.'

DC Tina Smales gave him her crooked, dimpled smile.

'This is Angie,' she said, indicating the uniformed officer in the front seat. 'Gav's new partner.'

'Excuse me, I forgot my manners,' Gav said.

'Wouldn't be the first time. Hi, Angie, I'm Sean.'

She twisted round in her seat as Gav accelerated off the kerb and Angie was forced to hang on to the headrest with one hand. She had a thin face and red hair.

'PC Boyce, nice to meet you. I've transferred from Barnsley.'

'Welcome to the madhouse.'

'Right, Mr Local Knowledge,' Gav said. 'Is there any other route that'll get us to the greyhound stadium from here? If we try to get back up on the ring road, we're going to hit the traffic and be here all night.'

'It's not a road as such,' Sean said. 'But as you're in the process of writing this car off, we should be all right. There's a track just beyond the shops, which comes out the other side of the greyhound stadium. We might have to climb over a gate for the last bit.'

They swung past the Eagle Mount flats and round the recreation ground. A boy standing on one of the swings looked up at the passing police car and flicked a V-sign.

'All units on the approach to Chasebridge Stadium, can I have your location and ETA please?'

'Three One, we're approaching via the shops on the Chasebridge estate. About three minutes. Over.'

'Three One, it looks like you'll be first on scene. Proceed with extreme caution until the firearms unit arrives. A neighbour has just reported a firearm has been discharged and we've lost contact with DS Knowles and CS Manager Morrison.'

'Oh my God,' Tina sat forward, as if urging the car to go faster.

Sean felt a new surge of energy and Gav put his foot down on the accelerator.

'Here, turn up the track,' Sean yelled.

'I'm on it,' Gav said and swung the car into a narrow gap.

Grass grew between cracked concrete slabs and when the concrete ran out, the car bumped onto a stony path, worn down on one side by dog-walkers. Brambles from the overgrowing hedges scratched the paintwork, like nails down a blackboard.

'What the hell is Lizzie doing there?' Sean said.

'Khan's plan was to send those two ahead,' Tina said. 'Lizzie was taking samples to match to the grit in the work boots and Knowles was going to talk to Derek O'Connor about the doctored CCTV. The rest of us were supposed to watch and wait. If necessary we'd back off, but if Knowles had enough to consider arresting those lads, we were to go in.'

'And now a weapon's been discharged? Lizzie's a civilian for God's sake, she shouldn't be put at risk like that.'

Gav yanked the wheel to avoid a pothole and Sean's shoulder hit the window. Tina was thrown against his side. He felt his muscles tense and she moved away. He stared out of the window at the old stone wall, the only remnant of the farming history of Chasebridge. He tried to clear his mind. Lizzie was in danger. His father was dead. The speed of it all made him feel sick.

The stone wall gave way to corrugated sheeting, topped with razor wire. Gav slowed down. To their left stood a large wooden gate with a chipped sign above it.

Levi Heron: Commercial Vehicles tel: 567092

The gate hung slightly open. Ahead of them, ten metres up the track was a newer, five-bar gate, with a huge chain and padlock wrapped around the gatepost, and beyond it the tarmac road that curved in to the entrance of the stadium car park.

'What do you reckon?' Gav said. 'Shall we take it from here on foot over that metal gate, or turn the car in through Mr Heron's vehicle emporium?'

'You won't get the car through there, it's ram-packed with old lorries and junk,' Sean said, unbuckling his seat belt. 'I'll go through the scrapyard on foot, you go round the front. With extreme caution, obviously. We just need to keep this exit secure and make sure nobody leaves.'

'Okay,' Gav said. 'I'll park in front of the gates.'

'I'll go with Gav, Angie can go with you, Sean,' Tina said. 'Have you got any extra kit in the car, Gav? I'm not sure one extending truncheon between two of us is going to be enough to fight off an armed assailant.'

'In the back,' Gav said. 'And a spare set of cuffs in the glovebox.'

'Thanks.'

'Right,' Tina said. 'Let's go.'

'Hang on,' said Gav. 'Sean, there's a vest in the boot. You take it. I'm assuming PC Boyce is wearing hers.'

'What about you?'

'It's too hot and, if you must know, I can't get the bugger done up around my middle-aged spread. Go on, I know what you're like, far more likely to get yourself in the line of fire.'

'Let's hope you don't mean that literally,' Sean said.

Angie Boyce already had the boot open and was handing Sean a large bullet-proof vest. He put it on over his shirt. Gav was right, it was going to be far too hot, but at least he was slightly safer.

CHAPTER FORTY-FIVE

Friday afternoon

Sean stepped through the high panelled gate and into the scrapyard. He noticed how the gate had caught in the long grass and scored a path of pulled-up roots. He moved forward, PC Boyce beside him, towards a rusty single-decker bus, sitting on the rims of tyreless wheels. Nothing moved. They looked into the bus and saw row upon row of plastic flower pots, each containing a leggy, leafy cannabis plant.

'They can keep until later,' Sean said quietly.

Moving around the front of the bus, Sean hesitated, listening and watching, but there seemed to be no one around. To his left there was a pile of copper pipes, sinks and cookers. To his right, a dented red pickup truck was parked next to the fence. He bent down to look into the driver's side window.

'Someone's left the keys in,' he said. 'Careless.'

He opened the door. The pickup looked like it had seen better days, but it still had four tyres and the keys looked clean, as if they'd come out of someone's pocket quite recently. If someone was planning to leave in a hurry, opening the main gate and leaving the car ready was a smart move, or it would have been if Gav hadn't parked right outside.

PC Boyce was behind him. He felt a trickle of sweat run between his shoulder blades.

'We'll keep to the edge,' he said. 'No need to draw attention to ourselves, until we have to.'

In his earpiece, the calm voice of Lisa-Marie, back in Dispatch, told him that the firearms unit was four minutes away. He watched as Angela quickly turned the volume down on her own radio.

'Don't know who else is listening,' she said.

'*Victor Charlie Three One, what is your location?*'

Sean and Angela stood still. He took his earpiece out. The sound wasn't coming from his radio, or Angie's. It was coming from the undergrowth at the foot of the corrugated metal fence that surrounded the yard. Sean moved quickly along the fence towards the sound. Gav was replying now, confirming that he was in the car park approaching the main building. Sean crouched down and there, nestled among the roots of a rosebay willowherb, he spotted the radio and a little further away, a mobile phone in a brown leather case.

'Have you got gloves?' he said. Angie already had them out of her pocket and was holding them out to him.

'I'll get an evidence bag from the car,' she said.

He put the gloves on and picked up the radio but left the phone where it lay. The last time he'd seen this phone, and its expensive cover, was on DS Knowles' desk.

'*Victor Charlie Three One receiving,*' Gav's voice on the radio was almost a whisper. '*There's a static caravan near to where the scrapyard opens out into the car park. I can hear voices, possibly DS Knowles.*'

'*Received, Three One. Maintain your position and await support.*'

Sean turned the radio off and put it in the evidence bag that PC Boyce was holding open. Then he picked up the phone. He looked around. There were two static caravans positioned at right angles to each other. The nearest offered three rear windows of opaque, scratched plastic, but from the other van there was a direct line from the front door. Someone with a good overarm throw could have hurled the radio and phone from there. They would have hit the fence and fallen into the undergrowth.

'Take these back to the car,' he whispered to Angie.

Using the nearer of the two static caravans as cover, Sean crept round the back until he was facing the end of the second van. He crept up to the window, positioning himself at the corner and looked in.

An explosion threw a flock of sparrows up into the sky. He dropped down and for a few seconds he went deaf. The explosion had come from inside the van.

From his position near the ground Sean ducked lower still, until he could see under the caravan. He could see the steps up to the front door. He was about to creep round to the door, when there was the sudden movement of an animal, feet skittering on the steps, then racing away towards the car park. A large dog, heavier than a greyhound, but too fast for him to see properly. It was followed on the steps by a pair of human feet in work boots. The same sort of work boots as in the CCTV images, worn by the man they now knew was Abbas. The boots that had been missing in their search of the school and the detritus left behind. The wearer of the boots turned right at the foot of the steps, away from the car park. Sean stayed low, making sure he couldn't be seen through the windows and crept forwards, hoping to have the element of surprise on his side. He extended the baton he'd taken from the patrol car and held it ready.

To his right, in the vicinity of the old bus, he saw a flicker of movement. Angie. He willed her to stay out of sight. Lying almost on his belly in the dust and dry grass, he watched the boots slow to a standstill, pause for a moment, then take off at a run, like the dog had done. Sean had guessed correctly; whoever was wearing the boots was heading for the pickup, but Sean had the keys.

Now there were sirens, getting closer, their tones rising and falling, interweaving and then coming together. The static caravan shook with the vibration of two people running up the steps and inside. Gav and Tina, he guessed. An image of what casualties they might find flashed through his mind, but he forced himself to concentrate on the suspect.

Now, he said to himself, and ran out from his cover, round the other static caravan, over a patch of dead, flat grass, just in time to see a young woman wearing men's work boots jump into the pickup and slam the door. PC Boyce shot out from behind the bus and they both arrived at the same moment.

He looked at the girl in the driver's seat, her hand clutching at the space where the keys should be. It was the girl from the kitchen, the one who'd given him the DVR, but it suddenly hit him that he knew her from somewhere else. Her face was all over the incident board, although the hair was shorter now. The make-up and false eyelashes in the photo gave her a completely different look, but you couldn't disguise those disappointed eyes, that turned-down mouth. They hadn't changed since she'd had her photo taken as a five-year-old.

'Bethany Winters?' he said.

She looked down at her knees and her shoulders crumpled.

CHAPTER FORTY-SIX

Friday afternoon

The air was full of sirens and voices. There were two ambulances, two response cars and a cub van. They spilt through the gate and into the car park. Sean watched them come, held in the moment, unsure of what to do next. PC Boyce moved first, leading Bethany towards one of the police cars and putting her in the back seat. Sean looked around, but he still couldn't see Lizzie.

Derek and Lou O'Connor were crossing the car park towards the scrapyard, clutching one another, as if they had escaped a fire.

Tina stepped towards them. 'Perhaps you should come with me, Mrs O'Connor.'

Mrs O'Connor looked past her, as if she wasn't there.

There was movement and the sound of low voices beyond the fence. From the scrapyard two paramedics emerged, wheeling a stretcher. An oxygen mask was over the victim's face, and the blanket was soaked in blood. Mrs O'Connor ran forward, a howl of anguish tearing the air. Tina took her arm to steady her.

Ivan Knowles walked beside the stretcher, his suit covered in blood and dust, as if he was emerging from a war zone.

'I take it you've got the girl,' Knowles said, when he reached Sean.

'Bethany Winters? Yes, she's in the car. PC Boyce is with her.'

Ivan looked at him. 'What did you just say?'

'Bethany Winters. Didn't you recognise her?'

'No, I bloody didn't,' Ivan said. 'That's your dyslexic advantage playing out.'

'I didn't realise I had one,' Sean said.

'Observational skills.'

'Hardly. I didn't recognise her when we came before, did I?'

'That's because you weren't looking for her.'

'So what are we charging her with?'

'You can start by arresting her for false imprisonment and attempted murder. Then let's see what she can tell us about the other murders.'

The ambulance doors were closing. It left the car park with sirens and lights on full. Derek and Lou got into the Jaguar and followed it out of the entrance, under the vinyl banner.

'Where's Lizzie?' Sean said.

'I don't know,' Ivan said, looking around him, bewildered. 'Isn't she here?'

Sean shook his head.

'She went with Derek O'Connor,' Ivan said. 'To look at something on the building site.'

At that moment Lizzie emerged around the side of the main building, walking with a tanned young man, deep in conversation. When she got closer, she led the man to DI

Khan, who had just arrived in a black Land Rover Discovery.

'This is Joe Heron,' Lizzie said. 'He's just showed me something very interesting in the vet's office. A supply of dog tranquillisers that's been looted. He said he'd only tell me because I'm not an actual copper. While we were on that side of the building, we heard the gunshots, and he was most solicitous, ensuring that I was okay. He took some persuading that it was finally safe to come out. I'm not sure if we're going to overlook the issue of the illegal disposal of the dog, but I think his behaviour should be seen favourably.'

Joe Heron looked sheepish. Sean stepped towards him, wondering exactly what Lizzie meant by solicitous. His fists were clenched and he was ready to unleash all the built-up pain of the day, smack in the middle of this handsome, gypsy-boy's face.

'Denton?' Khan's voice broke the chain between Sean's thoughts and actions.

'Sir?'

'Excellent work today.'

'Just wish we'd got here sooner. Is the lad going to be all right?'

'Too soon to say,' Khan said, softly, ensuring Joe couldn't hear. 'I want you to break it to the brother, gently, that Tommy's been shot in the neck, by the girl who was working here, Sarah Sutton.'

'AKA Bethany Winters.'

If Khan was surprised, he didn't show it. The briefest flicker of an eyebrow was all he gave away. Then he ran his fingers slowly through his beard.

'Of course,' he said.

'She's in the car. I'm just going to read her her rights and arrest her for false imprisonment and attempted murder, if that's all okay with you.'

'She's all yours,' Khan smiled. 'But see to Mr Heron first.'

Sean did as he was told, watching Joe's face register anger and fear, but he said nothing in response.

'Would you like to talk to my colleague, DS Knowles? He was with your brother when it happened.'

Joe shook his head. 'Where's my truck?'

'A red pickup?'

Joe nodded.

'It's in the yard, but I'm afraid it's part of a crime scene.'

'I need to go to the hospital.'

'One of my colleagues can take you.'

'I'm not getting in a police car.'

'I'll take you,' said Lizzie. 'I'm a civilian.'

'Hang on a minute,' Sean said. 'Is that wise?'

'I'll be fine,' she said. 'Come on, Joe, let's see if we can catch up with the ambulance.'

CHAPTER FORTY-SEVEN

Friday evening

If the air outside had begun to cool, it hadn't reached the ops room yet, despite all the windows being open.

'If you could guarantee this weather,' Tina was saying, 'you could save a fortune on foreign holidays. It's the kind of evening to sit out in the dark, sipping chilled white wine.'

'Plenty of time for that once we've wrapped up here,' Khan said, coming into the room with a stack of pizza boxes and the overwhelming smell of tomato, cheese and pepperoni.

He was greeted with a round of applause as the pizzas were handed round.

'Hey! Am I missing the party?' Lizzie said.

She stood in the doorway, cheeks flushed and damp hair sticking to her temples. Sean could have kissed her right there and then.

'Here, you can share mine,' he said.

She pulled up a chair next to him.

'You survived a car ride with Joe Heron, then?'

'Are you jealous? Just because he looks like a young David Essex.'

'Don't tell Nan that,' he said. 'She'll get a season ticket to the dogs just for the chance to see him.'

'Well, she may have to wait. I have a feeling our Joe Heron is going to be going away for a while.'

'Anything you want to share with the rest of us, Lizzie?' Khan said.

'Only a nice sweaty handprint on my car door, which I've just brushed down. Exact fingerprint match with the marks on the hairdressing stall. Fresh sweat makes a great sample!'

'Excellent,' Khan's eyes twinkled above his beard.

Ivan Knowles put his feet up on his desk and rested the pizza box on his lap. He let out a loud sigh.

'I would just like to say, boss, this pizza makes me glad I came up north, in fact it makes me glad to be alive.'

Another round of applause broke out.

Sean caught the expression on Ivan's face and detected a watery look in his eyes, but it soon vanished as he began to talk through the events leading up to Tommy Heron's shooting.

'Derek was expecting us,' Ivan said. 'The girl had told him we'd called yesterday, and he was very helpful, but it was taking him ages to find the section of CCTV I was interested in. I'd told him it had been doctored and I thought it was by someone with some knowledge of computers. He said they were all pretty old-fashioned, except the girl. She helped him and his wife out sometimes, with online bookings and suchlike.'

He took a bite of pizza and wiped a string of cheese from his chin.

'Then,' he said, his mouth still full, 'I asked where she

340

lived and made an excuse that I needed to get something from my car. I don't know what I was expecting to find, but I was curious about her. She wasn't family, but she was living on-site. Derek said she turned up out of the blue, looking for work, a few months ago. The boys took to her, especially Tommy, so she stayed.'

He paused for some more pizza.

'I let myself into her caravan with a quick tug of a very poor lock, but I hadn't bargained for the dog. He wasn't pleased to see me and was definitely guarding the door that led to the bedroom. I soon realised that he was just a noisy bugger and had no intention of biting, so I slipped past him and opened the door. Hey, is anyone recording this? I could save myself a load of work by getting admin support to type it up for me, before I forget what I said.'

There was laughter, but Sean didn't think Ivan would forget this story in a hurry.

'So there's this big lad stretched out on the bed. The room stinks of sweat and farts. He doesn't stir, even though the dog's barking his head off, so I go to the side of the bed and feel for a pulse. That's when I notice a couple of objects in the room. There's a Frankenstein mask hanging off the mirror and a bolt gun on the dressing table. I'm trying to understand the context of both objects. The mask belongs to the school murder and the bolt gun finished off Xavier Velasquez, but it seems too neat, them being there like that, as if someone's meant to find them. Meanwhile, the boy's got a pulse but I can't wake him. I lift his eyelids and his pupils are different sizes. I'm just wondering if he's been fitting, when the girl bursts in, pointing a double-barrelled shotgun at me.'

He drinks from a can of lemonade and catches his breath.

'She shoots a hole in the ceiling first time, and I'm thinking about asbestos and wondering how old the bloody van is. I know I'm going to have to talk her into handing the gun over, and it starts off all right. She's apologising, saying she thought I was hurting Tommy, thought I was Joe. I ask her to put the gun down and explain to me why Tommy's in her caravan and why can't I wake him? That's when she quietly turns the gun round to my face and tells me to hand over my phone and my radio. She throws them out of the window without shifting the aim of the gun on my head. She gets really weird then and kneels on the other side of the bed, still holding the gun, re-cocked and ready to fire the second barrel. She says we should pray for him, because he's done terrible things, but he did them to protect her. He's tried to take his own life, she says, but he's failed, so she's going to help him. She says he won't survive prison, so this is kinder. It's to put him out of his misery. She lays the gun on the bed next to him and tries to get his hand round the trigger. She's pushing the gun up under his chin.'

He paused.

'And then I make my move. The gun goes off just as I nudge it to one side. She runs and I'm trying to staunch the bleeding from his neck. By this time, I'm praying, and I'm a bloody atheist. Gav and Tina come in and we manage a bit of first aid before the paramedics arrive. That's it.'

There were murmurs around the room.

'Good work,' Khan says, in his most understated manner, but Sean can tell he's impressed. He wouldn't be surprised if Khan doesn't recommend Ivan for a bravery award. 'And to

DC Denton for apprehending Bethany Winters. We'll have a word with her when her lawyer gets here. The parents are on their way too, but she's an adult, so they don't have any immediate right to see her.'

'If we can match her DNA to one of the masks,' Sean said, 'and Tommy's to the other, we've got our intruders in the school. My guess is that they were targeting Homsi because of something that happened on the building site. Something that was cut from the CCTV footage. Velasquez is a revenge attack, but I don't understand the motive for the first murder.'

'They were all revenge attacks,' Tina said quietly. 'Bethany Winters was a damaged child who'd been abused by her foster brother. As her parents said, she'd made false accusations before. I find this really hard to get my head round, because false accusations are very rare, and I spend my life on the other side of this particular fence, but I think there's a case for challenging whether she didn't administer her own date-rape drug, before Velasquez had sex with her . . .' She hesitates before continuing, to let her words sink in. 'Maybe Homsi made an advance on her too, or she thought he did. It fired up the anger and hatred she has for men, particularly dark-skinned men, and somehow she persuaded Tommy to take her to see where the men lived. Either she, or Tommy, beat him to death.'

'I don't see how you can say it's all about dark-skinned men,' Steve Castle said.

'I'm mixed race, Steve, so I can say what I like, but look at the boy in the picture. We can only see his hand and his arm, but he's darker-skinned than her. It's obvious. She's gone beyond acting out the abuse itself, and she's been living out her revenge fantasy. Somehow she's manipulated Tommy and Joe into helping her. I just hope Tommy survives, and Joe gets over his dislike of the police, in time for them to tell us how she did it.'

'Hope this isn't a bad time.' Janet Wheeler came in, holding up a clear plastic bag containing a pair of pink trainers. 'But these turned up in the very last bag of clothes from the school. Pink satin trainers, women's size six, blood in the treads and soaked into the fabric.'

'Which explains why she was wearing Abbas' boots,' Denton said.

'I think she meant to leave the boots in the room with Tommy and the other stuff,' Ivan said. 'She was still following her plan, to pin the blame on him. She's been waiting for us to find him. I bet she wonders what took us so long.'

CHAPTER FORTY-EIGHT

A week later

The weather finally broke and the rain soaked the parched earth. It was the perfect day for a funeral.

Sean and Lizzie got out of the car. Sean opened the door for Nan and held an umbrella over her newly styled hair. Chloe had made her own way to the crematorium chapel with her boss from work, Bill Coldacre, and his wife Brenda. They had brought the flowers, all cut from the gardens at Halsworth Grange. In the back of Bill's old Land Rover, Wolf was waiting for Chloe. Sean had met Derek O'Connor in the hospital, a few days before, and made him an offer for the dog. He wouldn't take any money for it, just said he was glad it had a home, it would make a good guard dog for a young lass living on her own.

Inside they made a small party on the front row. Johnny Cash sang 'I Walk the Line' through the tinny crematorium speakers and Sean choked back tears. Chloe read a poem, her voice faltering in places. Sean didn't follow the words, just kept his eyes on her face, willing her to be strong. They listened to the first verse of the Rolling Stones' 'Jumpin' Jack

Flash' while a beige curtain juddered to a close around the coffin, and Jack was gone.

Later, after a pub lunch, when the rain had stopped, they walked along the canal towpath for a breath of fresh air. The sun came out and lit up the stones and the calm flat water. Bill took Nan's arm and Brenda walked with Chloe, Wolf close to her heel. Lizzie took Sean's hand and squeezed it.

'Ivan would have come,' she said. 'But he's up to his neck in the pretrial statements.'

'I can imagine,' Sean said.

He hadn't been back to work since Friday night. Khan had insisted that now he'd got his collar, Sean must take the compassionate leave he was due.

'Ivan's done a great job with Tommy Heron,' Lizzie said. 'The poor lad told him everything, about hearing Bethany screaming and how he came out to find Homsi standing in front of her by the trench. Tommy believed her when she said Homsi had molested her. He took her to the school, but he didn't see her kill him. His job was scaring the others to run away. Which wasn't hard, since he and his brother Joe had been in there to "tax" them a few days earlier. He even told us where to find the murder weapon, a metal pole, covered in blood, stashed in the ditch they'd filled in, next to all the cables.'

'Thanks for letting me know,' he said, although he wished he'd been there at the interview.

He'd picked up bits and pieces from the pub the night before, but it was mostly about Velasquez, and Joe finally admitting to helping Bethany hang the body over the stall, not realising, he claimed, that the boy was still alive. She'd twisted him into thinking it was Tommy who'd killed Xavier, and he was just helping move the evidence and confuse the police. Meanwhile, Kathy Edwards had handed herself in, admitting through tears that she'd stayed in the market hall to let in her old friend, Bethany Winters, the girl she'd known all her life from church. She'd believed what Bethany told her about the hairdresser, Greg Smart, although she swore she had no idea anyone was going to get hurt. Bethany had said she just wanted to do a bit of graffiti on the walls and door of the shop, to teach Smart a lesson.

'You know, Sean,' Lizzie said, 'I think it's okay to bring work home sometimes.'

He smiled and squeezed her hand.

'We're part of a team,' he said, 'and I'm happy about that.'

'Are you happy with Ivan as your mentor?'

'He's a good copper.'

'One of the best,' she said.

'I didn't like him at first. Thought he was stuck up, but he's not. He's offered to help me write up the case for my portfolio. Yeah, he's all right.'

'Is that the only reason you didn't like him? Because you thought he was stuck up?'

'What are you getting at? Okay, I was a bit jealous at first. I thought you and he were getting close, you seemed to have a lot in common.'

'Oh, Sean,' she said, 'even if Ivan was straight, I wouldn't trade you in for him.'

'What do you mean, "even if Ivan was straight"?'

'You didn't realise?'

Sean shook his head. 'Turns out I am thick, after all.'

'No, you're not. You just don't judge people – that's a good thing. Anyway, if anyone's going to be jealous, it should be me. You and Tina Smales have been getting on very well, haven't you? What was she giving you in a plastic bag outside the pub last night?'

'A surprise, for you,' he said. 'Something I saw and she offered to pick up for me. You'll have to wait until we get home.'

He hoped she'd like it, the picture of a purple house, the yellow light shining from its window. A landscape they could escape into, together.

ACKNOWLEDGEMENTS

I would like to thank my family, especially Josh, Isaac and Reuben, for being brilliant and wonderful and funny, and not minding when I hid myself away, with my notebooks and laptop, trying to get this book finished.

I'm enormously grateful to my agent, Laura Longrigg, for her continued encouragement and insight; to Susie Dunlop at Allison & Busby for seeing the potential in the Sean Denton series and giving it a home; to Lesley Crooks and the team for editorial feedback and enthusiasm for the series; and to all those who have been part of *Race to the Kill*'s production, from proofreaders to designers, sales people to booksellers. Writing may look like a solitary activity, but reaching an audience is a huge team effort. Thank you.

Big thanks to all the wonderful people who run and take part in online book groups, especially Tracy Fenton, Helen Boyce and the TBC community, Llainy Swanson at Crime Book Club and Dave Gilchrist at UK Crime Book Club. Thank you to Clare Malcolm and Will Mackie at New Writing North for everything, especially sending me to libraries across the north of England as part of the Read Regional project and to all the library staff who have welcomed me to give talks. Thank you to Wendy Kent at York Explore for making *To Catch a Rabbit* the Big City Read for 2017, and thank you to the tireless organisers of festivals, in particular Rob O'Connor at York Literature Festival, Jacky Collins at Newcastle Noir, Quentin Bates at Iceland Noir and Nick Quantrill at Hull Noir. For me, meeting readers, both in the real world and online, is one of the greatest pleasures of being a published writer.

Many, many thanks to all those who have helped me with research questions, read early drafts and given me all kinds of amazing support along the way, especially Mark, Dave Nicholson, Alyson Shipley, Lisa-Marie, David Harker, Rebecca Bradley, Donna-Lisa Healy. Thank you to Jackie Watson for taking me to the dogs, and Jez Wells for introducing me to Walter the lurcher; and last, but by no means least, thank you to the best bunch of crime-writing friends a girl could wish for. The crime fiction community is truly one of the most warm, kind and generous groups of people I have ever known and without them, I would never have written this book.

Last, but by no means least, thank you to Ben Mancey-Jones, Andy Proctor and all the staff at York District Hospital Magnolia Centre and Ward 31.